Susanne O'Leary

Daughters
of
Wild Rose
Bay

Bookouture

Published by Bookouture in 2020

An imprint of Storyfire Ltd.
Carmelite House
50 Victoria Embankment
London EC4Y 0DZ

www.bookouture.com

ISBN: 978-1-83888-262-4
eBook ISBN: 978-1-83888-261-7

For Maud

Chapter One

It was dark when Jasmine drove down the main street of the village and pulled up at the gate. She turned off the engine and sat there, looking up at the house. It stood on an incline with imposing views of the village and the sea beyond. The lights glowed through the windows and she could nearly feel the warmth of the logs burning in the fireplace, smell whatever mouth-watering food her mother had cooked for supper. But she couldn't bring herself to go inside. She gripped the steering wheel and tried to breathe slowly, in and out; tried to slow her heartbeat and gather up enough courage to get out of the car and walk up the path to the front door and open it, but found she couldn't move.

It had been cold in Cork when she drove off the ferry from Brittany, but here the winds were soft and balmy, as spring came early to this part of the west coast of Ireland. Jasmine knew that the rhododendron and camellia bushes in the back garden would be in bloom and that even the daffodils her grandmother had planted along the path up to the house would be showing their yellow heads. She had been here a long time ago, when her grandmother was still alive, but only for short visits. She had a sketchy memory of her grandmother sitting on a blanket on the beach watching

Jasmine build sandcastles. Sandy Cove had become a distant place in Jasmine's mind, somewhere she would visit again when she had the time. And now she found herself with all the time in the world, feeling that she needed somewhere safe and peaceful to rest and heal. Sandy Cove, with childhood memories of being cared for and loved, seemed the perfect place to run to.

Jasmine had been longing to step into the warm, bright living room and into the welcoming arms of her mother, sit at the kitchen table and tuck into a plate of something delicious, but now that she had arrived, she felt suddenly paralysed. How would her mother react when they met again? Would she be hurt that Jasmine hadn't been in touch for nearly a year? Or would Sally be so happy to see her daughter she'd brush away the past and forget all the bad times? Most of which were Jasmine's fault and not her mother's. It was all so complicated, she thought while she sat there trying to gather up the courage to go inside the house.

A year ago, she had decided to distance herself from her mother's concerns and fussing about what she was doing and the choices she was making. She wanted to prove she could manage by herself and be a success through her own efforts without her mother constantly asking questions and passing comments, warning her about taking risks. She had finally told Sally that she needed some space and that she would be in touch when she felt she was ready. Sally had said she understood and promised not to meddle any more. The silence after that had been deafening and Jasmine felt deep down that her mother wasn't happy about their separation.

She had wanted to prove that she had succeeded before she saw her mother again and she had been nearly there, all the boxes ticked, all the chips falling into place and her life a glorious success. At the age of thirty-three, she had finally achieved what she'd dreamed without help from anyone. That was before it all came crashing down.

No, she couldn't bear thinking about it. She was here and this had to be home for the next few months, even if she had to beg. The last few days in Paris had been traumatic to the point of unbearable and now Jasmine found herself sitting here wondering if recent events had really happened. It all seemed like a bad dream. Things like that only happened to other people, not to her, Jasmine Delon with the perfect job, the perfect soon-to-be husband and the perfect apartment in the best part of Paris.

She glanced in the rear-view mirror but in the darkness only saw a white face and huge frightened eyes. Her poker-straight brown hair perfectly cut at Salon Carita gleamed when she moved her head and that gave her a tiny dart of confidence. 'There is never an excuse for a lady not to be well-groomed,' her French grandmother had always said, and that had resonated with Jasmine ever since she was in her early teens. Looking good at all times sent the right signals and provided her with an armour, a sense of power, of confidence. But that was the glossy surface that hid her insecurities, her desire to be loved and the rootlessness Jasmine struggled with every day of her life. Nobody knew who she really was. She wasn't even sure she knew that herself.

There was a movement in the back seat. Jasmine straightened up and turned. 'We can't sit here all night, can we?' she said. 'And you need a pee and a bowl of something tasty, I'm sure.'

The white fluffy dog sat up and yawned. Then he wagged his tail and whimpered softly.

Jasmine sighed and patted the little terrier on the head. 'Okay, Milou. We'll get out. Mam will be happy to see *you*, at least.'

Jasmine got out, opened the door to the back seat and the little dog jumped out and stretched. Then she opened the gate, and with the dog trotting beside her walked up the garden path.

After having stopped while the dog sniffed something behind a bush, Jasmine arrived outside the front door of the house. The garden was dark and silent, but she could hear a strange noise from inside the house – an eerie humming sound. She could also see that the light coming through the glass panel beside the front door had a blue hue and was flickering on and off. That, combined with the humming sound, sent shivers up her spine. Something strange was going on in there – but what?

Jasmine took a deep breath and pushed the door open, Milou pressing himself against her leg, shivering. She walked through the hall and stepped into the living room where she stopped and gasped, staring at the figure sitting on a cushion in the middle of the floor. She peered through the dim bluish light at the woman who was sitting in the lotus position, her eyes closed, humming loudly.

Jasmine coughed as the smell of lavender hit her throat.

'Mam?' she said in a near whisper, her eyes glued to the woman. Was this really her mother? The woman looked like she was in some kind of trance. Her light brown hair, streaked with pink, blue and purple, hung down her back in loose curls and she was dressed in yoga pants and a soft blue sweater that slid off one shoulder. 'Sally?' Jasmine asked, remembering that her mother preferred to be called by her first name.

The woman's eyes slowly opened while she let out a last 'oooom-mmm'. She looked at Jasmine and smiled. 'There you are.'

'Yes,' Jasmine said, rooted to the spot. She couldn't believe what she saw. The change in her mother's appearance was startling. Sally had always been an eccentric woman but this lithe ageless creature sitting with her legs crossed as if she was made of rubber, looked nothing like her mother. Her face was devoid of make-up and she looked so relaxed. What had happened to her?

'I knew you'd come,' Sally said without getting up.

'Of course you knew. I told you when I called from the ferry.'

Sally's laugh sounded like little bells. 'I knew before that, my sweet girl. The stars told me. It's in the plan of the Universe that you would come here. Mother Nature wanted it to happen.'

'Mother – who?' Jasmine sniffed the air. Was Sally smoking something? But all she could smell was the lavender that seemed to come from the smouldering logs in the fire. Essential oils, she thought.

'But why are you standing there? And who is that little person hiding behind you?' Sally jumped to her feet and stretched. 'I have dinner ready, so we can eat whenever you've unloaded the car.'

'Oh, lovely,' Jasmine said, her stomach rumbling at the thought of Sally's delicious home cooking. She picked up the dog. 'This is Milou. My West Highland darling. Isn't he lovely?'

'He's beautiful.' Sally approached and patted Milou on the head. Then she kissed Jasmine on both cheeks. 'Welcome, darling. I'm happy to see you. It's been too long, don't you think?'

'My fault,' Jasmine said with a dart of guilt. 'I should have—'

'Nobody's fault,' Sally interrupted. 'Just life getting in the way. I was crowding you and not letting go. Bad karma here and there too. Kamal always says you have to be patient and wait for it to get better.' She stepped back before Jasmine had a chance to ask who this Kamal was. 'But look at you. So chic and polished.' She touched Jasmine's cheek. 'But your eyes are sad and your cheeks pale. What's happened?'

Jasmine pulled back. 'Nothing,' she said. 'I'm just a little stressed and tired. I've taken a sabbatical from work. I thought I'd come here and stay with you for a rest.' *And to lick my wounds and be taken care of*, she thought but didn't say out loud. She suddenly noticed a glimmer on the ring finger of her left hand. Oh, God, the ring. She had forgotten to give it back. Jasmine quickly took the ring off and stuffed it in her back pocket. She'd get it back to him somehow.

'You've come to the right place,' Sally said, looking pleased, not appearing to have noticed the ring. 'This village is becoming the go-to place for the stressed and burnt-out. Kamal teaches them to find themselves again. He's a wonderful teacher.'

'Who's Kamal?' Jasmine asked, intrigued by the blissful look in Sally's eyes.

'Oh,' Sally said airily as her face turned pink and her eyes sparkled. 'He's… a friend, a… soulmate. He's changed my life in many ways. But you have to meet him to really understand.' She clapped her hands, making Milou jump. 'But hey, get your bag and settle in. We'll talk over dinner. I want to know everything that's been going on in your life since last year. And' – she held up a hand – 'no recriminations or accusations about not keeping in touch. You're here now and that's all that matters. We'll move forward and not look back. Deal?'

'Uh, yes,' Jasmine replied, bewildered. What was all this forgiving and moving on? Jasmine had been anticipating the reunion with trepidation, ready to eat humble pie and take the blame. Sally had always been the one to ruminate over old hurts and never wanted to move on until she had expressed her feelings and they had had a good row about whatever it was they had fallen out about. But this new Sally was breezy and bright and all sweetness and light, talking about the Universe and Mother Nature. What on earth had happened to her mother during the year they'd been apart?

Jasmine blinked and shook off the thought. Whatever it was could be discussed later. She had to get her case and get settled, but most of all have something to eat. 'I'll go and get my bag,' she announced.

'Lovely,' Sally said. 'Are you staying for a week or so?'

'I'm planning to stay for a bit longer,' Jasmine replied, not daring to say it could be for a very long time as the memories of what had happened in Paris came back with a vengeance. Better to drip-feed her mother slowly with the facts.

'Wonderful,' Sally chanted from the kitchen. 'Stay as long as you want, pet. And I love the dog.'

Jasmine put Milou on the floor and he immediately trotted toward the kitchen. 'I'll get his food, too,' she said as she turned to walk back outside. As she went down the path, she tried to sort out her thoughts and make a plan.

Firstly she needed to get settled: have dinner and try to get used to her mother's new behaviour. Then she needed to tell her a little about what happened, editing out the most horrible details. And lastly… Jasmine stopped. No, that was something she had to keep secret for a while, the real reason she was here.

Chapter Two

Dinner was not what Jasmine had hoped for, nor was Sally. She had expected to find the mother that she'd said goodbye to over a year ago, a mother who was a little unconventional, outspoken and feisty, but her whole demeanour had changed. She seemed distant and serene in a way that unnerved Jasmine.

Jasmine sat at the kitchen table staring at the bowls of lettuce, chopped vegetables and nuts. 'Is this the starter?' she asked, hoping a casserole or an Irish stew might come out of the oven.

Sally laughed. 'No, this is dinner,' she said. 'I've adopted the raw food diet. I started it six months ago, at the same time as yoga came into my life. I realised that what I put into my body had to be pure and clean and not cooked and covered in sauces. Much better for you. It's very easy to do. The only thing that's cooked is bread, but then it has to be sourdough. Olive oil instead of butter and no wine. It was hard at first, but now I love it. I've lost four kilos and sleep like a baby every night. And my blood pressure and cholesterol levels are down to normal, my doctor tells me.' She smiled at Jasmine as she sliced a huge loaf of bread. 'Go on, help yourself. Your body will thank you and your spirits will soar.'

'I'm sure they will,' Jasmine muttered as she picked at the carrot sticks and baby spinach on her plate. Her spirits felt more like a damp squid as she chewed her way through the dinner of raw food, her own heavily doused with olive oil that helped make it more palatable. At least the bread was delicious and she ate three big slices in order to fill her very empty stomach, washed down with elderflower cordial that Sally had made herself, she said proudly.

Jasmine sighed and thought with longing of the gourmet dishes and wonderful wines Sally used to serve. What was so wrong with a plate of coq au vin and a glass of Bordeaux? She glanced at her mother's glowing face and had to agree that this new healthy living had rejuvenated her beyond what any cream or lotion could achieve. But there was still a flicker of sadness in her eyes at times, as Jasmine talked about Paris and her childhood home in that gorgeous apartment on the Left Bank.

'So how is the shop going?' Jasmine asked in an attempt to find the old Sally.

'It was hard work to get it started,' Sally replied, brightening as she talked about her shop. 'But now it's really going well. All thanks to Cordelia, who came here from America two years ago. She helped me start a whole new concept and that turned things around amazingly. She and her cousins, Maeve and Roisin, have been wonderful friends. And Nuala, of course. The salt of the earth.'

'Maeve and Roisin McKenna?' Jasmine asked. 'The Willow House family?'

'That's right. Lovely girls. Younger than me, but true friendship has no age, does it?'

'Not at all,' Jasmine agreed.

'You'll love them too.'

'I'm sure I will. And… yoga,' Jasmine started. 'It seems to have changed you a little.'

Sally smiled. 'More than a little. Oh, God, I don't know how to explain it. But it was as if Kamal was meant to come here to show us a different way of living. Yoga tunes you into your body and teaches you to look at yourself in a whole new way. It makes you accept yourself as you are and not how others want you to be.'

'Oh,' Jasmine said, startled by the light in Sally's eyes. 'That sounds difficult to achieve.'

'It is. I'm not there yet. But I think the whole lifestyle suits me. The diet is hard at first, but once you get used to it, you begin to feel the benefits. Body and mind and all that, you know.'

'Uh, great,' Jasmine said. 'Must be lovely.'

'You should try it. At least come to yoga. It's very calming.'

'I'll give it a go,' Jasmine promised only to make Sally happy.

'You should. It'll help with all the stress you must be going through. I mean,' Sally continued, 'I'm guessing you've come for a bit of a rest?'

'Yes,' Jasmine mumbled. 'Something like that.'

'Your job must be very stressful.'

'Uh, yes. Sometimes.' In order to avoid more questions, Jasmine changed the subject to something more neutral and they kept chatting as they ate, talking about this and that and reminiscing about the old days. There was no mention of Jasmine's father, Matthieu, but Jasmine felt his presence all the same as the conversation touched on family matters.

The divorce of her parents when she was only six had affected Jasmine badly, turning her into an angry little girl who scowled at the world around her. Her relationship with her mother had always been strained as she grew up, but they had finally become closer and their relationship improved, even if Sally's fussing was a bone of contention. The fact that they hadn't been in touch for a whole year had little to do with the divorce. It was more because of Sally hovering over Jasmine at all times, handing out advice on everything – her career, her clothes, her choice of boyfriends. It had felt stifling and the year apart had made her feel free to do what she wanted. But after the shock of what had happened so recently, Jasmine's first thought had been to run to her mother and hide from the big bad world. She smiled at Sally and felt suddenly that coming here had been a good move. Despite the raw food and the absence of wine, it was comforting to be with someone who cared about her and wanted only her best. Sally's fussing had been irritating at times, but now it seemed silly to have stayed out of touch for a whole year.

'Dessert,' Sally said and placed a bowl of fruit in front of Jasmine. 'And then bed, I think.'

'Bed?' Jasmine checked her watch. 'But it's only nine o'clock.'

'Yes, but I get up early. An hour's yoga before I go to the shop I've found to be so energising.'

'Of course,' Jasmine mumbled, looking at Milou, who had just got up from his place by her feet. 'But you don't mind if I stay up? I need to walk Milou and then I want to check some stuff on my laptop. You have broadband here, don't you?' she asked, hoping that hadn't been ditched along with meat and wine as part of the healthy living plan.

'Yes,' Sally replied. 'We got fibre last year, which was a huge relief. I'll write down the password for you.'

'Great. Thanks, Mam,' Jasmine said without thinking. 'Sorry, I mean Sally.'

Sally smiled. 'I like you calling me Mam, actually. I know I used to hate it, but I have been released from all those negative thoughts and feelings. I have to embrace my whole being and go with the karma of the day, good or bad, whatever the gods send us.'

'Oh, okay,' Jasmine said, wondering if she'd be able to find a shop open at this time of the evening or if she could sneak into her mother's stash of wine when she'd gone to sleep. She knew there were racks of it in the larder in the utility room off the kitchen.

'I feel so free now,' Sally said as she cleared the table. 'Free from all the old hurts and concerns. You know, I sold all my wine to the new restaurant just the other day. It felt fantastic.'

Merde, Jasmine thought, *why did she have to do that*? 'New restaurant?' she said out loud. 'What new restaurant?'

'It's a little gourmet place on the main street,' Sally replied. 'Opened by a young chef who's been on television quite a bit. A kind of Irish-style Jamie Oliver. This village has become very trendy. Good for my business, too. The shop is doing very well.'

'That sounds fun,' Jasmine remarked. 'I'll have to check it out some day.'

'Yes, you should. He's around your age and I think he's even lived in Paris at some stage. It'd be good for you to meet young people around here. I'll introduce you to Cordelia tomorrow. She's my business partner and about your age, too. You'd get on really well, I think.'

'Is she into the yoga lifestyle, too?' Jasmine asked.

'She comes to yoga classes, but I don't think she has embraced the lifestyle yet. I'm sure she will, though. Kamal is very persuasive and so charismatic. A lot of the people in the village follow his health plan. You'll see how wonderful he is when you meet him.'

'Can't wait,' Jasmine said with a fake smile. 'I'll go and walk Milou now. Could you give me a key so I won't disturb you when I get back?'

Sally laughed and waved her hand. 'You don't need a key around here. Nobody locks their doors. I don't think there has ever been a burglary in Sandy Cove. In any case, who'd dare break into an O'Rourke house?'

'You mean because they were rebels in the eighteenth century? Haven't they become respectable since then?'

'Yes, but that rebel spirit is still there, and everyone knows it. It's in you, too. You just need to find it.'

'I could do with some of that,' Jasmine said, wishing she had been able to conjure it up when everything exploded in her face.

That O'Rourke rebel spirit, she thought as she walked into the dark night, *I wish…*

Chapter Three

Jasmine looked up at the velvety sky studded with glimmering stars and felt the salt-laden breeze on her face, suddenly happy she had come – and knowing this was the best place to recover from what had happened to her.

With Milou trotting beside her, Jasmine walked along the dark street, illuminated by old-fashioned street lights. The street was lined with a mishmash of old cottages and Victorian houses, many of which housed shops on their lower floors. She could see light through slits of curtains and hear televisions and music here and there. She walked past her mother's shop and stopped to look into the window with its array of curiosa that Sally had collected from markets and artisan shops in all parts of Ireland and even France and Germany. It was such a lovely collection, she thought, admiring her mother's sense of style and artistic streak. She continued past a flower shop, a small country grocery store, a chemist's and the local library housed in a former rectory.

When she was younger, she hadn't been interested in small country villages. It hadn't seemed a lot of fun to spend any time in this remote part of Ireland among country bumpkins. Apart from the odd week during her childhood, she hadn't explored the village, preferring to meet her mother at seaside resorts in France where the weather was more reliable. The outdoorsy surf-shack kind of holiday had not been her thing at all and her mother had complied, happy to go anywhere to pamper her spoilt daughter. What a little princess she had been, Jasmine thought with a pang of regret and guilt. She had missed out on so much. But now she had a chance to repair what she might have broken and to get to know her Irish roots. And find that O'Rourke spirit.

In any case, this village had suddenly become trendy, she had read in the travel section of *Vogue* the last time she'd had her hair done. As that thought hit her, she came to a stop outside a restaurant that looked interesting. 'The Wild Atlantic Gourmet', it said on a simple sign over the door. This must be the place Sally had mentioned. Jasmine studied the menu in a little glass case by the door. Expensive but oh, that food… Grilled goat's cheese with a honey and mustard dressing, *gambas* with garlic and thyme, fillet of beef with… Her mouth watered as she read, and without thinking she pushed the door open, praying that they would still be serving dinner. It was only a little after nine.

Jasmine stepped inside, finding the restaurant empty but with a delicious smell of food wafting around. The dining room was small and intimate with only around ten tables covered in blue-and-white checked cloths. The wooden floor gleamed in the warm light of the little lamps on the tables and a fire still flickered in the fireplace. This room was enchanting, Jasmine thought, the décor a mixture of Paris bistro and beachcomber seaside chic. But there was no one here and they were probably about to close. She jumped as someone entered through a door behind the counter at the far side and Milou gave a little yelp.

'We're closed,' a man's voice said. 'And dogs are not allowed here.'

'Oh, sorry,' Jasmine mumbled. 'I just wanted to—' She stopped, staring at the man. That voice, the floppy brown hair, those sloping blue eyes and the strong chin were all so familiar. Was it—? 'Oh my God!' she exclaimed, recognising the man in a flash. 'Aiden?'

The man stared at her looking startled. 'Who—'

'It's me,' Jasmine chortled. 'Jasmine Delon. From school in Paris?'

He kept staring at her. 'School in Paris? You mean…'

'Yes,' she said. 'Don't you remember me? We got drunk at the prom and you ended up in the fountain. Come on, you can't have forgotten that.'

He blinked and then his face brightened as the penny seemed to drop. 'Oh Jaysus, it's you!'

'Finally,' Jasmine exclaimed. 'Am I so forgettable?'

'No but maybe I was in denial,' Aiden suggested. 'I might be suffering from post-traumatic stress after that event.'

Jasmine laughed. 'Post-traumatic what? Just for that little thing? I thought you were stronger than that.'

He smiled and shook his head. 'You're right. It always makes me laugh when I remember it. And you. It was just that seeing you here all of a sudden was a bit of a shock.'

'I know. I got a bit of a fright myself.'

They looked at each other in silence, Jasmine trying to take in that this tall man was really that Aiden she remembered. The Aiden who had been the class nerd, who had teased her and then become her friend. She had helped him with his French homework and he had taught her to speak Irish-English. She had been chubby then and he had hugged her as she sobbed when the mean girls in her class had jeered at her. They had gone to the graduation ball together because neither of them had been able to get a date and they had spent the evening talking and laughing, feeding each other cake and getting drunk. All those memories flowed through Jasmine's mind as they stood there, neither believing their eyes.

'You grew up very nicely,' Aiden finally said.

'And look at you,' Jasmine said, 'all polished and smart-looking. Where are your glasses?'

'Laser surgery,' Aiden said. 'But I kind of miss them. They were good to hide behind.'

No need to hide now, Jasmine thought and smiled, more from nerves than anything else. 'I can't believe it's really you.'

'Weird, isn't it? But yeah, it's me all right.' Aiden held out his arms. 'But hey, I'm really happy to see you. How about a hug, old pal?'

Jasmine laughed and fell into his arms, hugging him tightly. How nice it was to meet an old friend like this, especially an old friend like Aiden, her very best friend at school. He felt solid and strong.

She pulled back and looked at him. 'And I heard from my mother that you're a celebrity chef. How did that happen?'

'Celebrity?' Aiden shrugged. 'That's a bit of an exaggeration. I cooked a few meals on TV on one of those afternoon shows and then I got a job at a top hotel in Dublin. While I was there, I met a guy who was investing in restaurants in the west and as this village is now one of those gems of the Wild Atlantic Way that's becoming trendy, we decided we'd give it a lash. It's worked very well so far, thank you very much.'

Jasmine laughed at his turn of phrase. 'You sound just like the old Aiden. Always so modest.'

'Sure I'm still him, aren't I?' He studied her for a moment. 'And you haven't changed a bit. All glitter and glam as always with your lovely shoes and handbag. And a dog with a collar to match. Not to mention that hair. Not the dog's, of course. He's nice, too, though. I like dogs. Except in my restaurant.'

'I know.' Jasmine twitched at Milou's lead. 'I just came in here to see if I could get something to eat. The menu looks so enticing.' She looked down at her designer trainers with the Chanel logo and was suddenly painfully reminded of the life she had left behind. 'I'm staying with Sally, who's converted to this raw food diet, you see. It's a bit hard to take, especially when you're hungry.'

'Sally?'

'Yes. My mother. Her name's Sally O'Rourke.'

He looked at her and blinked. 'Sally O'Rourke is your mother? How come I never knew that?'

'Well, we never met each other's parents, did we?'

'That's true. God, I can't believe Sally's your mother. I wish I had met her back then. She's great.'

'If she's not your mother,' Jasmine said without thinking. 'I mean… you know…'

Aiden laughed. 'Oh yes. Irish mothers, eh? Mine is the same, can't stop asking if I've changed my socks and stuff like that. She phones me nearly every day. Drives me nuts. Can't imagine Sally being like that, though. She seems a lot more laid-back.'

'She is now,' Jasmine remarked. 'Yoga seems to have made her more relaxed.'

Aiden nodded. 'I've always found her to be dead sound, as we say in Dublin. She helped me a lot when I first came here. She steered many of her customers to my restaurant and that helped get my place off the ground. I think this new lifestyle is a bit of a fad, actually. But if that has made her more relaxed, why knock it? All Irish mammies should take up yoga.'

Jasmine laughed. 'I can't imagine that happening. I don't know your mother, though. All I know about your parents is that your dad worked in Paris and was an economist.'

'Still is,' Aiden cut in. 'But now he is doing it in Dublin, where I trained as a chef.' He smiled suddenly, his eyes crinkling. 'Hey, why don't I give you something to eat? I was going to grill myself a steak and heat up a dish of potato gratin and eat it all on my own.'

'Oooh,' Jasmine sighed, her eyes filling with tears. 'Steak *and* potato gratin…' She was suddenly aware of a movement at her feet. 'But what about Milou?'

'Your dog?' Aiden shrugged. 'Only you and I know he's here. And neither of us will tell, will we? Except if a health inspector should come by, but at this time of night that's not very likely.'

'I must be dreaming,' Jasmine said as Aiden locked the door. 'Meeting you and then getting real food. Can't be true.'

'You want me to pinch you?'

'No, it's okay. I know I'm not dreaming. You can't feel hunger in dreams.'

'Hunger? Well, I'd better get weaving then. Come with me to the kitchen. I'll just turn off the lights here and lock up.'

'You had guests tonight?'

'Yeah. A bunch of Dubliners rolled in around seven demanding to be fed. About ten of them. That was all, but it's great for low season. No idea how they knew about the place, I think we might be on some kind of tourist trail.'

'This village was mentioned in a travel article in *Vogue*,' Jasmine said, still standing in the same spot while Aiden switched off the little lamps. 'Not sure if it said anything about this restaurant, though.'

'These people wouldn't be reading the likes of *Vogue*,' Aiden replied. 'I think word of mouth has kicked in. A friend tells a friend who tells another friend, that sort of thing. It's beginning to take and I might have to hire more staff. I only have one sous-chef and a waitress. Works fine right now but once we get more into spring, it might be very busy.'

'I'm sure you'll find someone,' Jasmine said, thinking that anyone working in this restaurant would love a boss like Aiden.

'Hope so.' Aiden turned off the last of the little lamps. 'Come on. Let's go and eat. Try not to trip in the dark.'

They walked across the dark restaurant and went into the bright state-of-the art kitchen, where a big fridge-freezer and a huge dishwasher hummed in unison. There was a little alcove beside the stove with a pine table and two chairs under a small window. Aiden pulled out one of the chairs. 'Here. Sit down. I'll get going on the food. Won't be long. How do you like your steak?'

'Kind of charred but pink in the middle,' Jasmine replied, her mouth watering. She sat down on the chair Aiden had pulled out for her, Milou settling at her feet.

'Coming up.'

In no time at all, Aiden put a plate with a charred fillet steak and a pile of golden potatoes that smelled of garlic and onions in front of Jasmine. After having placed a saucer with a few scraps on the floor for Milou, he got a bottle of wine from a rack beside the fridge and opened it, filled two glasses and brought them to the table. 'Nice little Bordeaux from your mum's collection. I bought the whole stash.'

'I know,' Jasmine sighed and took a swig of wine before she attacked the food. She closed her eyes in ecstasy as she chewed the tender meat and savoured the velvety garlic potatoes. 'Mmmm,' she mumbled through her mouthfuls.

'Orgasmic, is it?' Aiden asked, his voice bubbling with laughter.

'Nearly.' Jasmine sighed and sat back when she had finished. 'Oh my God, that was wonderful.' She picked up her glass and took a sip. 'And I'll have to come here to drink my mother's wine. I had been hoping I'd be having it at home with her. We'd eat her fabulous coq au vin or some other fantastic dish and get slightly sloshed and get to know each other again. But instead I find this new-age woman with purple hair sitting on a cushion *humming*. I couldn't believe my eyes. She told me she's met this guy who's changed her life.'

Aiden let out a laugh. 'Yeah, it seems yoga and mindfulness have hit town with a vengeance. All thanks to Mr Bendy.'

'What?' Jasmine exclaimed. 'I thought his name was Kamal.'

'It is, but I call him Mr Bendy. I've seen him doing his yoga on the beach. I swear that man is made of rubber.'

'Is he Irish?' Jasmine asked.

'On his mother's side. His dad's Indian, Sally said. And he grew up over there and came to Ireland about ten years ago. He was teaching in Dublin before he came to Sandy Cove.'

'Oh,' Jasmine said, intrigued. 'Sounds interesting.'

'I'm sure he is.' Aiden studied her for a moment. 'But what about you? What have you been up to? How many years has it been? I haven't seen you since that mad night at the prom when we got legless and you pushed me into the fountain near the Eiffel Tower.'

'You fell in,' Jasmine said with a giggle. 'God, you looked so funny. And then *les flics* arrived and nearly arrested you until I pleaded with them and said it was an accident and that you were my brother and my dad was a *fonctionnaire* in the Élysée Palace. That's more than ten years ago.'

'You haven't lost ze French accent,' Aiden teased. 'But your English is better than way back then.'

'I went to London to study economics,' Jasmine replied, topping up her glass from the bottle. 'Then I worked in Dublin for a year and then I went to Toulouse to work in my dad's firm. But I found it hard to be the boss's daughter so I left and went to Paris and got a job in a bank. Stocks and bonds and stuff like that.'

Aiden let out a low whistle. 'Impressive. My old friend Jazz an investment banker.'

'I'm not quite that, but I find the stock market fascinating. Watching shares go up and down and trying to figure out what'll happen next.' Jasmine smiled at the memory. 'I really felt I had landed there. I rented this cute little apartment near Boulevard St Germain and really loved living in Paris again.'

'What about your dad? Is he still in Toulouse?'

'No, he decided to move back to Paris a year ago and sell his business. He's half retired now but has a consultancy firm with a friend, which gives him the chance to play golf and have a good time with his friends. It was lovely to have him around again. We used to have lunch somewhere nice every Sunday and then walk around Paris and browse in the markets. Happy times.'

'And then?'

'What do you mean?'

'I have a feeling something happened. Something that made you pack up and leave, no?'

Jasmine looked away, still not yet able to admit the truth. 'I just felt like a break. I thought staying with my mother for a bit would be a good thing. We've been apart for a while and I wanted to reconnect.' Jasmine added bleakly, 'But now…'

'Ah, she hasn't changed, you know,' Aiden soothed. 'This yoga thing is just a way of living, Jazz, not a way of being. She's still the same woman, the same mum.'

Jasmine smiled at the old nickname he had invented for her when they were at school. 'When did you become so wise?'

He smiled and sighed at the same time. 'I've had my heart broken a few times. That teaches you a few things about life.'

'Your heart was broken?' Jasmine asked, not sure if he was joking.

'Yeah. But I survived and moved on.' He picked up the plates and rose from his chair. 'You want something to follow? Cheese? Or dessert? I could have a look in the fridge and see if there's any left.'

'I'm stuffed,' Jasmine said and surreptitiously eased open the top button of her jeans. 'Thank you so much for that amazing dinner, Aiden. I still can't believe we're sitting here together.' She kept looking at him to make sure he was real and not a dream. She was surprised at how little he had changed. He was still that honest, true friend, down to earth, with a dry sense of humour and not a bit boastful about his own success. 'Incredible,' she said as if to herself.

'It's a small world.' His face broke into a grin. 'But I was really happy to see you walk in through the door, even with that dog.'

Jasmine lifted Milou onto her lap. 'He's the best little dog in the world. Aren't you, Milou?' She dropped a kiss on the dog's head, which made him wag his little tail furiously.

Aiden laughed. 'I'm sorry. I didn't mean he wasn't a good dog. I'm sure he's highly intelligent and could get a degree in engineering or something if he tried. There. Does that make me look better?'

'Only if you meant it.'

'Of course I did.'

'Hmm, I'll pretend to believe you.' She patted Milou's head. 'So, tell me, how long have you been here?'

'Nearly a year. It took about three months to get the place finished and then I opened up in late June. Didn't take long for customers to turn up. There's only one other restaurant here, by the harbour, but they serve a completely different menu to us and they're more of a family place. So we complement each other. The owners – a great couple called Nuala and Sean Óg – even come to my place for a quiet dinner on their own when they need a break.'

'Seems like a good place for couples to spend an evening,' Jasmine remarked.

'And for people who want to eat something a little different,' Aiden continued. 'This place is beginning to trend, which could be bad for the village. I mean, the quiet life and the time-warp feel would disappear if it were to turn into some kind of Irish South Hampton. Designer boutiques, spa hotels, posh delis… Ugh.'

'That'd be horrible.'

Aiden nodded. 'It would. But I don't think it's going to happen. We have the Irish weather in our favour. Nobody knows when a storm will hit. Except our very own weather guru – Mad Brendan.'

'Who's he?' Jasmine asked, forgetting her tiredness. 'He's mad?'

Aiden laughed. 'Not mad at all. Just a little eccentric. He keeps donkeys on his little farm at the end of the village and is some kind of wise old man who knows everything about these parts. If you want to know anything about the people in this village, you go and ask him. He's old but has a memory like a steel trap. He can tell you about all the families around here and what they were up to centuries ago. I think I heard him say he's written it all down in notebooks. Anyway, he's quite reliable when it come to the weather.'

'Maybe he can tell me about the O'Rourkes,' Jasmine mused. 'My mother keeps telling me bits and pieces about them and how they were into all kinds of stuff hundreds of years ago.'

Aiden nodded. 'If you want to find out about them, Mad Brendan's your man.'

'I'd love to meet him.' Suddenly exhausted, Jasmine got up and put Milou on the floor. 'We'd better get going. I'm really tired after my trip and the wine has made me sleepy. Thank you so much for the fabulous food, Aiden. It was heavenly.'

'Oh, I wouldn't go that far.'

'It was to me.'

'Great,' he replied, getting up. 'I hope you'll settle in with your mum. And you'll love the village, even if it's a little tame for a city slicker like you.'

Jasmine bristled even though she knew he was teasing her. 'What if I'm not as much of a city girl as you think?'

'That'd be the surprise of the century,' Aiden replied with a grin. 'But what do I know? You might take to this village like a duck to water. Wonderful bunch of people here, you know. It's like a little time warp in a way. If you don't listen to the news or read the papers, you'd think nothing really bad ever happens. A real home away from home, you'll discover, if you like that sort of thing. But whatever floats your boat, right?'

'And what floats yours?' Jasmine couldn't help asking.

'Windsurfing,' he replied with a glimmer of joy in his eyes. 'And hiking. Best place in the world for that is right here. What about you?'

'Me?' Jasmine stood there, holding Milou's lead, wondering what really did make her happy. 'I could say shopping, but that isn't really my thing any more.'

'No?' He eyed her shoes. 'You could have fooled me.'

'Well, maybe a bit,' she had to admit to her annoyance. 'But that's part of living in Paris. I like museums and antique shops, too. And I love history and reading and ballet and music and…' She stopped.

'Those are interests,' Aiden remarked. 'But what's your passion?'

'Money,' she said without thinking. Then she laughed at his shocked expression. 'Oh, not like that, not money to spend on shoes and yachts. I meant money as in stocks and shares. I love playing the stock market trying to figure out what will be the next big thing. It's the futures market really. I worked in investments at the bank. And I was good at it,' she ended with a touch of pride.

'I bet you were. So why aren't you there playing the markets?'

Jasmine avoided his eyes and looked down at Milou. 'I needed a break. It was getting a little… hot.'

'Too stressful? You crashed and burned?'

'Something like that. I got involved in…' She stopped abruptly. 'Sorry. Can't really talk about it.'

'No need,' Aiden reassured her. 'Better to look forward than back, eh?'

'Yes.' She stifled a yawn.

'You should get some sleep.' Aiden went to the door and helped Jasmine with her jacket. 'I'll walk you home if you like.'

'No need for that,' she said. 'You must be tired.'

'A bit, yeah,' he confessed. 'I'll lock up and get to bed if you're sure you're okay.'

'Of course I am,' she assured him. 'Where do you live?'

Aiden pointed up to the floor above the restaurant. 'I have a flat up there. Small but quite comfortable. I don't need much space right now. I keep my car and my windsurfing board in the garage next door. I might look into buying a house when I've been here a bit longer. If I decide to stay. I'll see how it goes before I put down roots. Not sure I want the rural life just yet.'

'I see.' Jasmine opened the door. 'Well, good night and thank you so much for the delicious dinner.'

'You're welcome. Nice to see you again, Jazz,' Aiden said and gave her a brief hug. 'Sleep tight.'

Jasmine smiled. 'Night, Aiden.'

She walked back up the dark silent street, her mind full of what had happened that evening. First her mother turning into some kind of new-age hippie, then meeting her old school friend Aiden who had turned into a top-notch chef running his own restaurant. She had a feeling there were more surprises around the corner, but she felt ready to tackle them. It would help turn her mind against the disaster she had run away from.

Chapter Four

The sun poked fingers of light through a slit in the curtains as Jasmine slowly got out of bed. She pulled them back and opened the window to the mild spring air. She could see all the way to the beach and beyond in the bright light, the shimmering water of the bay and the waves crashing against the rocks. She sighed and closed her eyes, breathing in the fresh air, feeling the soft wind touching her face and ruffling her hair. What a clean, fresh day to wake up to and how lovely to be here at last. She had avoided coming here in the past but now she realised just how wrong she'd been. Maybe this was the perfect place to heal her broken heart. *Time will heal the wounds*, she thought, *and help me start again.* Meeting Aiden had been like a small miracle. A friend and, she felt, an ally who would help her get used to her new surroundings. She turned as there was a knock on the door and her mother came in carrying a tray, Milou trotting at her heels.

'Good morning, sweetheart,' Sally said with a bright smile and put the tray on the bedside table. 'I thought you'd like breakfast in bed this morning as you came home so late. Milou and I have been up since six greeting the sun. Must say he's a very peaceful animal. He sat in the window all through my yoga session without so much as a whine. I think he has great karma, you know. Dogs often do.'

Jasmine laughed. 'I never knew Milou had any kind of karma, but I'm not surprised.' She shivered suddenly as the wind from outside made her feel cold in her flimsy nightgown.

'Come on, get back into bed,' Sally ordered. 'And have your breakfast and talk to me.'

'Okay,' Jasmine said obediently and got back into bed, putting the tray across her legs. 'Ooh, toast and coffee and an egg.' She smiled at her mother. 'I thought we were only allowed raw food.'

Sally shrugged. 'Normally, yes. But I thought I'd ease you into the new way slowly. Last night was maybe too much of a shock. Sorry about that.' Sally tucked a strand of Jasmine's hair behind her ear. 'And… I'm worried you're not well. You're so pale and thin. And you have such a sad look in your eyes, even when you smile. What's the matter, my darling? Can you tell me?'

Jasmine picked up a slice of sourdough toast 'I'm fine, Mam, don't worry. Just a little overworked and stressed.'

Sally sat down on the bed with Milou on her lap. 'It's that job at the bank, isn't it? That awful stock market and all the shares going up and down. It has to be a nightmare trying to keep up.'

Jasmine nodded while she chewed on the slice of toast 'It's not easy. But I've… I'm on a long break. A very long one,' she added. 'I was due some leave and…' She stopped. Oh, God, what was she doing? Telling her mother a pack of lies to avoid having to reveal that she…

'Actually, I've quit,' she said.

'Quit? Your job?' Sally asked, looking shocked.

'My job, yes. I resigned.'

'What? Why? I mean… Isn't that a little drastic?'

'Maybe,' Jasmine mumbled and put her piece of toast back on the tray. 'I can't talk about it right now, Mam. Do you mind?'

Sally patted Jasmine's leg. 'It's all right. Tell me when you're ready.'

'I will. Soon.' Jasmine paused. 'But there is something else I want to tell you. I walked into that new restaurant last night and realised that the chef you spoke so highly of is a friend of mine. Aiden, from school.'

'Aiden Daley? You know him from school? In Paris?'

Jasmine nodded, smiling. 'Yes. You didn't know him but he was the guy I went to the graduation ball with. Remember how I told you I'd been rescued by a very nice boy? I was living with Mamie Clotilde at that time, so you didn't meet him. Mamie Clotilde didn't really approve but I managed to convince her and off we went together and had a great time despite it all. We got a little drunk and Aiden fell into the Trocadéro fountain on the way home and nearly got himself arrested. It was hilarious.' Jasmine laughed at the memory.

Sally smiled. 'I think I remember something like that. But it was a hard time for me. You were about to move away and go and live with your father. And you had been living with your grandmother for over a year.'

'Yes, that was your idea, don't forget,' Jasmine said. 'You felt I needed peace and quiet to study and someone to look after me. You couldn't do that because you had to travel around for your job and then organise all those fashion shows. And you were dating whatshisname, too. That handsome man with the deep voice.'

'François,' Sally said, looking slightly guilty. 'God, I know my life was pretty wild at that time. I wasn't very happy, looking back at it now. And I know I wasn't fair to you either. You needed me and I wasn't there for you.'

'I thought you were so glamorous,' Jasmine said wistfully. 'And I wasn't.'

'And then you turned into a swan,' Sally said and smiled fondly at Jasmine. 'All thanks to your granny Clotilde.'

Jasmine nodded. 'Yes. She helped me find myself and become who I am today.'

'I should have been there to help you,' Sally said with a sigh. 'But then you disappeared to Toulouse with your dad. I didn't protest, but I hated it. Your dad said that it was his turn to have you, and he wanted to get to know you.'

Jasmine sipped her coffee. 'I needed to get to know him, too. I also needed to understand what happened between you both and why you split up.'

Jasmine looked at her mother over the rim of her cup, remembering how wonderful it had been to live with her father, who had been supportive without being too judgemental. He had taught her a lot about business and finance and always shown her how much he trusted her to succeed.

'But it didn't tell me anything. Papa was so great and such a support to me when I was studying. But he didn't want me to go off and do that course at the London School of Economics, or that internship in Dublin. He was happy when I came back to work for him, only I didn't like being the boss's daughter. In any case, I wanted to do investment banking and not accountancy. The job in Paris was the best break for me. That's when we clashed a bit. But he gave in in the end and wished me luck.'

'And now he's back in Paris, too?' Sally asked.

'Yes.' Jasmine broke off a bit of toast and threw it to Milou. 'He's working at the consultancy firm and playing golf at the weekend.'

'And dating?' Sally asked casually.

'Not that I know. But he seems…'

'Happy?' Sally asked casually.

'As happy as he can be,' Jasmine replied, trying to gauge her mother's mood. 'But not quite like you. He hasn't really landed and found his groove. I think he's looking for something. Or someone,' she ended, studying her mother surreptitiously. Sally appeared disinterested but there was something in her eyes that said the opposite. Maybe there was hope after all?

'Finished?' Sally asked after a few minutes' silence.

Jasmine gave a start. 'Finished what?'

'Breakfast,' Sally replied. 'What else would I mean?'

'Yes. Thank you. Lovely breakfast, Mam.'

'You seemed to need it. But lunch will be—'

'I think I'll go for a walk and get a sandwich somewhere,' Jasmine interrupted, feeling she needed to get out of the house and away from the atmosphere that was becoming too heavy with unspoken conflicts. Sally didn't appear to want to discuss the past even if that would help to clear the air, so a little time spent away from each other seemed like a sensible idea.

Sally took the tray. 'Good plan. You need fresh air and sunshine.'

'I think I do. Can I leave Milou with you? I don't think he could cope with steep hill paths and he might start chasing sheep.'

Sally patted Milou on the head. 'Of course he can stay. I can take him to the shop with me. Cordelia would love to meet him.'

'Thanks. I think he loves you already.' Jasmine drained her cup. 'Where do you think I should walk today?'

'Take the path around the headland, but don't go over the hill on the other side. It's dangerous because the cliff face has subsided. It runs along the very edge of the cliffs and there is a steep drop to the sea.' Sally hesitated for a moment. 'There is something about that side of the hill I don't like. A vibe, something I can feel in the wind. Nothing I can explain in a rational way. It's just a feeling. But in any case the path is rough, too, and difficult if you're not an experienced hiker, so stay away from there.'

'Okay, I will,' Jasmine promised even though that side of the hill suddenly seemed very enticing.

Chapter Five

Wearing her pink trainers, a waterproof jacket and a small rucksack borrowed from Sally for the sandwich and bottle of water she planned to buy on her way to the coast walk, Jasmine set off, waving goodbye to her mother and Milou. It was a heavenly morning of the kind only Kerry could provide in early spring, with bright sunshine, clear blue skies and a fresh breeze that smelled of the sea. Jasmine felt a surge of energy as she walked down the main street, momentarily forgetting all the pain and heartbreak she had left behind in Paris. She knew it would take a lot of time before she could deal with what had happened and move on, but right now she was determined to enjoy this beautiful day. It felt like the first day of a new life, a new way of being.

Jasmine was a big-city girl, but as she looked out over the sea, Paris and its delights seemed far away and she began to understand why her mother had chosen to come back to this little village, perched seemingly on the edge of the world. Energised by the thought that nobody would think of looking for her here, she walked faster and was soon at the end of the main street. She continued up the road, taking the first lane down towards the beach, where she would find a café called The Two Marys', Sally had said. They would make her a sandwich to take on her coast walk.

Jasmine made her way down to the beach where she could see wetsuit-clad people dragging their windsurfing boards to the water. She walked on towards the opposite incline where she could see a thatched cottage and a sign that said 'café' pointing at it. But before she had reached the path, a voice called her name. She stopped dead, her heart beating, but then turned and saw Aiden running after her. *How silly to be so nervous*, she told herself. Of course it was him and not anyone from Paris having found her. How could it be?

'Hi, Jasmine,' Aiden panted.

'Hi.' She smiled at him standing there, his hair windblown and his cheeks pink. The wetsuit clung to his body and she noticed how well it fit. 'Nice to see you. Thanks again for the lovely dinner last night.'

'You're welcome. It was a blast. Couldn't believe we'd meet again like that.' He paused. 'So what are you doing here? Are you going for a walk?'

'Yes, I am. I'm going to get a sandwich up there at the café and then I'll walk along the cliff path and maybe up the mountain if I have the energy.'

'Mind if I come with you?' Aiden asked.

She looked at his wetsuit. 'Dressed like that?'

'No, I'll change. I have my clothes and walking boots in my car. I'll just drag the board up the beach and leave it there until I get back.'

'No windsurfing today, then?'

He shrugged. 'Not much wind. The forecast said the wind would increase but it hasn't. So a walk would be nice while I wait. If you don't mind me tagging along.'

Jasmine smiled. 'Of course not. I'd love some company. Especially yours.' It was true, she thought, Aiden would be the best company. Even though they hadn't seen each other for more than a decade, they had immediately fallen back into the relationship they had enjoyed during the last year at school. He was someone that she found both comforting and endearing. *The fact that he he's grown into a very attractive man is an added bonus*, she said to herself. 'Tidy yourself up, then,' she ordered. 'I'll go in there and get us some sandwiches and water. See you up by the café when you're ready. And brush your hair, will you?'

Aiden smoothed his hair. 'You haven't changed a bit, Jazz. Still the cheeky girl you were back then.'

She laughed. 'Oh, I've grown up in ways you might not realise.'

'I dread to think what those ways are,' Aiden said. She knew he was only teasing her but something flashed in his eyes, gone before she could figure out what it was. 'See you in a few minutes,' he said and walked back down the beach.

Jasmine returned to the path and walked the rest of the way to the old cottage. She could see that it had been turned into a café, serving both coffee and cake, by the look of the menu, and something more substantial for lunch. She stepped into the bright interior, where the smell of coffee and newly baked bread made her feel hungry again. Apart from two women at a table near the window and a man with a small boy, the place was nearly empty. A smiley woman with red hair looked at Jasmine as she approached.

'Hello. What can I get you this fine morning?' she asked.

Jasmine eyed the display. 'I was hoping to get some sandwiches,' she said. 'Do you make them to order?'

The woman nodded. 'Yes, my partner makes them up in the kitchen.' The woman peered at her with curiosity. 'Haven't seen you around. Have you just arrived?'

Jasmine nodded and held out her hand. 'Yes. I'm Jasmine Delon, Sally O'Rourke's daughter.'

'Sally's daughter, eh?' The woman shook her hand. 'Hi there, Jasmine. I'm Mary O'Rourke. Same name, different branch of the old clan. You don't look a bit like your mum. I suppose you take after your dad?'

'So they tell me. He's French.'

'And you live in Paris, I heard.'

'I did. Until now,' Jasmine said without thinking.

'So you've moved here, then?' Mary asked.

'Oh, no,' Jasmine replied, startled by the very idea. 'But I'm staying with my mam a bit anyway. It's a break from work. Like a sabbatical,' she added, feeling this was the best way to explain why she was there, even if it wasn't quite true.

'Ah sure, it's a lovely place up there on the hill.'

'That's true.'

'So, sandwiches, you said,' Mary continued. 'What would you like? We can do chicken with stuffing, or ham and cheese with pickles, or a tuna wrap, or…' She paused. 'We even have what Mary B calls a "yoga sandwich" for the health freaks that have taken up the new lifestyle. Grated raw vegetables on sourdough bread with a soya cream dressing, if that takes your fancy.'

Jasmine made a face. 'Oh, uh, no. I'll have one chicken and stuffing sandwich, and one with ham and cheese with pickles, please. I'm going for a long walk with a friend, you see.'

'Lovely day for it.' Mary opened the door behind her. 'Sandwiches on order, Mary,' she shouted. 'One chicken and stuffing, one ham and cheese with pickles.'

'Okay,' a voice shouted back. 'I'll get on it right away.'

'She'll have them ready in a tick,' Mary said. 'That's the other Mary, by the way. My cousin. We run this place together.'

'So my mother said,' Jasmine replied with a smile. 'I love the idea of running a café with a cousin. Does it get confusing having the same name?'

'We don't get confused, but the customers do sometimes,' Mary replied. 'But I'm Mary O and she's Mary B, so that helps. Anyway, the sandwiches shouldn't take long. Would you like a coffee while you wait? And maybe some of our walnut and carrot cake? On the house as you're Sally's daughter.'

'Yes, please,' Jasmine said, suddenly hungry again. She sat up on one of the high stools by the counter, looking on while Mary busied herself with the coffee machine. 'So what about this new lifestyle that's getting so popular around here?' she asked. 'Are you one of the fans?'

Mary snorted as the coffee machine hissed. 'It's not for me at all. I do a bit of line dancing at the Harbour pub on Friday nights, but that yoga is beyond me. Tying myself in knots isn't really my thing. And all that breathing and chanting, what's that all about?

You can hear them from yer man's yoga studio at the other end of the village every morning. A terrible racket it makes, enough to scare the sheep up on the hills. But a lot of the women around here love it. They say it's changed their lives and it has made them feel good about themselves. And all that raw stuff Kamal says you should eat would make me all windy and bloated.' Mary paused for a moment and smiled suddenly. 'I have to say that yer man with the long hair is a sight for sore eyes all the same. He's glammed up the village no end.'

'Really?' Jasmine said. 'I haven't met him yet.'

'I'm sure it won't take long before you do.' Mary placed a cup of coffee on the counter. 'There you go. Carrot cake coming up.'

'Thank you,' Jasmine said and added sugar and a dash of milk from the jug on the counter. 'We're going to take the trail around the headland ' she said. 'Are there any other walks from there?'

'Well,' Mary said as she cut a slice of carrot cake and put it on a plate. 'You could go up the mountain from there or take the path from the ruins of the old village. Lovely views over Wild Rose Bay. But it's a bit tricky if you're not used to hiking.'

'Wild Rose Bay?' Jasmine asked. 'I've never heard of that.'

'It's a bit out of the way, I suppose,' Mary remarked. 'And kind of forgotten these days.' She put the plate in front of Jasmine. 'And the bay is no more than a cove, really. But it's beautiful in the summer with the Kerry roses in full bloom. Those ruined houses are where the old village used to be. Well,' she added, 'it wasn't a village as such. More like a hamlet. Just a few cottages grouped together before the bigger houses in Sandy Cove were built. There isn't much left of the houses now, just a few piles of stones. But in the old days, it was very lively I've heard. Lots of things going on,' she said with a wink.

'Like what?'

Mary shrugged. 'Oh, you know. Things that nobody talked about. They all pretended to be sheep farmers and fishermen, behaving themselves and pulling their forelocks to the lords that ruled here then. But they were laughing behind their backs and making a little bit of extra cash on the side.'

'Doing what?'

Mary shrugged. 'Oh, this and that. Things that weren't quite legal in those days.'

'When was this?' Jasmine asked, so intrigued she forgot to eat her carrot cake.

'Hundreds of years ago,' Mary replied. 'The houses and the people are long gone, but the legends live on. I don't know much more than that. We don't talk about it much. We don't want people going down there looking for treasure or something. Wild Rose Bay must stay the way it's always been: wild and forgotten.'

'Oh,' Jasmine said, wondering if Mary was having her on. 'But I'd love to go and have a look.'

'Nothing much to see,' Mary remarked. 'Only a few piles of rocks. And the path is treacherous.'

'That's what my mother said.'

'Maybe you'd better stick to the trail up the mountain,' Mary said as the door opened. 'Here's your friend now, I think.'

Jasmine turned and smiled at Aiden. 'Hi there. I ordered sandwiches for us both. Ham, cheese and pickles for you. That's what you used to order in the school canteen, if I remember right.'

'Spot on,' Aiden replied, walking to the counter. 'And hold the pickles for yours?'

Jasmine laughed. 'Yes, of course. I'm impressed that you remember I'm not too fond of anything pickled. I ordered chicken as I prefer that to the tuna or cheese.'

Her phone pinged in her pocket, giving her a start. He glanced at it. A message from Monique, her friend from work in Paris. *He's been asking about you*, the message said. Jasmine froze for a moment, suddenly transported back to the bank, the city and – him. She pulled herself together and turned her phone to silent.

'You okay?' Aiden asked. 'You look a little pale suddenly.'

'I'm fine,' Jasmine replied. She pushed the plate with the cake towards him. 'Do you want some carrot cake? I thought I wanted it but I don't feel like it any more.'

'Sure,' Aiden said and stuffed some of the cake into his mouth.

Mary put a steaming cup of coffee in front of him. 'Coffee to go with that, Aiden?'

'Thanks,' he mumbled through his mouthful. 'Put it on my bill, will ya, Mary?'

'Of course. How's the cake?'

'Terrific,' Aiden said and wiped his mouth. 'Very moist and crunchy at the same time. Love the walnutty taste. Have you considered that idea I floated with you?'

'About the chocolate cake?' Mary looked thoughtful. 'Yes. I think we'd like to accept your offer and deliver it to you whenever you need it. It can be frozen with the sauce without ruining it. We tested it yesterday. But I can get you a sample if you like.'

'That'd be terrific,' Aiden said as he devoured the rest of the cake. 'I'll be in touch about that later today.'

'Grand.' Mary nodded. 'I'll get you the sandwiches so you can get going.'

When they had put away their sandwiches and paid, Aiden and Jasmine walked out of the café and took the path at the side of it, following it to the edge of the cliff on the other side of the beach. Jasmine looked at the narrow trail following the cliff face as far as she could see. 'It's a bit steep,' she remarked.

Aiden nodded. 'Yeah, but it's quite safe. The path is paved in most places – I think it was used to connect the main village with the old road to Killarney. Imagine going along on horseback or with donkeys and carts on that narrow track.'

'Amazing,' Jasmine mumbled as she looked along the path. She could see that parts of it were raised and had been secured with paving stones. 'I'm trying to imagine how hard they worked to make this path.'

'All by hand, too,' Aiden filled in. 'Must have taken them ages.' He gave Jasmine a little push. 'Come on, you chicken, let's do it.'

'Okay.' Jasmine started walking, tentatively at first, but then increased her speed as she felt how solid the path was under her feet. The paving stones had been laid in such a way that the path was slightly raised above the grass, which made it feel more secure. On she walked, glancing down over the sheer drop to the undulating blue-green waves hundreds of feet below her. It was hair-raising in parts but also exhilarating with the wind in her hair and the smell of the sea in her nostrils. She looked up at the sky and took a deep breath of the fresh air. There seemed to be more oxygen here, and something else that felt intoxicating. She turned to Aiden walking behind her. 'What is it?' she asked. 'This thing here that makes me feel so energetic?'

'Something to do with negative ions, I've heard. But I think it's more the amazing views, the clean air and the beautiful light on the green slopes and the deep blue of the ocean. It's all so exhilarating to me.'

'Oh, yes,' Jasmine agreed, looking up at the blue sky. 'Well, whatever it is, I love it.'

'I can see that,' Aiden said, grinning.

Jasmine turned back and concentrated on the path that now wound itself around a bend, where it continued up the mountain-side, joining a track that ran along a stone fence nearly all the way up to the top of the mountain above them. She could see white dots all over the steep slopes. 'What are those?' she asked Aiden, pointing up.

'Sheep,' he replied. 'Don't ask me how they manage to get up there.'

'Sheep? Oh, God, they must have glue on their feet.'

'Or maybe Velcro?' Aiden suggested. He wiped his forehead with the back of his hand. 'How about we stop for lunch? We've been going for over an hour.'

'I just want to go a little bit further,' Jasmine said and pointed to where there was a group of boulders. 'We can sit there and eat. Looks quite sheltered from the wind and we'll have a great view of the ocean and the islands.'

'Good idea,' Aiden agreed. 'I've never come this far. I usually turn back at that tree stump behind us. Great place to sit and think.'

Jasmine glanced at the place they had just passed, where a tree stump provided a seat for one. 'I can imagine. But I don't want to think, I want to explore.'

'Explore what?'

'Wild Rose Bay,' Jasmine replied. 'I have a feeling it's a fascinating place.'

'I have a feeling it could have been a gruesome place,' Aiden said darkly. 'Mayhem and murder, I've heard.'

'From whom?'

'Mad Brendan. But he had had a few at the time so he might have embroidered his tale a little. In any case, Wild Rose Bay is not widely known. I only heard about it by accident that time when Mad Brendan was sitting beside me one evening last summer at the Harbour pub. We were both more than a little sloshed at the time. It's a miracle I remember what we were talking about. I'm sure he can't remember anything. I had to lead him up the lane to his house and help him get inside.' Aiden laughed and shook his head. 'The donkeys were running around making an awful racket. He had forgotten to feed them and lock them up. So I had to do that, too, which wasn't easy considering the state I was in myself.'

Jasmine laughed. 'I'd love to meet Brendan. He sounds like a great character.'

'That he is,' Aiden agreed as they reached the boulders. 'Let's sit down here. I'm shagged.'

'What?' Jasmine asked, startled.

'Tired in oirish,' Aiden said and ruffled her hair. 'Not what it means in English-English, so don't look so shocked.'

'Oh.' Jasmine laughed and sat down on one of the boulders. 'You Irish have the weirdest expressions. I can't understand a thing sometimes.' She tried to smooth her hair but gave up. What did it matter anyway?

'Sure, aren't you Irish yourself, girl?' Aiden said as he sat down beside her. 'You just need to brush up on the lingo and you'll be grand.'

'Grand,' Jasmine said. 'I love that expression.' She looked away from him across the deep blue ocean, where she could see the outline of the Skellig Islands shimmering in the distance. 'They look so magical,' she murmured. 'Magical and mysterious. Like Never-Never Land.'

'"Second star to the right, then straight on till morning,"' Aiden quoted.

'Ohhh.' Jasmine sighed. 'I wish I could go there right now.'

Aiden leaned closer to her. 'But you are, dear girl, you are. This is the closest you will ever get.'

'You think?' Jasmine looked at him and felt a surge of affection for this sweet man who had been her friend when she'd needed one the most and was here again as if by magic. She felt her phone vibrate in her pocket and fished it out, looking at the message, gasping as she saw the name on the screen. *No*, she thought, *not him, not now, not ever.* The spell was broken and she was suddenly gripped with fear.

'What's the matter?' Aiden asked. 'You've gone that funny colour again.'

'I…' she started, still looking at the screen. 'It's… Oh, God.' Then as if driven by an inner force, she pulled back her arm and threw the phone away from her with all her might, making it fly in the air, bounce against the cliff and then disappear over it down into the water hundreds of feet below. 'There,' she said with satisfaction. 'All gone. No more frights. No more calls or messages.'

Aiden stared at her. 'Are you mad? You threw away that expensive phone, just like that?'

'Yeah,' Jasmine said defiantly. 'Just like that. And oh, God, it feels fantastic.'

'But… I mean… Your phone?' Aiden asked, sounding horrified. 'How will you call people now? How will they call you? How will you manage?'

Suddenly ravenous, Jasmine took her sandwich from her backpack, undid the wrapper and took a huge bite. 'I'll manage very well. It's possible to survive without a phone, you know. It's not life-threatening at all. It's liberating and cleansing.'

'Not for me. I couldn't do without mine. I don't know many who could.'

'I probably won't either,' Jasmine said, sobering up after her attack of rage. 'I'll get one of those old-fashioned button phones tomorrow. New number, new SIM card and a whole new me.' She looked at Aiden defiantly. '*He* won't know anything about it.'

'He, who?'

Jasmine looked down at her sandwich. 'Nobody. Just someone I never want to see again.' She took another bite of the sandwich. 'Gosh, those Marys do great sandwiches.'

Aiden looked at her strangely and opened his mouth as if to speak, but then seemed to change his mind and attacked his own sandwich with gusto and nodded as he ate. 'They sure do. They're the sandwich queens.'

'The Queen Marys,' Jasmine said with a giggle, grateful he hadn't asked any awkward questions. It wasn't really funny, but her giggle turned to laughter and when she had finished, she sighed and looked up at the sky. '*Magnifique*,' she said and put her hand on Aiden's knee. 'I can't believe I'm here with you. It's like a dream.'

He smiled at her. 'I couldn't believe it when you walked into my restaurant yesterday. Why didn't I know you were Sally's daughter? How stupid. I knew she had lived in Paris and that she had a daughter who lived in France. She has mentioned you a few times but I never put two and two together. Probably because Sally never said your name.'

'Yes.' Jasmine looked back at him and knew she could trust him. But his words had given her a jolt. 'My mother really never mentioned my name? That makes me feel really good.'

His face fell. 'I didn't mean to upset you, I just wanted to explain why I had no idea Sally was your mother. I didn't know you two were having problems.'

'We're not having problems,' Jasmine replied, her voice cold.

'No, of course not,' he said, sounding annoyed. 'I just made a stray remark. I'm sorry if I upset you.'

'Never mind,' Jasmine said, feeling a little guilty at having snapped at him. It wasn't his fault, and he was right that she and her mother had issues that needed to be sorted out. 'Let's not talk about it any more.'

'Fine by me,' Aiden replied and touched her shoulder reassuringly. 'No need to talk about stuff like that at all. Let's just go with the flow.'

'The flow,' Jasmine repeated. 'Oh yes. Let's go with that.' She drank some water, stuffed the sandwich wrappings and the bottle into her rucksack and got up. 'Let's get going, okay?'

'Up the mountain?' Aiden asked.

'No.' Relieved he had cheered up, Jasmine pointed down the steep slope ahead of them. 'Down there. I can see that there is a lot of heather and bushes, but I want to see if I can find where the houses were. If we go a bit further we might see Wild Rose Bay. It's a tiny bay, Mary said, more like a cove.'

Aiden put his bottle into his pocket and got up. 'That sounds interesting. But we have to be careful. The path is very rough and it's steep.'

'I'll go slowly,' Jasmine said and started down the rough track.

It soon became nearly invisible because of the thick heather that grew there. She had to feel with her foot before she took a step forward and stumbled over stones and down potholes while holding on to the branches of the bushes as she slowly made her way down the slope. She stopped for a moment to catch her breath and looked up at Aiden stepping carefully, walking sideways as the path dropped steeply at one point. 'How are you doing?' she called.

'Fine,' he replied. 'It's a bit rough here and there. Don't look down whatever you do.'

But Jasmine couldn't help herself. She looked down the slope to where the path stopped at a natural platform with something that looked like piles of rocks. *Must be the remains of the ruins*, she realised, her heart beating faster. She was so excited she walked too fast and started to slide down the muddy track, shouting as she tried to grab onto heather plants. She came to a sudden stop as her bottom hit one of the rocks and she was able to scramble to her feet, rubbing her behind. 'Ouch,' she groaned.

Aiden had managed to get down the slope without falling and soon stood beside her. 'Are you okay?' he asked.

'Apart from a very sore derrière, I think I'm fine. Nothing damaged except my dignity.'

'Ah sure, then you're grand,' Aiden said and brushed her back with his hand. 'A bit of mud on your anorak, but that'll come off when it's dry..'

'Thanks.' Jasmine straightened her clothes and gave her jeans a brush, but stopped as she caught sight of the view. From here, she could see the lower slopes covered in emerald green grass that ended in a half-moon-shaped beach where the waves lapped gently over white sand. 'Look,' she exclaimed, pointing down. 'The bay. Isn't it beautiful?'

Aiden looked and took a deep breath. 'Wow! It's stunning. How come I've never been here before? How come nobody told me about it?'

'I suppose not that many people would want to venture down this way,' Jasmine suggested. 'The path is not easy to find, and if they did they wouldn't think to go down here. You don't see the bay or the beach until you're at this spot.'

'That's true,' Aiden said, looking down at the beautiful sight. 'But gee, this is truly awesome.' He wiped his forehead with the sleeve of his shirt, glancing at the pile of rocks beside them. 'Hey, this looks like the ruins you were talking about. See how the rocks go in a line and then end over there?'

Jasmine squinted in the sunlight. 'Yes, and then there is another pile and a slab that could have been the base of a fireplace. And look,' she continued, pointing ahead. 'There's part of a stone fence just at the edge of the plateau. Must have been the fence that ran around the houses to protect them from the winds. But it's overgrown with brambles and thorny bushes. This is where the wild roses bloom, don't you think?'

'Looks like it,' Aiden agreed. 'It'll be fantastic to see it in the summer.'

Jasmine walked over to the fence and looked over it down the slope to the beautiful bay. 'It's such a steep slope. I can't imagine anyone walking down to there. But I can see a faint outline of a path. They wouldn't have moored their boats down there, would they?'

Aiden looked down. 'The path is nearly perpendicular. They can't possibly have walked there from here.' He looked up at the hill opposite the bay. 'But look,' he continued, pointing, 'there are paths there, too. And something that looks like it could have been a small tower. Maybe that's where they lit a fire to lure ships into the bay. They would have crashed onto the rocks at the entrance.'

'You mean they were shipwreckers?' Jasmine asked with shiver of excitement.

'Oh yeah, and smugglers. This bay would have been perfect for that. Hidden away, not accessible for anyone with a faint heart. I'd say this was a well-kept secret in those days.'

'What days?' Jasmine asked, unable to tear her eyes away from the ruined tower at the other side.

'Early eighteen hundreds or so,' Aiden replied. 'I'm not a historian so I can't tell you exactly, but I think there was a lot of stuff like that going on in these parts. The locals would have been a cagey lot, that's for sure.'

'Oh, God, this is so exciting,' Jasmine exclaimed. 'I want to go down there and look for buried treasure, or at least bits of old ships or—'

Aiden laughed. 'There would be nothing like that left. It was over two hundred years ago. Besides, today the slope will be muddy and wet after all the rain we got a few days ago. It'd be foolish to go down there now.'

'I suppose,' Jasmine said with a dart of disappointment. 'But the next day it's dry, I'll be down there.'

'Not by yourself,' Aiden said sternly. 'We could get walking sticks and do it together.'

'You're such a chicken,' Jasmine teased. 'It doesn't look that steep.'

'I think it's more dangerous than it looks. Promise you won't come here on your own, okay?'

'I promise,' Jasmine said, touched by his concern. And he was probably right. It would be foolish to go down that steep slope alone. 'Funny,' she said as if to herself. 'My mother didn't say anything about the stuff you were talking about. She just said this part of the village had bad vibes or something.'

'Vibes?' Aiden looked around. 'I feel something melancholic here, but that's just the abandoned houses.'

'Yes,' Jasmine agreed. 'There is always this sad whisper in the air at places like this. But that's all. I'd love to find out more, though. Maybe I could ask that old man – Mad Brendan? Didn't you say he knows a lot of stuff about the history of this village?'

'Yes,' Aiden replied. 'His folks have lived here since time began.'

'Where do I find him?'

'Easy. He usually sits on a bench outside the old thatched cottage on the road to Ballinskelligs. Sometimes he has a donkey beside him. It's all for the tourists. They love taking photographs and then they pay him for posing with the donkeys. Grey beard, flat cap,

Aran sweater, the whole auld Ireland shebang. He must have made a fortune by now. He also plays the fiddle in the Harbour pub on Saturday nights. Great character and as crafty as they come.'

Jasmine laughed. 'Oh, God, I don't believe it. Are you pulling my leg?'

'Not at all, I swear. You'll know what I mean when you see him.'

'I'm looking forward to meeting him.'

'You'll love him.' Aiden checked his watch. 'It's getting late. I have to get back. The restaurant isn't open tonight as it's Monday, but I have to do the accounts and meet the owner, who's arriving this evening. He lives in Cork, but we meet once a week to take stock of how the business is going.'

'How is it going?' she asked, cautiously.

'Great so far. And now we're looking at the new season and trying to look into the future, so to speak. I have a feeling Easter will be busy and that'll be the start of the season. Nuala at the Harbour pub tells me that's the way it works around here these days.' Aiden zipped up his jacket and started back up the slope. 'Let's get going. I'm sure you have stuff to do as you haven't been here more than a day.'

'Oh yes. I haven't even unpacked yet.'

Jasmine started walking behind him, holding on to boulders and heather plants as she went, only now realising how steep and dangerous the path was. When they had reached the crest, she looked down at the grassy platform and the piles of rocks that had once been the houses of the people who had lived there so long ago. Further down, the water of the tiny bay glittered in the sunlight and she felt she had found something special, something that would help her forget what had happened to her. She vowed to come back if only just to sit on a rock and look at the pretty bay for a while. There was something there that spoke to her in a way she couldn't explain.

Chapter Six

The main street was busy when Jasmine walked back to Sally's cottage. Lots of people were wandering along, walking into shops, greeting each other and chatting animatedly, and smiling at Jasmine, even though they didn't know who she was. She stopped at Sally's shop at the end of the street and peered inside, wondering if she was still there. But there was no sign of her. A tall pretty woman with short dark hair was wrapping a parcel for two customers. She looked up from her task and smiled at Jasmine. 'I'll be with you in a second,' she said as she handed the women their parcel and took the payment. Jasmine waited while the purchase was finalised and the women left to cheery goodbyes and thank yous.

The young woman turned to Jasmine. 'Hi. Welcome to our shop. How can I help you?'

'Oh, I'm not going to buy anything,' Jasmine replied, smiling. 'I was looking for my mother.'

The woman laughed. 'You must be Jasmine.' She held out her hand. 'Hi, I'm Cordelia, your mother's business partner.'

Jasmine smiled back, liking Cordelia instantly. Even her voice, with the soft American accent, was charming. They shook hands and Jasmine stepped further into the shop, looking around at the array of items for sale that were scattered on little tables and shelves. There were silk scarves, earrings and necklaces, candlesticks, ceramic bowls, books with beautiful covers, silver frames, antique ornaments, small framed watercolours and lots of other items that would make lovely gifts for tourists to take home. A lot of the things had been made with a Celtic touch, Jasmine noticed.

'Mostly handmade by local artists,' Cordelia remarked as Jasmine picked up a small wooden bowl. 'That one is made of yew.'

Jasmine ran her finger over the smooth surface. 'Beautiful. What a gorgeous shop.'

'Sally's baby, really.' Cordelia laughed. 'I mean, you're her real baby, of course. But this is her creation. Except I might have given her a few ideas.'

'I'm sure you did.' Jasmine looked on as Cordelia straightened the array on one of the shelves. 'This lovely selection is typical of my mother. She has such an eye for unusual things. But you would have inspired her to get started.'

Cordelia shrugged. 'Oh, I wouldn't say *inspired*. I just told her about this little shop in the States that my mother and I used to love browsing in. Sally liked the whole concept so she adapted it to here. She's great at picking up quirky little things in markets all over the place and I'm sure I don't have to tell you how great she is at haggling for a good price.'

Jasmine had to laugh. 'Yes, I know. I've cringed many a time in shops while she tried to get the price down on even the most expensive haute couture item. And to my surprise, she usually got a few euros knocked off the regular price. Sometimes she even managed to get them down by ten per cent.' Jasmine shook her head as she remembered the feeling of embarrassment shopping with her mother when she was a teenager.

'It's amazing to watch her,' Cordelia said. 'I wouldn't have the nerve, but she does it like a pro.'

'She *is* a pro,' Jasmine filled in. 'I wish she'd been with me when we bought the apartment in Paris.'

Cordelia looked impressed. 'You have an apartment in Paris?'

'Not any more,' Jasmine said, regretting letting it slip out.

'Oh.' Cordelia looked at her with sympathy in her bright blue eyes. 'I see. Sorry about that. Breaking up is hard, isn't it?'

'Yes.' Jasmine met Cordelia's kind eyes, wondering how she knew and wishing suddenly she could tell her everything. She looked like someone who'd listen and not judge or gossip. But they had only met a nanosecond ago, so that kind of conversation was impossible. 'So,' she breezed on. 'Have you lived here long?'

'Two years,' Cordelia said. 'I'm from America, as you might gather from my accent.'

'Yes. New York?'

'No, New Jersey.'

'And how come you landed here?'

'Long story,' Cordelia said with a laugh. 'And that's the understatement of the year. I came here because of family connections. It was a kind of a miracle, really. And then I fell in love. First with the village and then with a wonderful man. We're still together, which is another miracle.'

'Lucky you,' Jasmine said with a dart of envy. Cordelia looked so happy and grounded, like someone who had truly found her place in life.

'Yes,' Cordelia said with a happy sigh. 'I'm very lucky.' She looked at Jasmine across the counter. 'I'll be closing the shop soon. Would you like to meet me for a drink sometime when you're settled?'

Jasmine nodded. 'That'd be great. But I'd better get home. Mam will be wondering where I got to. And I have to take Milou for a walk.'

'He's a gorgeous dog,' Cordelia said. 'He sat by Sally's side the whole time she was here. Seems like they've made great friends.'

'I think she's started spoiling him already. He's such a little flirt.'

Jasmine walked to the door and stopped, looking at Cordelia, feeling she would get an honest answer to the question she had been dying to ask. Cordelia was a stranger to her, but her mother's close friend despite the age difference. And she was roughly the same age as Jasmine, which could bridge the gap between mother and daughter.

'What about this yoga guy? Are you one of his followers, too?'

Cordelia let out a sound halfway between a laugh and a snort. 'Followers? You make it sound as if he's some kind of cult figure. Kamal is a yoga teacher and a very good one, too. I go to the classes because they make me feel relaxed and at peace with myself. But I find his diets and other lifestyle ideas a bit extreme, to be honest. Raw food? Nah. Give me a good hamburger or a slice of pizza and I'm happy. I like a glass of wine or two as well from time to time. I don't believe in extremes in food, or life. A little bit of everything is better for you, I think.'

Jasmine grinned. 'Me, too. But my mother seems to believe this Kamal guy is some kind of saviour.'

Cordelia looked thoughtfully at Jasmine. 'I have a feeling you're right. It worries me a bit. She seems so swept up in it all. But I think it's because she's having a hard time.'

'With what?'

'It's not my place to say,' Cordelia said. She started to sort a pile of scarves on the counter. 'She's not my mom, just a very dear friend.'

'Did you mean to say she has problems with me? With our relationship?' Jasmine asked, feeling guilty. 'Please tell me, I won't be offended.'

Cordelia nodded. 'Yes. I think that's one of her issues. But there are other things, too. One of them is about her age. She's dreading turning sixty.'

'Oh, but I thought…' Jasmine paused. 'She is always saying she doesn't care and that age is just a number. Is that just bravado, do you think?'

'Yes, I think she says it to convince herself. But deep down she is terrified of old age. Of growing old alone.'

'But she's not alone,' Jasmine protested. 'She has me.'

Cordelia looked doubtful. 'Does she?'

'Yes, of course she does. And I'll make sure she knows it,' Jasmine said, feeling that this was something she hadn't thought about – her mother's fear of growing old.

Cordelia nodded. 'I'm glad you're here. Sally needs you. She's facing a very tricky milestone in her life. That's why Kamal has been such a lifeline to her.'

'I see. That's why she's a little absentminded, I suppose,' Jasmine suggested. She began to understand that Sally's new lifestyle was her way of distracting herself. 'The yoga and new diet and everything that goes with it must be quite seductive,' she said. 'Especially taught by someone who seems so – charismatic.'

'I think so. You'll see when you meet him. He is very…' Cordelia paused, looking for the right word. 'Powerful,' she ended.

'I see,' Jasmine said, even though she didn't understand a thing. So many questions hovered on her lips, but she didn't feel she could voice them. But right now she needed to get back to the cottage and sort out her things. She hadn't really settled in yet, but so much had happened since she arrived – she had only been looking for a safe haven and a shoulder to cry on, but things in Sandy Cove were more complicated than she realised.

'Come to yoga this evening,' Cordelia suggested. 'Then you'll meet Kamal and you'll see what he's like. And,' she added with a smile, 'it'll make you feel better.'

'That's a good idea,' Jasmine said. 'I can't wait to meet this man.' She opened the door. 'Bye for now. See you this evening.'

She walked away from the shop, her mind full of what Cordelia had said. Her mother was clearly going through some kind of crisis, but how could Jasmine help when she was trying to cope with a massive crisis of her own?

Chapter Seven

Sally was sitting on the front step with Milou beside her when Jasmine arrived. 'Oh, thank God, you're here!' she exclaimed and flung herself at Jasmine, wrapping her arms around her. Milou barked and tried to jump up on them both while Sally laughed and cried at the same time.

'I'm fine, Mam.' Jasmine pulled away from her mother's frantic embrace. 'Were you worried?'

'Of course I was,' Sally chided. 'You went for a walk hours ago. It's nearly five o'clock and it's getting dark. I tried to phone you but there was no answer. And then I called the two Marys and one of them said you had gone off walking with Aiden but that he had come back and had loaded his windsurfing board on his car but there was no sign of you. Then I phoned him and he said you had lost your phone and would be home soon, but you weren't. Where have you been all this time?'

'I stopped at your shop on the way back and started chatting with Cordelia. I suppose I lost track of time. Sorry,' she added, feeling like a five-year-old. 'I should have phoned you.'

'But you lost your phone?' Sally said. 'What happened?'

'It, uh, fell over the edge of the cliff,' Jasmine replied.

Sally looked puzzled. 'How is that possible? Did you try to answer a call when you were walking?'

'Something like that.' Jasmine gathered Milou into her arms. 'Come on, let's go inside. It's getting cold.'

'And we need to talk,' Sally declared. 'Really talk, I mean.'

They went inside, where – to Jasmine's delight – Sally had lit a fire and there was that smell of woodsmoke she remembered from her childhood, when her grandmother had lived here. The curtains were drawn against the darkening skies and the lamps were lit, casting a warm glow on the wool rug and the polished wooden floor. The only thing missing was the smell of Irish stew, but she supposed that would be too much to expect.

'I'll make some tea and toast some of my sourdough bread,' Sally said behind Jasmine.

'Great.' Jasmine put Milou on the floor and watched as he trotted to the sheepskin on the floor in front of the fire and lay down with a contented little sigh. 'He's happy there,' she remarked. 'I'll go and change while you make the tea and toast.'

'Do you have anything to change into?' Sally asked. 'You didn't pack a lot into that tiny suitcase, did you?'

'Not much,' Jasmine confessed.

'I'll get you some leggings and a T-shirt,' Sally offered. 'Will you come with me to yoga later?'

'I thought I'd give it a go,' Jasmine said. Seeing her mother so worried, she realised just how stupid she was to have thrown her phone away, but she had felt so cornered and fed up at that moment. She realised that there was someone else who might want to contact her, who could help her, but maybe she could send them an email.

When Sally had handed her a pair of black leggings and a pink T-shirt with the Eiffel Tower picked out in glitter on the front, Jasmine rolled her eyes, but she went into her room and put them on. She glanced down at the front of the T-shirt, thinking that her mother's new look was a great improvement on this kind of outfit. Sally's choice of clothing before had been eccentric and over-the-top, with all kinds of cast-offs from the fashion houses she worked for. She had worn them with a flamboyance that suited her personality, but they would have been a disaster on anyone else. *Especially on me*, Jasmine thought as she caught sight of herself in the tall mirror beside the door. Even though she and her mother had the same shape and height, they didn't share the same taste in clothes. Jasmine had been taught French chic by her grandmother in Paris and by now it was tattooed into her soul. But as she looked at her pink cheeks, her Parisian hairdo ruffled by the wind, her designer trainers covered in mud and the glittering Eiffel Tower on her chest, she couldn't help letting out a chuckle. What would Mamie Clotilde say if she saw her now? She'd say that Jasmine was turning just as wild and Irish as her mother. Mamie Clotilde, being from an aristocratic French family, had never approved of Sally, and Jasmine had realised as she grew older that it had been part of what had broken up her parents' marriage.

Jasmine sighed and turned away from the mirror. Well, Mamie Clotilde was dead, her father, Matthieu, was all alone and miserable in his big apartment in Paris and Sally was living in her mother's old cottage and was looking for solace through yoga and raw food. And their daughter? Where was she? All lost and confused after having been betrayed by someone she thought loved her. Three people who had once been a happy family, now all damaged and lost, trying to cope with their sad situations. Could they ever come together again and heal what had been broken?

Jasmine took her laptop from the bag, sat down on the bed and turned it on. She knew there would be emails she didn't want to see, but she wouldn't open those. She'd just send a quick message to her one and only confidant, who she knew she could trust. Once her emails came up, she skimmed through the list in her inbox. There were eight messages from an address that made her shiver. Having deleted them, she quickly opened the compose page and started to type, writing in French.

> *Cher ami, she wrote, I arrived safely yesterday. Sally was happy to see me and it was lovely to be here after all the drama in Paris. But there have been some drastic changes in her life which worry me.*
>
> *But despite all this, it's wonderful to be here. Spring has arrived and the sea air is truly intoxicating. Milou loves it, too, and Sally has totally seduced him the way she does with most people and animals. I know you will be lonely now that I'm gone, but I had to leave. Have you thought about what we discussed last time we saw each other? Please consider what I suggested before I left!*
>
> *Love,*
>
> *Jasmine*

Jasmine pressed send and closed the email with a content little sigh. It felt good to send that email off. As she turned off the laptop and put it back in its bag, she heard a noise from the door and went to open it to Milou, who trotted inside and jumped up on the bed. 'Hey, are you allowed there?' she asked.

Milou wagged his tail and licked her hand.

Jasmine laughed and kissed him on the top of his head. 'I suppose you are, you big chancer. This is not a swish apartment in Paris, it's a cottage on the edge of the Atlantic coast. We don't have strict rules here for dogs, do we?'

Milou didn't seem to think so. He yawned and lay down on his side, closing his eyes.

Jasmine patted him and went out to the living room for that tea and sourdough bread. Her legs ached after all the walking and her mind was full of what had happened during her walk with Aiden. It had felt good to turn her mind to other things and she knew that coming here to the relative peace of this little village was the best remedy for her heartbreak. She sat down on the green velvet sofa, relaxing against the soft cushions, enjoying the warmth of the fire. She smiled at her mother when she came from the kitchen carrying a tray. 'What kind of tea did you make?'

'Green tea,' Sally replied, placing the tray on the antique coffee table in front of the sofa. 'It'll give you energy for the yoga practice. And I found a jar of my plum jam from last year, so I decided we could relax the rules a little and have some of it.'

'Lovely.' Jasmine took one of the mugs from the tray.

Sally joined her on the sofa and took the other mug, gazing at Jasmine over the rim. 'Yoga is not until seven.'

'Great,' Jasmine said. 'Then we have plenty of time to talk.' She looked sternly at her mother, trying to convey that she didn't intend to skirt the issue any longer.

'Okay.' As if to gain time, Sally sipped some tea and put the mug back on the table. She nibbled at the bread, looking as if she was savouring the taste of the plum jam. 'This is delicious, even if it's not quite part of the diet.'

'I'm glad you're taking a little break from it.' Jasmine took a slice of bread. 'I'll eat while you talk.'

Sally looked sternly at Jasmine. 'Me? I think you should start the talking. I thought we could pick up where we left off but you can't walk around as if your whole world has collapsed without explaining. You seem sad, Jasmine, different from before.'

'I know,' Jasmine muttered through her mouthful of bread and jam.

'You haven't been in touch for nearly a year,' Sally continued as if she hadn't heard. 'Except for a short text message here and there saying life is "great" and that you'll be in touch "soon" with "some amazing news". Is this why you're here?'

'I know,' Jasmine said again, guilt mixed with relief that her mother finally wanted to break the silence and really talk instead of being all forgiving and sweet. 'I know, I know, I know!' she all but shouted, staring at Sally. 'Please don't make me feel even more guilty than I already do. I know I should have called you and come to see you, I know it was terrible of me not to even ask how you were and what was going on in your life. But…'

'But what?' Sally asked. 'Tell me.'

Jasmine drank some more green tea, hoping it would give her a little courage. Then she put the mug on the table and faced her mother. 'But you were always hovering over me, like a big bird, calling me every day, fussing and worrying as if I was a teenager. I felt you didn't trust me to make my own decisions.'

'Oh,' Sally said, looking taken aback. 'I had no idea. I was worried about you, that's all. Being too much of a mother hen, I suppose.'

'Exactly. I was going to tell you when it was all decided. When I could give you the amazing news that I had not only been promoted at the bank, but also that I was getting married to this wonderful man and that I wanted you to come over to help me organise the wedding. It was going to be a huge big explosion of good news that would make you so happy. A big, big surprise, you know?'

'You were getting married?' Sally said, looking shell-shocked. 'To whom?'

'To a man called Damien de la Force.'

Sally gasped. 'Damien – de la Force? Of the famous de la Force family?'

'That's right.'

'And you didn't tell me?'

'I was going to. He had just presented me with the ring and we were going to buy a lovely apartment on Île Saint-Louis. I was planning to call you just after that.'

'Did your father know about this?' Sally asked with a sharp edge to her voice.

'No. I was going to tell you first. Nobody knew. Damien didn't want me to say anything until we had seen his family. That was his story, anyway,' Jasmine ended bitterly.

'But? Something happened?'

Jasmine clasped her hands in her lap. 'Yes. It all came crashing down like a house of cards. That was all it was, actually. A beautiful, Technicolor house of cards with glitter all over it.'

'Can you tell me what happened?' Sally asked, her voice softer.

Jasmine closed her eyes for a moment as Damien's handsome face flashed before her eyes. Oh, that face, those eyes, that lopsided smile… And the way he had looked at her, as if she was the most precious thing on earth. 'I'll try,' she whispered. 'But it's so painful, and I'm still so raw.'

Sally put her arm around Jasmine. 'I understand. But maybe it would be good to talk about it? To let it all out? I'll just listen and you tell me as much as you can.'

Jasmine leaned her head on her mother's shoulder. 'Okay,' she mumbled, tears stinging her eyes. 'I met Damien a year ago at a party at the Ritz in Paris. One of those corporate parties where you drink nothing but champagne and eat those little canapés from Fauchon, you know?'

'God, yes,' Sally said with feeling. 'Those things are lethal.'

'Irresistible,' Jasmine said with a dreamy smile. 'The shrimps you dip into that pink sauce, and little slices of smoked salmon with a dollop of sour cream with chives, and the tiny squares of paté with cornichons and—'

'Stop,' Sally said with a hint of laughter. 'You'll make me fall off the raw food wagon.'

Jasmine laughed through her tears. 'I was there for a while, nearly tasting all that food.' She sniffed and sat up. 'Anyway, that's where I met him. He was smiling at me across the room and I smiled back and before I knew it, he was there at my side, and then later, when was a little tipsy, we went out on the balcony and looked at the lights of Paris and talked. It was a cold night and he put the jacket of his suit around my shoulders.' Jasmine sighed as that night played in her mind like a film. 'We talked and talked and he was so fascinated by my job at the bank. Then when the party ended, we went to a little restaurant in the Latin Quarter for *steak frites* with Béarnaise sauce.'

'You're doing this on purpose,' Sally chided. 'I'm drooling here.'

'I knew you would,' Jasmine teased. 'I was only joking. I don't remember what we ate, to be honest. But anyway, we kept talking and then we kissed and then…'

'Then you went to bed with him?' Sally asked, sounding shocked.

'No. He walked me back to my apartment and asked me to have dinner with him every night the following week. So I did,' Jasmine said, the memory making her heart ache.

'What was he doing at the party? Is he in banking, too?' Sally asked.

'No. He just saw there was a party in the Ritz and went in and when he said his name, they didn't even check if he was on the list. That's how famous that family is. Only he isn't really one of them,' she ended. 'I mean, he is, but he's not one of the famous de la Forces, but I didn't know that at the time – or that he's addicted to gambling. I only found that out last week.' Jasmine suddenly burst into tears.

Sally hugged her and let her cry, making soothing noises. Jasmine kept crying, as the comfort of her mother's arms calmed her. It was such a relief to finally let out all her pain and sorrow after having held it in for over a week. The tears finally stopped coming and Jasmine pulled away. 'Have you got a tissue?' she asked in a near whisper.

'Of course.' Sally jumped up and went to her bedroom, appearing with a box of tissues seconds later. She handed the box to Jasmine. 'Here.'

Jasmine pulled a wad of tissues from the box and dried her eyes, blowing her nose noisily. 'Oh, God, I'm sorry, Mam. I'm sure I drenched your lovely kaftan.'

'That's okay. I'll be changing for yoga later anyway.' Sally sank down on the sofa and looked at Jasmine with concern. 'So what happened next? Can you tell me?'

Jasmine nodded. 'Of course I have to tell you.' She sighed and put the wad of tissues on the tray. 'I'll try not to cry like that again.'

'Go ahead if it helps.'

'I'm all cried out. And he doesn't deserve my tears.' Jasmine pulled herself together and looked back at her mother. 'I always wondered how women could possibly allow themselves to be conned by men like that, and then here I am having been conned big time. How stupid I was not to see through him.' She sighed. 'But he was so gorgeous, so perfect, I thought, and I was so in love.' She grabbed a tissue as the tears threatened to well up again. She blinked and cleared her throat.

'So, what happened? Lots of things. After three months of dating and, yes, sleeping together, he moved into my apartment. A bit small for two, but we managed. I loved having him there, with all his gorgeous clothes and the silk ties and all that he brought with him. We went to glamorous parties and we had so much fun. It wasn't easy to go to work every morning and sometimes stay late at the office, but it was as if being in love helped me cope with all that was going on in the bank. I didn't really know what he did all day. He said he was between jobs but would soon be working at his uncle's firm. They were property developers. He said he had a business degree from Harvard and his qualifications would be a great asset to the firm. I swallowed all of that. So I went to work at the bank and hadn't a clue what he did all day. I trusted him. And when he proposed and gave me this enormous diamond ring from Cartier, I thought I was the luckiest girl in the world. We started to plan our wedding and found the perfect apartment we had been saving up to buy. I had just been promoted at the bank, too, so it looked like my life was suddenly perfect. That's when I was planning to call you and go, "Tada! Look at your wonderful, successful daughter."'

'And then?' Sally asked, staring at Jasmine with big eyes.

'Then it all crumbled. Only last week, I found out that the money in our joint account was gone. He'd never paid his part of the rent and it took everything I had to get out of that debt,' Jasmine said, feeling her heart breaking all over again as the memory of the total bewilderment and hurt came hurtling back. 'And then, to end this tale of misery,' Jasmine continued, 'I called his family to ask if they knew where Damien was. His uncle told me that Damien had a gambling addiction and had been cut off by his family years ago. So then everything fell into place.'

'You realised the suits and shirts had been bought with his money from gambling?' Sally asked, having put two and two together all on her own.

'Yes. And my engagement ring. He must have been on a winning streak then. Before he lost it all and disappeared.'

'So why did you rush over here?'

Jasmine sighed and slumped back against the cushions in the sofa. 'I just wanted to take a break and go somewhere peaceful. I felt so ashamed. I didn't want anyone to look at me. So I decided to disappear for a while. I packed up my things and asked a friend to store them for me. I quit my job and came here,' she ended bleakly.

'Oh, sweetheart,' Sally said and hugged Jasmine. 'What a terrible thing to go through.'

'I feel so ashamed,' Jasmine whispered into Sally's shoulder. 'How could I have been taken in like that?'

'Oh, well, he sounds like he was irresistible. Handsome, charming, glamorous, sexy – and loving, yes?'

Jasmine nodded. 'He could have any woman he wanted, but he wanted *me*.'

'I can understand that you'd be swept away by all of that.'

'Oh I was. But it wasn't the money I thought he had, or the family connections, it was someone loving me and making me feel so special. And then I found out that it was all a lie and that he had been *pretending* to love me, lying to me every single day. It makes me feel like a total idiot.'

'Don't blame yourself, Jasmine,' Sally soothed. 'I'm sure he was good at pretending and would have fooled anyone.'

Jasmine nodded. 'That's for sure. He's very hard to resist. Like some kind of delicious sweet that you can't help tasting, even if you know it's laced with poison.'

'But you didn't know,' Sally argued. 'How could you? You have to stop thinking it was your fault. It wasn't. Not in any way.'

'Maybe.' Jasmine let out a deep, ragged sigh. 'I know you're right, Mam. But how can I trust a man ever again?'

Sally patted Jasmine's hand. 'I'm sure you will in time. But right now, you have to put it behind you and move on.'

'I'll try. But it'll take a long time.' Jasmine sat up and finished her tea. 'Oh, Mam,' she exclaimed, suddenly overcome with love for her mother. 'I'm so happy to be here with you.'

'I'm really happy you're here, too,' Sally said, looking at Jasmine with tears in her eyes. 'I'm so sorry you had to go through all of that. But now you just have to turn your mind away and try to heal from all the hurt.' She checked her watch and got up. 'I'll just get ready and then we should head off to yoga.' She paused. 'If you still feel like it, that is?'

Jasmine dried her eyes got to her feet. 'I think it would be good for me. And I can't wait to meet this Kamal.'

'You'll like him.' Sally gathered up the tea things and put them on the tray.

'I'll go and tidy myself up,' Jasmine said. 'Do you have something for me to wear that'd be better for yoga?'

Sally laughed. 'I suppose that T-shirt is a little OTT. It was a bit of a fashion mistake, I suppose. I'll get you a plain top.'

'Thanks, Mam.' Jasmine hovered at the door to her room. 'And thanks for – being there, for listening, and not judging.'

Sally smiled. 'How could I judge you? I'm your mother, and I'm not perfect either. Come on, shake a leg and let's go. Meeting Kamal will take you out of yourself.'

Jasmine stood there as Sally disappeared into the kitchen with the tray. She hadn't told her mother the real reason she had fled from Paris in such a hurry. Damien was trying to get in touch with her, saying he wanted her back. And even after all he'd done, she wasn't sure she could resist him if they met again.

Chapter Eight

The yoga studio had once been a cowshed attached to an old farmhouse, but nobody would believe any cow had ever been near it. It was a bright, airy room with large windows and skylights in the ceiling. The windows overlooked the ocean which could be heard as a faint whisper in the distance, but at seven o'clock it was too dark to see. The walls were painted white with a hint of pink and the room smelled of lavender from scented candles on a shelf in front of a small Buddha statue. Most of the yoga mats on the floor were occupied by women sitting cross-legged chatting softly to each other. Sally found two mats side by side and sat down on one of them, telling Jasmine to take the other one.

'He'll be here, soon,' she murmured. Jasmine sat down and crossed her legs awkwardly.

'Okay like this?'

'Perfect.' Sally turned to the woman on the mat beside Jasmine. 'Hi, Nuala. This is Jasmine, my daughter.'

The woman, who was tall with dark hair tied back in a ponytail, smiled broadly at Jasmine and grabbed her hand in a strong handshake. 'Hi. I'm Nuala. Used to be two stone heavier, but now I'm half the size I was before this yoga lark kicked in. Nice to meet ya, Jasmine. You're lovely, by the way. So French-looking and chic.'

'Hi, Nuala,' Jasmine replied with a grin. 'Nice to meet you. I've never done yoga before, so please don't look at me.'

'Sure, it'll be a breeze for a young thing like you,' Nuala replied. 'But shh…' she added as the door at the far side of the room opened. 'Here he is. No talking.' She sat up straighter, turned her hands up and placed them on her knees and closed her eyes. Then she opened one of them. 'How about a drink after the torture?'

Jasmine nodded. 'Would love to,' she whispered back.

Nuala winked and closed her eyes again as someone glided into the room.

Jasmine looked at the man who had just entered. He was tall and slim with dark shiny hair tied back in a ponytail. Dressed in yoga pants and a tight black vest, his body was clearly defined. Jasmine had never seen such a perfect body, or such a beautiful face on a man. He had dark, nearly black eyes and dazzling white teeth. She stared at him as he walked around the room, greeting the women, touching their shoulders or simply smiling at them. The atmosphere in the room had suddenly become still and calm and she could see the women visibly relax.

When Kamal reached them, Sally smiled at him and made a gesture towards Jasmine. 'My daughter,' she said.

Kamal smiled at Jasmine, crouched down beside her and took her hand in both of his. 'Jasmine,' he said in his husky voice. 'Welcome to yoga practice. I know you're new to this, but don't worry. You'll be fine. Just listen to your body and do what it tells you to do. If you feel yourself getting too tired, just go into child's pose and take a break.'

'Child's pose?' she asked, looking into the dark eyes.

'It's a pose where you lie on your knees with your bottom on your heels and stretch your arms in front of you. Like a child. Easy and relaxing.'

'Oh.' Jasmine felt the warmth of his hands soothe her and breathed in his warm, spicy scent. His touch, voice and the accent, halfway between Irish and Indian, were hypnotic. 'Thank you. I will,' she whispered.

'Good.' Kamal let go of her hand and rose gracefully. When he had dimmed the lights to a soft glow, he walked to a mat in front of the class, sank down into cross-legged position and closed his eyes. 'Thank you for coming to yoga today,' he said. 'Sit for a moment and let your mind drift away from all the stress and bad thoughts that might crowd it. Send them all away and replace them with peace and tranquillity…'

His words were followed by a long breathing session then by everyone humming for several minutes. Jasmine felt herself relax as she slowed her breathing. She fell in with the chants and felt all the stress of the past week floating away.

Then came the yoga practice, starting with turns and twists of the spine, which felt difficult but eventually wonderfully beneficial deep in her muscles. The rest of the practice was hard, but she listened to her body like Kamal had told her and only did half of what the other women managed to do. As she stood in her very first downward-facing dog pose, she glanced at her mother, amazed at her suppleness and grace. As the class progressed, yoga was no longer a series of stretches like she had thought, but a gruelling workout for every part of the body that required strength, flexibility and balance. She had felt stiff and clumsy at first, but finally quite proud of herself that she had managed at least some of the poses, even if she had collapsed into child's pose more times than anyone else in the class. By the time they all lay in the corpse pose, also known as shavasana, and she heard the tinkling of bells from the sound system and breathed in the scent of lavender, she felt her mind floating away like a cloud into the starlit sky she had glimpsed through the skylight before she closed her eyes.

The stress and worries about Damien, her job, her father and her life in Paris all disappeared and were replaced by the memory of the beautiful hidden bay she had seen earlier that day. The soft sand, the blue water, the green slopes... Wild Rose Bay was beckoning her, and she wanted to go back there and find its treasures and the secrets that had been hidden away for such a long time.

Jasmine slowly came back to reality and sat up, bowing like everyone else as Kamal said his 'namaste' and rose gracefully from the floor. She sat there in a daze as he disappeared through the door. Her whole body felt relaxed and her mind calm.

As the door closed behind him, Jasmine tried to figure out the relationship between Kamal and Sally. She wasn't sure if it was romantic, or a deeper spiritual connection. Kamal seemed to be able to read people, as if there was an extra dimension to him, some kind of intuition that gave him the ability to tap into people's feelings, the way he had just done with her. She had overheard stray comments here and there in the village this morning about them, but now she felt foolish for having listened.

'So how did you like it?' Sally asked as she helped Jasmine up.

'It was amazing,' Jasmine mumbled, still slightly dazed. '*He* is amazing, I mean.'

'Isn't he?' Sally said, beaming.

Jasmine looked around and spotted Cordelia at the other side of the room as she was getting up from her mat and putting on her jacket. 'Hi, Cordelia,' she called. 'See, I made it and I survived.'

Cordelia smiled and waved. 'Well done,' she said and joined them as they were leaving the hall.

'Who's coming for a drink?' Nuala asked behind them.

'But we haven't eaten yet,' Sally argued.

'I can feed you, too, if you like,' Nuala replied.

Sally shook her head. 'No, I need to get to bed early. But you go if you like, Jasmine.'

'I'll look after her,' Nuala promised. 'Are you coming, Cordelia?'

'Thanks, but Declan is waiting for me at home,' Cordelia said. 'He said he'd have dinner ready, so I'd better not be late.'

'Okay, then it's just the two of us.' Nuala put her arm through Jasmine's. 'It's this way,' she said and pulled Jasmine along down the next street. 'See you, Sally. I'll make sure she gets home before bedtime.'

Sally laughed. 'I'll believe it when I see it, Nuala. When you get chatting there's no stopping you. I'll take Milou out for his evening walk and leave the light on, Jasmine.'

'Thanks, Mam,' Jasmine said and kissed her mother on the cheek. She felt as light as air after the class, and her mood was improved. It was lovely to be here among people who were so ready to make friends.

Cordelia waved goodbye and turned into the lane that led to her cottage, promising to invite them for dinner there soon.

'So here we are,' Nuala said as they walked along the road to the harbour. 'You, me and the heavenly bodies up there in the universe.'

Jasmine looked up at the stars that studded the black sky. 'How amazing. They're much brighter here than anywhere else.'

'No light pollution,' Nuala said with a touch of pride. 'This area is what is known as a dark sky reserve. And to make things even more amazing, we have been told it's a Gold Tier reserve, the only one in the northern hemisphere. There are only three Gold Tier reserves on the planet. How do I know all this? Because of my son, the astronomer. He's not actually a real astronomer as he's only fourteen and still in school. But that's his passion and he wants to be one when he grows up.'

'You must be so proud of him.'

'I'm totally chuffed and amazed. He must have been switched at birth,' Nuala said with a chuckle. 'I wasn't exactly a genius at the science subjects at school and neither was my husband. But Turlough, who now uses his middle name, is a top student. We look at him in awe and wonder where he came from. I bet there are some genius parents out there somewhere looking at a stupid kid wondering what happened.'

Jasmine laughed. 'I'm sure he's all yours.'

'That'd be a miracle. Could be a throwback to ancient times or something. But we're grateful he landed with us. It's fascinating to hear him talk about the stars and planets.' She pointed at the Milky Way which ran like a wide, glittering band across the velvety sky. 'See that tight cluster up there? That's the Andromeda Galaxy. And further away are the star clusters and nebulae. This is the only place they can be seen with the naked eye. If you know where to look,' she added.

Jasmine craned her neck and looked up, feeling nearly dizzy at the thought of the enormity of the universe. The stars glimmered and glinted, as if they were trying to send messages down to Earth. 'What a wonderful sight,' she murmured in awe.

'You never get tired of it.' Nuala increased her speed. 'But come on, let's get inside and have that drink and something to eat. It'll be quiet tonight as it's Monday, so this is a good time to get to know each other.'

Jasmine fell into step with her. 'I didn't bring any money,' she said, feeling foolish.

Nuala laughed. 'Hey, I'm inviting you. It'll be all on me this time. Just like a little welcome gift or something.'

'Thank you. That's very kind.'

They had arrived at the harbour, where the pub stood on its own, the windows glowing and the smell of turf from the fire coming from the chimney. Nuala opened the door and Jasmine followed her into the cosy pub, where a tall man was drying glasses behind the counter.

'Hi, darling,' Nuala said. 'I brought a guest. This is Jasmine, Sally's daughter. And this gorgeous hunk is my husband, Sean Óg. That means "young Sean" in Irish just to save you asking questions. Not so young any more, but the name stuck just to distinguish him from his dad, who was also called Sean. They had no imagination in those days.'

'Hi, Sean Óg,' Jasmine said and shook his hand.

'Hello there, Jasmine,' he said. 'Sally's daughter, eh? You do look a little like her around the eyes and when you smile.' He stepped back and studied her for a moment. 'Oh, yeah, that's an O'Rourke face, even if the colours are different.'

Jasmine smiled at him. 'That's the nicest thing anyone has said since I came here. Thank you, Sean Óg.'

'You're welcome.' His eyes crinkled as he smiled. He turned to Nuala. 'I suppose you're starving after the contortions. I prepared a raw food platter for you and any guest you might bring.'

'How about slipping a wedge of pizza onto that platter?' Nuala suggested, taking off her jacket. 'And get Jasmine here a glass of Guinness, so she can taste the local brew.' She sat on one of the high stools at the bar. 'Is it okay for you to sit here, Jasmine? I need to keep an eye on the customers and give Sean Óg a hand if he needs it.'

'That's fine,' Jasmine said and sat on the stool next to Nuala. She glanced down the bar counter at the customers enjoying a drink and spotted Aiden on the table next door with another man deep in conversation.

Aiden glanced up and noticed her, smiling and nodding.

She smiled back, not wanting to interrupt their conversation.

But Aiden said 'Hi' and gestured at the other man. 'This is Connor, the owner of the restaurant. And this, Connor, is Jasmine, an old friend from my school in Paris, whose mother just happens to live here.'

'It's a small world,' the man said. 'Hi, Jasmine. Lovely to meet you.'

'Hi, Connor,' Jasmine said, noting that he was very nice-looking with a shock of blonde hair and green eyes.

'We'll join you in a minute,' Aiden said. 'We're just finishing our meeting.'

Sean Óg put a tall glass in front of Jasmine. 'Glass of Guinness for you while you wait for your food. Let me know if you like it and if not, I'll get you something else.'

'I've tasted Guinness in France,' Jasmine explained and sipped the black brew. 'It's nice,' she said, taking another sip. 'Better than the Guinness I've had before.'

'Of course it is,' Sean Óg said. 'This is draught Guinness. Completely different to the stuff in cans.'

'It really is,' Jasmine said and took another sip. 'I could get used to this.'

Nuala had gone behind the bar and pulled herself a whole pint. She laughed as she saw Jasmine enjoying her first draught Guinness. 'I knew you'd take to the black stuff. That's the Irish in you coming out.'

'Ah sure, an O'Rourke would never say no to a glass of stout,' Sean Óg remarked, putting a plate with salad, grated carrots and a big slice of pizza in front of Jasmine. 'Homegrown veg and pizza made in our pizza oven.'

'Thank you, it looks delicious.' Jasmine breathed in the smell of tomato, cheese and oregano from the pizza and dug in.

Nuala followed suit beside her, chatting between bites of pizza and sips of Guinness from her tall glass. 'Oh my God, this is heaven,' she said with a sigh. 'I haven't had pizza for weeks. I started Kamal's raw food diet to lose weight, and then I kept going because it made me feel good. But I thought we'd break you in slowly. Or not at all,' she said, as Jasmine licked her fingers. 'No need for you to take anything off. You're perfect the way you are.'

'Gosh, no,' Jasmine protested. 'I'm at least three kilos overweight and I have a bit of wobble here and there. But this was too good to miss. That's the best pizza this side of Naples.'

Aiden and his boss had finished their conversation and joined Jasmine and Nuala. Aiden nudged Jasmine with his elbow. 'You look happy and relaxed. They say Guinness is good for you. Looks like it works in your case.'

'That and yoga made me feel really good,' Jasmine replied.

'So the yoga was a hit, then?'

'Definitely,' Jasmine said with a happy sigh. She wiped her mouth with a paper napkin and drained her glass. 'I was stiff after our walk this morning, so I needed to loosen up. I never knew yoga was so tough. But at the end I felt so relaxed and now with this pizza, I think I have everything anyone could need for a good night's sleep.'

'How about another glass of Guinness?' Connor asked.

Jasmine laughed. 'Yes, please. It's a strange drink, but I like it. Goes well with pizza.'

'Ah, but you should try it with oysters,' Connor said. 'That's a match made in heaven.'

'That sounds weird but I'm sure it works.'

'You could try it tomorrow at the restaurant,' Aiden suggested. 'We're putting oysters on the menu for the next month as they're in season right now. Irish oysters are the best in the world.'

'I'd love to try that,' Jasmine said. She turned to Nuala. 'Why don't you come with me? And I'll get my mother to come, too. Oysters are raw, aren't they?'

'And alive,' Aiden said with a laugh.

'It's a date, then?' Connor asked, looking at Jasmine with a glint in his green eyes.

'Date?' Aiden said. 'But I thought you were going back to Cork tomorrow morning.'

'I might stay around for a bit,' Connor replied, smiling at Jasmine. 'Just to see if the oysters with Guinness take your fancy, Jasmine.'

'Are you hitting on my old friend, Connor?' Aiden asked.

'She doesn't look that old to me,' Connor retorted. 'Sorry, Jasmine. I hope you don't mind me. I'm not in the habit of trying to pick up girls I've just met. It was your enthusiasm for Guinness that piqued my interest. And then one thing led to another, and here I am looking like an eejit in front of a beautiful Frenchwoman.' He sighed and picked up his glass. 'Another pint to drown my sorrows, Sean Óg. And a glass of Guinness for the lovely Jasmine.' He slapped his forehead. 'Shite! I did it again. That was way too forward. I do apologise. I think I might go back to Cork in the morning as planned. You probably never want to see me again, Jasmine.'

Jasmine looked at his eyes sparkling with mischief and burst out laughing. 'I'm not offended at all. Please don't beat yourself up. I'm from France, remember. Frenchmen don't worry too much about flirting with women in bars and restaurants. We can take it. And if we don't like it, we let the men know.'

'How?' Connor asked, looking intrigued.

'We slap them hard in the face and walk away. They usually get the message.'

Connor nodded. 'The direct approach. I like that. Irish women are pretty sassy as well. I was only messing, really.'

'Flirting with a woman while pretending you hate yourself for it,' Aiden remarked. 'Clever, that. And I can see it works. Go to the top of the class, Connor.'

'Gosh, it's only Monday, and people are misbehaving already,' Nuala said with a laugh, having listened with interest. 'But that oyster party sounds great. Count me in, Aiden. Sean Óg,' she called, 'how about you? Oysters and Guinness at the Wild Atlantic tomorrow night? We can get the lads to mind the pub for a few hours.'

'You're on,' Sean Óg called from further down the bar, where he was serving fish and chips to a couple. 'We haven't had a night out for a long time.'

'We'll get Cordelia and Declan to join us,' Nuala suggested. 'Then you'll meet nearly the whole gang, except Maeve and Roisin. But Roisin and her husband are gone to get their sons for the mid-term break and Maeve might not be able to get out from under the kids. She has twin baby boys and a three-year-old,' she added. 'So she hardly ever has the energy to go out in the evenings.'

'I'm sure I'll meet her soon anyway,' Jasmine said. She finished the last of the pizza and smiled at Aiden. 'I'm going to Killarney tomorrow to get myself a pair of good walking boots.'

'And a phone, I hope,' he filled in.

'That too,' Jasmine replied.

'You don't have a phone?' Connor asked with a shocked expression when Aiden had turned to say something to Sean Óg and Nuala.

'I lost mine in a kind of accident,' Jasmine told him. 'So now I have to get a new one. And a new SIM card, of course.'

'That's a pain,' Connor remarked. 'Losing your phone, I mean.' He pulled his out of his pocket. 'Mine is physically attached to me at all times. It's like a mini office. And of course my means of contact, banking and' – he held the phone up – 'a camera.'

Jasmine held up her hand in front of her face. 'Oh, no, please don't.'

Connor lowered his phone and looked at her in surprise. 'Why not? You look so cute sitting there.'

'God, no,' Jasmine exclaimed, hear heart racing. 'Not Instagram or any social media. Please delete that photo,' she pleaded, panic making her break out in a cold sweat. It hadn't struck her that she might meet people who wanted to take photos of her when she was out in public. Then they'd be shared on social media with hashtags that might be clicked on by the person she was trying to hide from. He must never get the slightest hint of her whereabouts. 'Is it gone?' she asked, her voice shaking.

'I didn't take it yet,' Connor said reassuringly, looking at her with curiosity. 'And I shouldn't even have attempted it without asking you first.' He pushed his phone into his pocket, looking contrite.

'No harm done,' Jasmine said, smiling at him. He was so beguiling sitting there looking embarrassed and she felt terrible for snapping at him.

'Another Guinness?' Aiden asked.

Jasmine shook her head. 'No, thanks. I'd better get home. I'm really tired after all the physical activities today. And yoga made me sleepy.'

Nuala yawned beside her. 'Me, too. Sorry, lads, but I think I'll go home and get some sleep. The school run starts early tomorrow.' She got up from her stool and put on her jacket. 'Come on, Jasmine, we'll walk home together. My house is near Sally's.'

'I'm ready.' Jasmine smiled at Aiden and got off her stool. 'Bye, Aiden. Nice to meet you, Connor. See you tomorrow night.'

Aiden stood up and kissed her cheek. 'Night, Jazz.'

'Good night, Jasmine,' Connor said beside him. 'Sorry about the messing earlier. And trying to take your picture. Won't happen again.'

'It's okay,' Jasmine said with a laugh. 'I had forgotten about it already.' She waved at them both and followed Nuala out of the pub.

As she opened the door, she glanced over her shoulder and caught Connor looking at her. As their eyes met, she felt a tiny dart of something that made her heart beat a little faster. Then she turned away, chiding herself. She had only just come out of a disastrous relationship and shouldn't embark on something new so soon. She needed peace and time to heal. And she needed to make sure Damien would never find her.

Chapter Nine

It turned wet and windy the following day, but the bad weather didn't deter Jasmine. She woke up early and set off to Killarney after breakfast, leaving Milou with Sally, who was delighted to have him. 'He's such great company,' she said and bent down to pat the dog lying at her feet under the kitchen table. 'I want to introduce him to Kamal. I'm sure he'll say Milou has a wonderful aura.'

'No shop today?' Jasmine asked.

'Oh yes, and I'm on my own. Cordelia has the day off. But it'll be a quiet day so I can do some stocktaking and tidy up the shelves. Kamal will drop in during the day, he said.'

Jasmine looked thoughtfully at her mother. 'You and Kamal seem to be getting close.'

Sally coloured slightly. 'Close friends, yes. Nothing more at all.'

'He's…' Jasmine hesitated. 'Interesting.'

'Did you like him?'

'I only exchanged a few words with him, so I can't say whether I liked him or not. He's a good teacher, though. I found myself following his instructions without thinking.'

Sally nodded. 'Of course. You need to get to know him better. He says you seem to be under some kind of stress and you feel hunted.'

'Hunted?' Jasmine said. 'Are you sure he didn't mean haunted?'

'No, hunted. As if you're looking over your shoulder at someone behind you.' There was a worried look in Sally's eyes. 'Is there something you're not telling me?'

Jasmine looked at Sally with an innocent air. 'No, Mam. I have no idea what he means. But maybe he overreacted. I might give out stressful vibes and he gets them wrong.'

'Kamal never gets anything wrong. He can see into people's minds and souls,' Sally said darkly.

'Scary.' Jasmine bent to look at Milou under the table. 'Look after Mam, Milou. I'll be back in a few hours.' Milou lifted his head and wagged his tail.

'He'll be fine,' Sally said.

'I'm sure he will,' Jasmine said with a laugh. 'You spoil him with treats and kisses. He's in seventh doggy heaven with you.' She gathered up her bag and jacket. 'I'll be off. Looking forward to exploring Killarney.'

'Get yourself a new phone,' Sally ordered. 'I don't like not being able to contact you.'

'I will. And I'll call you when I've bought one. I promised Aiden I'd call him, too. He wrote down his number for me. I know yours by heart, of course.'

'It's amazing to think you two were friends at school and now you meet again right here,' Sally said, smiling.

'Unbelievable, isn't it?' Jasmine threw her and Milou a kiss from the door. 'Bye, *mes amours*. I'll be back in the afternoon.'

'Be careful on the roads,' Sally warned. 'It's wet and windy today.'

'I'll be fine,' Jasmine reassured her. She ran down the slope of the front garden, her head down against the rain and quickly got into her car and slammed the door shut. The rain driven by the wind smattered against the windscreen and her car shook. She realised the drive would be far from pleasant. Her Toyota Yaris, so perfect for Paris traffic, might not be suitable for Irish rain and wind. But she had to go and get those boots, and a phone, both of which were essential for a long stay in Sandy Cove.

Jasmine jumped as someone knocked on the window. She saw a dark shape and heard a muffled voice asking if she was okay. She wound down the window and discovered the good-looking man she had met in the pub the night before, dressed in an anorak with the hood up. 'Connor?' she said, only then remembering his name.

'Hi. Just thought I'd come by and see if you'd like a lift to Killarney in my car. This one seems a little flimsy for a drive down country roads in this weather.'

'Oh,' she stammered.

'Is that a yes?' he shouted against the sound of the wind.

'Yes, sure, thanks,' Jasmine said as she caught sight of his sturdy SUV.

'Great.' He opened the door to her car while she scrambled out with her bag, putting up the hood of her jacket.

When she had slammed the door shut, he held the door open to the passenger seat of his car and she climbed in, smiling as he settled behind the wheel, having taken off his jacket. 'This is much better than struggling with my car against that wind,' she said. 'Thanks for giving me a lift.'

'I saw you getting into your little car and thought it might be a bit of a challenge to drive it in these conditions. I felt it was a practical solution as I'm going to Killarney myself today. I have to pick up some kitchen equipment and call into the bank.' He started the engine and they drove up the deserted main street, turning off towards Killarney at the crossroads. 'The road isn't bad, but it twists and turns a bit,' he announced. 'It can be a bit uneven in bits as well, which might be tricky in a small car in this weather.'

'I remember that it was a bit bumpy when I drove here on Sunday,' Jasmine agreed, suddenly realising that she had only arrived the day before yesterday. It seemed more like weeks ago. So much had happened and she had been hurtled into village life in an instant.

'So you only just arrived?' Connor asked, echoing her thoughts. 'It must have given you a bit of a jolt to bump into Aiden like that. He told me how you were friends at school in Paris years ago.'

'Yeah, we were,' Jasmine said, smiling as she thought of Aiden. 'Great friends. We were the class nerds. At least he was. I was just the girl nobody wanted to hang out with.'

Connor glanced at her. 'I find that hard to believe.'

'Well, I've grown up since then,' Jasmine replied, blushing slightly under his admiring gaze.

'You certainly have. And now you're in banking, I hear.'

'Was,' Jasmine said, staring into the rain, as her mind turned to her job and why she had quit. 'I'm thinking of changing careers.'

'To what?'

Jasmine shrugged. 'Not sure yet. Something to do with investments but in a different way.'

'Oh.' Connor glanced at her again and seemed to sense her change of mood. 'But you're taking a break now?'

'That's right. I want to stay here for a bit. Get to know my mother's place and connect with my Irish relations.'

'You have lots of those around here?'

'Yes,' Jasmine said, trying to remember her O'Rourke relatives. 'I have aunts and uncles somewhere in other parts of Kerry. And cousins. I haven't seen any of them since I was around ten, but I'd like to get to know them, wherever they are.'

'Sounds great.'

'What about you?' Jasmine asked, glancing at his profile in the dim light, as the rain continued to beat against the windows. 'What's your story? You seem to know a lot about me, but all I know about you is your first name and that you own a chain of restaurants.'

Connor laughed without taking his eyes off the road as they continued into the driving rain. 'Me? Not much to tell. My last name is Flanagan and I'm thirty-seven years old. Originally from Dublin, but now I live in Cork. I don't own a chain as such, only three restaurants so far, in Kinsale, Sandy Cove and Lahinch. The Kinsale one is the flagship, but I have great hopes for Sandy Cove.'

'Oh? That's your work. But what about your early life? Do you have brothers and sisters? Where did you go to school? And university?' She was dying to ask if he was married, but that might be going too far.

Connor shook his head and chuckled. 'That's a lot of questions.'

'Just answer the ones you're comfortable with.'

He took a deep breath. 'Oh, okay. Well… I went to a boarding school just outside Dublin run by the Jesuits. Tough, and heavy on the rugby. You might say it's an elitist school, but life there was pretty frugal. Bland food, early morning prayers, jogging around the school grounds every morning, rain or shine. It was all supposed to make men out of us.'

'Did it?'

Connor flexed his biceps, laughing. 'Yeah, sure it did. At least it made us hate our teachers forever. Anyway,' he continued, 'I went to Trinity College in Dublin and studied politics and history. Got a master's degree and then I was flung out into the world to make a living. My degree wasn't much use and I ended up working in pubs and restaurants and had a lot of fun. I learned about the restaurant business and decided to get into that line of work. My dear old dad helped me invest in my first little restaurant on the quays and that did very well. I sold it and made a good profit and then I started the one in Kinsale four years ago.' He paused. 'And to wind the clock back, I have two sisters and a brother and my parents are both lawyers from quite prosperous families. You could say I'm a spoiled brat who was born with a silver spoon in my gob. But apart from my parents investing in my first venture, I've done everything else on my own.'

'Impressive,' Jasmine said, feeling the question of his marital status hanging in the air.

'Isn't it?' Connor revved the engine as they drove up a steep hill. 'And, no I'm not married. Not any more,' he added as an afterthought. 'I'm newly divorced. My wife didn't want to move to Cork. I suppose she didn't love me enough. What about you?'

'Me?' Jasmine asked, startled.

'Yeah. Married, divorced or…?'

'None of the above. I—' She stopped for a moment. 'I've just broken up with someone.'

'Didn't he love you enough either?'

'No.' *Not enough not to wreck my life*, she thought, the memory of Damien's betrayal making her wince. 'Do you have children?' she asked to take the spotlight away from her relationship status.

'No.' He shrugged. 'Maybe that was lucky. But we had been talking about having children shortly before we… before it all went sad and wrong and we started to hate each other.'

'I'm sorry,' she said, touched by the pain in his voice. 'It must be hard.'

'I'm slowly getting over it.' He smiled suddenly at her. 'Being here with you helps. You have a very soothing presence. Do you know that?'

Jasmine shook her head in disbelief. Was he joking? 'No,' she said. 'I was a bit of a troublemaker when I was small. Always scowling and throwing tantrums. I don't think that was soothing in any way.'

'Ah but you grew up to be someone who doesn't take shit from anyone.'

'Sometimes you get it thrown at you despite being confident,' Jasmine said with a touch of bitterness in her voice. It seemed odd to talk about such personal things with a perfect stranger, but in the confines of the car with the rain beating against the windows she had felt secure and oddly close to this man. She looked out the window at the windswept landscape. 'I think it's stopped raining. And I can see a patch of blue sky. I'm sure the sheep in that field are happy to see the end of the rain.'

'They're used to it.'

'I suppose.' They were quiet while they continued down the road, through green fields dotted with sheep, and then the road went through a dense forest with huge oaks and tall pine trees. 'Killarney National Park,' Connor said. 'There's some great hiking here, especially up the mountains past the waterfalls. Stunning views.'

'I'd love to see it all,' Jasmine said. 'But I'm going to do some hillwalking around Sandy Cove first. There are some interesting trails up the mountains there. But first I need boots, and then I have to get fitter. I have never done much walking, really. Except around Paris where you end up walking for miles sometimes. But that's on pavements so it's not the same.'

'Certainly not.' Connor slowed down as they came out of the wooded area.

The road became more built-up and they passed huge hotels and then went through a roundabout and into a street lined with all kinds of shops and restaurants. Jasmine peered out the window at the people thronging the streets, going in and out of shops. 'It's very busy.'

'Not half as busy as on a Saturday,' Connor remarked. 'And this is low season. You should see it in the summer. Impossible to drive through town then.'

'I prefer it like this,' Jasmine declared.

'Me, too.' Connor pulled up outside a small café. 'I'll park here so you can find the car when you've finished shopping. I'll be at the bank further up the street. Oh, and the sports shop is down the next street. Maybe you could call me when you've finished shopping?'

'Uh, I don't have a phone,' Jasmine reminded him.

'No, but you'll get one, won't you? The phone shop is near the sports place. Hang on, I'll get something to write my number on.' He searched the pockets of his waxed jacket and extracted a crumpled receipt and a biro and scribbled on it. 'My number. Call me when you have a phone. We can have lunch in this little place if you like,' he said, gesturing at the café. 'Looks nice and not too crowded.'

'Thanks, Connor. That sounds great.' Jasmine took the piece of paper and put it in her pocket. 'I'll call you when I can.' She opened the door and climbed out of the SUV, smiling at him. 'See you later.'

'Have fun,' he said. He took his phone out of his pocket and was already deep in conversation when she closed the door and walked away.

He's obviously a busy man, she thought. *And nice and good-looking. What's not to like?* she asked herself as she looked up at the patch of blue sky. But she knew it was too soon. She was still trying to recover from Damien's betrayal which had felt like being hit by a sledgehammer. Better to give up men for a while, even the dishy ones, she decided, and concentrate on her other concern. Her new quest to get down to Wild Rose Bay and find out more about its history, made her heart beat faster and helped her turn her mind away from her worries. She found the sports shop easily and pushed open the door with a feeling of excitement at the adventures ahead.

Having purchased a cheap phone with a pay-as-you-go SIM card, Jasmine spent an enjoyable hour in the sports shop, trying on sturdy hiking boots, and after a long session with the shop assistant, an avid hillwalker, finally decided on a pair of Meindl boots in blue nubuck. 'The colour won't be visible after a few muddy hikes,' she said, 'but they're cute, aren't they?'

'I like them.' Jasmine wiggled her toes inside the boots. 'But they seem a little big.'

'You need socks,' the girl said. 'And maybe an insole. Let's see what we can find for you.' She went to a shelf stacked with wool socks and insoles and picked out a few.

Jasmine tried them all on and after several trips around the shop, decided on a pair of sheepskin soles and wool socks, which made the boots fit snugly. That done, she picked out a dark green waterproof jacket, a pair of walking trousers and a thin fleece and felt she was now equipped for hillwalking in any weather. The bill came to a considerable sum, which made her blink, but then decided it was an investment, and paid with the only credit card she had left with enough money to see her through the next few weeks. After that she'd have to look into getting a job, or return to Paris and try to get back into her old line of work.

'How about a baseball cap and some sunglasses?' the shop assistant asked, pulling Jasmine out of her thoughts. 'I know it seems unlikely we'll see the sun this side of Easter right now, but it can be blinding up on the mountain on a good day.'

'Good idea,' Jasmine said, smiling at the girl who had been so helpful.

The girl held out a bright green cap with a shamrock on the front. 'How about this one, as it's Paddy's Day soon.'

'Uh, maybe something more discreet,' Jasmine suggested. 'I don't want to scare the sheep. And... I'm not actually a tourist,' she continued. 'I'm staying with my mother in Sandy Cove at the moment.'

The girl laughed. 'Oh, God, I'm sorry. I thought… with your French accent and everything…'

'That's because I grew up in France,' Jasmine explained. 'I'm half Irish actually. My mother's name is O'Rourke.'

'Oooh,' the girl said, looking impressed. 'An O'Rourke from Sandy Cove. They're a legend around here.'

'Oh? Why?'

The girl shrugged. 'I don't really know. Just one of them old families that ruled the roost in the Middle Ages or something. And they were fierce in all of those rebel uprisings way back. I think we learned about them in Irish class, but I can't remember much about it, to be honest. Couldn't wait to finish school and get a job.'

Jasmine laughed. 'I know the feeling.' She threw the cap and sunglasses on top of the pile on the counter. 'That's it, I think. Unless you think I should buy ropes and tackle and binoculars and other stuff for survival in the mountains.'

The girl laughed. 'Nah, you have enough there, I think. You wouldn't want to blow all you have in one shop, would you?'

'Absolutely,' Jasmine said with feeling as she paid for the additional items.

The girl took a large paper carry bag from under the counter and put the purchased items into it. Jasmine pocketed the receipt and looked out the window to see if the weather had improved. The sky was brighter and the blue patch had widened and people walking past had taken off their hats and hoods. Good. That would mean the drive back would be a lot more pleasant.

She looked at the passers-by trying to guess where they came from. The couple, both tall and blonde, with rucksacks on their backs had to be either German or Scandinavian, and the woman coming up the street wearing a brown raincoat was obviously a local, and the man looking into the Irish knit shop had to be…

Jasmine froze as he turned around. *Oh my God*, she thought, her knees suddenly so weak she had to grab onto the counter. *It can't be. Not him, not here…*

Chapter Ten

Hiding behind a display of caps and gloves, Jasmine peered at the man, who was now nearly at the corner. She couldn't be sure, but it looked like him – Damien, walking around, peering in through shop windows.

'Someone out there you don't want to meet?' the girl asked, making Jasmine jump.

'Uh—' Jasmine mumbled, her eyes still on the man who looked so like Damien, as he turned into the next street and then disappeared from view.

The girl handed Jasmine the bag and craned her neck to see out the window. 'That guy who's just turned the corner?'

'Yes,' Jasmine croaked. 'Him.'

'He was in here before you. Looking around but not buying anything. I asked if I could help him, but he just grunted and left without bothering to close the door.' The girl rolled her eyes. 'Some people. So rude.'

'Horrible,' Jasmine said and fished the baseball cap and sunglasses out of the bag. She put the cap and sunglasses on. 'Thanks for your help. I have to get going now. If he comes back…'

The girl nodded and pretended to zip up her mouth. 'I'd never dare squeal on an O'Rourke,' she said and waved. 'Bye. Good luck. Be careful on the mountains.'

Jasmine left the shop and hurried down the street to Connor's car and found him sitting there talking on the phone. She got in with her bags and banged the door shut, pulling her cap further down.

Connor finished his call and stared at her. 'What's up? You didn't call me. Did you get a phone?'

'Could you drive off, please,' Jasmine pleaded.

'Right now?' Connor asked, looking confused.

'Like yesterday,' Jasmine said with panic in her voice.

'What about lunch?'

'I'm not hungry.'

Connor put away his phone and started the car. 'I suppose you'll tell me what's going on?' he said over the rumble of the engine.

'I will. Just go,' Jasmine urged, sinking down in the seat. She knew she was being rude, but she was terrified Damien would spot her. He had tried to contact her several times before she left Paris and tried to get into her apartment but she had changed the lock. She had been out, but the concierge had told her he'd been around. After that, she had moved in with Matthieu for a few days and then left for Ireland. She knew Damien had been trying to get to her and that if he found her he might try to get her back. She wasn't sure she trusted herself not to be seduced by him again and be pulled into another series of lies. Better to avoid him and not be tempted.

As if sensing her panic, Connor drove up the street as fast as he could and turned the corner on two wheels. 'I hope the Guards weren't watching,' he grunted. 'I'd get a speeding fine and two penalty points on my licence if they did.'

Jasmine looked around. 'No Guards,' she announced, 'and not much traffic.' She calmed down when they reached the outskirts of town and took off her sunglasses. 'Thanks, Connor. I'm really sorry about all of this.'

'Okay,' he muttered, looking ahead. 'You looked really scared back there, so I'm sure you have a very good reason.'

'I do.' Jasmine took off her baseball cap and smoothed her hair. 'It's my ex-boyfriend,' she explained. 'He's been trying to find me.'

Connor glanced at her, alarmed. 'Bloody hell, really? All the way from Paris? Maybe you should tell the police? Get a restraining order or something.'

'He hasn't done anything,' Jasmine said, feeling miserable. 'He's just tried to contact me a few times and then he tried to get into my apartment in Paris. But I had changed the lock.'

'So he didn't succeed?'

'No.' She stared ahead while they drove through the beautiful wooded area, wondering how she could explain her fear. She was still shivering after the shock of seeing him like that in a street in Killarney and it had brought it all back in a flash – the lies she had believed in and all the promises he had made and not kept. She didn't want to meet him again.

'And now he's here, looking for you? Are you sure it was him?'

'Nearly sure,' Jasmine replied. 'But of course I could have been mistaken. My nerves play tricks with me so that I see him everywhere.'

Connor glanced at her and slowed down. Then he turned and pulled up outside a pub.

'Why are we stopping?' Jasmine asked.

'Lunch,' he replied grimly. 'I'm hungry. And you need something hot and maybe a stiff drink. Don't worry, nobody is after us.'

'He wouldn't know your car anyway,' Jasmine said, feeling slightly calmer.

'Of course not.' Connor opened his door. 'Come on. Let's get something to eat.'

Jasmine put on her baseball cap and followed him into the warm pub. She looked at his broad back as he walked ahead and thought how kind it was of him to help her, not minding going out of his way.

After a bowl of vegetable soup, some soda bread and a cup of tea, Jasmine felt calmer and ready for the trip back to Sandy Cove. Damien would never find her there, she thought. He had somehow figured out that she had gone to Ireland and Kerry, as she had told him she had family there, but never said exactly where. He hadn't been that interested anyway, which had been disappointing at the time but now seemed like a lucky break. Kerry was a very big county and it would be impossible to find anyone if you didn't know where to go. But she was beginning to believe the man she had seen wasn't Damien after all, just someone who looked like him. She sighed and pushed away her bowl and smiled at Connor. 'Thank you for lunch. Just what I needed. I'm okay now. I just want to get back to Sandy Cove.'

Connor nodded. 'Me, too. I'll just pay and we'll be on our way. And hey, yer man isn't likely to follow you to Sandy Cove unless you told him you were going there.'

'I never did,' Jasmine declared. 'He wasn't very interested in my Irish relatives, anyway. He was only interested in himself, really.'

'He sounds like a bit of a narcissist.'

'What?' Jasmine stared at Connor as his words sunk in. Then she nodded. 'Well, that's a bit strong, but in a way you're right. Very egocentric, anyway.' She had never analysed their relationship or his behaviour, but now everything seemed to fall into place...

When Jasmine came home, she found the house empty and a note on the kitchen table:

Stocktaking at the shop. Aiden told me about the party at the restaurant. Will be home in time to change. Sally xx

Jasmine went to her room to put away her shopping and check her email. She sent a text to Aiden from her new number and also to her mother and Connor. That done, she sat down on the living room sofa with her laptop and checked her emails, deciding to open the ones from Damien that she hadn't had the courage to look at before. They were still in the trash folder. The first one said he was sorry about everything and they should meet so he could explain, the second said roughly the same thing, but then the tone changed when he hadn't got a reply. He just didn't want to give up. He wanted her to dance to his tune all the time, even now. Why hadn't she realised how manipulative he was? Because he had been so charming.

Jasmine shuddered and closed her eyes and then deleted all Damien's emails, blocking his address. Then she went into Google and typed 'narcissist'. The checklist that came up made her blink.

Not all the attributes fitted, and she felt calling him a narcissist was going a bit far. But still… Damien was charming and smooth, selfish and manipulative, had a filthy temper and a huge lack of empathy. He had also lied very convincingly about his family and about what he did for a living. How on earth had she allowed herself to be taken in by him? Because of his film-star looks, his talent for flattery and turning her head in such a way that she had been blind to his faults. He had made her feel special and cherished. But then, later on, he had shown his true colours. The proposal, the ring and his declaration of love for her were all a sham. Desperate for money, he had emptied their joint account and left her with all the bills.

Jasmine felt a wave of shame mixed with anger as she thought of how he had fooled her. She had loved him with all her heart and thought he did, too, and that was what hurt the most. As she remembered, Jasmine started to cry, softly at first, then harder until her whole body was racked with sobs and the tears streamed down her face. She grabbed a cushion and cried into it, letting out all her sorrow and anger until she had no tears left. Then she lay down, exhausted, staring at the ceiling.

Her new phone buzzed. She sat up, wiped her face with her sleeve and picked it up. Probably Sally asking if she'd got home. 'Hello,' she croaked.

'Hi,' Aiden's voice said. 'Thought I'd give you a call. How did the shopping trip go?'

'Uh, great,' she replied. 'Connor gave me a lift as the weather was so bad.'

'Did he? He's in the office here going through the accounts, but was probably too busy to tell me. The oysters arrived from the suppliers, so we're all set for the party. Your mum is coming and the yoga guru, too, which was a big surprise. Then we have Nuala and her hubby and Cordelia and Declan and a few other odds and sods. Should be a great evening.'

'Lovely.' With the phone to her ear, Jasmine got up to get a tissue from her mother's bedroom to blow her nose.

'Do you have a cold?' Aiden asked. 'You sound a little hoarse.'

'No, it's this new phone. Could be that the sound is wonky.'

'You got one, at least.'

'Yeah, I'm glad I did.' Jasmine entered Sally's bedroom and spotted a box of tissues on the chest of drawers. 'Nice to be in touch again, and—' She stopped talking and stared, not at the tissues, but what was beside it. Aiden was still talking, but she didn't hear what he said as the photo in a silver frame took all her attention.

'Hey, are you still there?' Aiden asked.

'Yes,' Jasmine mumbled and picked up the photo, staring at it. 'But I have to go. Bye for now. See you later.'

She hung up and sank down on the bed, still looking at the photo. It was of the three of them, her father, Sally and Jasmine, who must have been around four years old at the time. They were on a beach and sitting together in a kind of group hug. Jasmine sat in the middle with her arm around her mother's neck and her hand on her father's knee. But the two parents didn't look at their daughter; they were smiling into each other's eyes, looking like starstruck lovers. *How happy we were*, Jasmine thought. *And they look so in love…* She couldn't remember where they had been on holiday then, but judging by the blue sky and the palm trees in the background, it had to be somewhere in the South of France.

What had happened during the two years that followed this happy holiday snap? And why did Sally have it in her bedroom? Jasmine got up, put the photo back and pulled a few tissues from the box. She blew her nose noisily and walked around the large, bright room.

The window overlooked the front garden, the village street below and the bay in the distance. She could see dark clouds gathering on the horizon and knew another heavy shower was on its way. The cliffs looked dark and dangerous in the gloomy light but she could see a bit of the path they had walked and it seemed to hold a promise of a mystery to be solved. She smiled to herself as she thought of Aiden and the fun they had had. What a stroke of luck that she had come here after the disaster in Paris. She had run to her mother for comfort and love and found a dear friend as well. And then Connor… But right now she had other things on her mind, the first of which was her parents. She glanced at the photo again and wondered if there might be a tiny spark left of that love that was so obvious in that picture. And if the spark was there, could she blow it into life and make the fire burn again? She gave a start as the door opened and her mother, dressed in a dark blue kaftan, walked in.

'There you are,' Sally said. 'I was wondering if you were back yet. How did you get to Killarney? Your car was parked outside all day.'

Jasmine turned from the window. 'I got a lift with Aiden's boss. The weather was so bad that he thought I'd be safer with him in his SUV, which was a great idea.'

'Aiden's boss? Oh, you mean Connor. I met him when I sold the wine.' Sally frowned. 'I'm not sure you should be accepting lifts from a stranger, even if he seems nice.'

'He's lovely,' Jasmine said with a laugh. 'And I'm not five years old, you know. I had a great trip and bought some stuff for hillwalking. Aiden and I are planning to hike up the mountains around here.'

'Lovely. I like Aiden.' Sally sat down on the bed. 'What else happened? I have a feeling you're not telling me everything.'

'I don't know what you mean,' Jasmine replied. 'What else could happen in Killarney?' She walked to the wardrobe. 'What didn't happen was me buying any other clothes, so I think I'll have to raid your wardrobe tonight. I have nothing to wear for a party.'

Sally laughed and stretched out on the bed. 'No need to panic. We don't wear ballgowns for parties around here. Except for Christmas at Willow House, of course.'

'Willow House?' Jasmine asked. 'You mean the big Edwardian house at the other end of the bay? Isn't that where Maeve and Roisin grew up? And where your friend Phil lived?'

'That's right.' Sally sighed. 'God, I miss Phil. She was such a great friend. Both in Paris and here, just before she died.'

'I'm sad that I didn't meet her.'

'You did in Paris when you were a baby.'

'The happy days,' Jasmine said.

'The happiest of my life,' Sally filled in. She stretched out her hand and touched Jasmine. 'In yours, too, I think, my darling.'

'Yes.' Jasmine sat down on the bed. 'Until you decided to separate from Papa.'

'I know,' Sally said and looked down at her hands. 'That was so hard for a little girl. Hard for us all, really.'

'What happened, Mam?' Jasmine asked, her voice gentle. 'Why did all that happiness turn into such sadness?'

'Oh, it's complicated. We didn't get on for a long time and started to drift apart.' Sally sighed. 'It still upsets me to talk about it. Do we have to go over it now?'

'But I want to know,' Jasmine insisted. 'I want to try to understand.'

'Maybe another time,' Sally pleaded. 'I'm not in the mood to talk about it right now.' She patted Jasmine's shoulder. 'Let's have a look at something for you to wear.'

Sensing her mother's discomfort, Jasmine turned her attention to the evening ahead. 'Can we do casual chic?' she asked. 'Both of us? I love your kaftans, but could we synchronise our looks tonight and be just us?'

Sally's face broke into a smile. 'Okay, why not? I'm not a nun or anything. I can break out of the kaftans and show a leg, can't I?' She lay back and waved her legs in the air. 'These pins are still in good shape, don't you think?'

'Fabulous shape,' Jasmine agreed, admiring her mother's lovely legs. 'And the rest of you isn't bad either.'

Sally jumped up from the bed and peeled off her kaftan to reveal leggings and a lacy bra. Her midriff was flat and smooth and her arms were, too, even if they weren't quite as toned as they used to be. Her freckly skin glowed with good health and Jasmine couldn't help thinking that the yoga lifestyle was working wonders. Maybe she should try to go all out and do the whole diet and daily yoga practice herself? She dismissed the idea as soon as it had popped into her head, knowing she wouldn't last a day on raw food and water. Her French genes wouldn't allow it.

'I know,' she said, remembering the way they used to dress for dinner when they were on holiday in fancy hotels on the Riviera.

'Let's close our eyes and pick whatever we find in the wardrobe, like we used to do on holiday.'

'You mean that Russian roulette thing?' Sally asked, her eyes sparkling. 'Oh, yes, let's. That was such fun. Remember when you had to wear a swimsuit and a pair of capri pants to dinner at that restaurant n St Tropez?'

'God, yes,' Jasmine exclaimed, giggling. 'I was fifteen and mortified. But you made me do it and then you couldn't stop laughing.'

'I was in a sarong and one of your mad T-shirts myself,' Sally said, shaking her head. 'They nearly didn't let us in.'

'But then you smiled and winked at the head waiter and he gave us one of their best tables,' Jasmine said, remembering Sally's effect on men when she was younger. 'Cute guy, I remember.'

'Yes, he was sweet.' Sally opened the double doors of the large wardrobe. 'So, let's see… Tops on the left, skirts and pants on the right.'

'No kaftans,' Jasmine ordered.

'Okay. They're hanging on the far right, but if you happen to pick one up by mistake, you can start again. Deal?'

'Deal,' Jasmine said, scanning the colourful array of clothes in the wardrobe. 'Gosh, what a lot of stuff. Haven't you thrown anything out since you left Paris?'

'Not a thing,' Sally said, fingering a sequined top. 'Every item has its own history. I wore this one to a movie premiere ten years ago. Such a fun night. We ended up in a night club where we danced until five in the morning.' She sighed. 'That was with Philippe, I think. Or was it François? One of those glamorous fashion designers anyway. Arm candy, really, but such darlings.'

'Must have been fun,' Jasmine said, remembering being twelve years old and watching Sally get ready for those dates. The scent of her perfume, the rustle of silk, that twirling in front of the mirror, then watching her beautiful mother sail out the door on the arm of a handsome man and being left with a babysitter more often than she liked.

'The glory days,' Sally said as if to herself, running her hand along the line of clothes. 'All that's left are the memories, these rags, and my ageing body.'

'Stop it!' Jasmine snapped, suddenly angry at the display of self-pity. 'You're still lovely, Mam. Still the same Sally, only a little older. You're fit, healthy and lovely and now we're going to have fun.'

Jasmine was suddenly gripped with a wave of frustration. How was she going to get Sally to stop staring herself blind at the fact that she was getting older? And make her understand that even though her new lifestyle was hugely beneficial, it wouldn't cure all her insecurities. Jasmine's master plan was doomed to fail if Sally didn't change her way of thinking.

'Easy for you to say, standing there all young and gorgeous.' Sally shook herself. 'But yeah, you're right. There is only now, after all. And now is pretty good because you're here. I'm going to snap out of it, don't worry. And I might even ger rid of the clothes. Why live in the past?'

'Why would you do that?' Jasmine asked, feeling suddenly that she was the only adult in the room. 'Aren't they reminders of all the fun you had? Moving forward is a great idea, but you should cherish the memories of the happy days, too.'

Sally looked thoughtful. 'I never thought of it that way. But you're right. I've had so many happy moments all through my life, despite all the pain that followed. I should be grateful for those and forgive some of the old hurts.'

'Exactly,' Jasmine agreed, feeling slightly more hopeful. 'Now close your eyes, and pick a top. No peeking.'

Sally laughed and screwed her eyes shut. 'Okay. And don't worry, I don't really know where anything is. I haven't worn any of them for months.' She waved her hand in the air and then grabbed something towards the left and pulled it out. Then she opened her eyes and looked at what she had ended up with. 'Nooo,' she wailed. 'Not this shirt. I thought I had thrown it out.' She held out a pink and orange shirt with red heart-shaped buttons. 'I bought it in a sale and never wore it.'

'But it's cute,' Jasmine said and held it up in front of her mother. The colours, although strong, suited Sally's freckly face and colouring and even matched some of the streaks in her hair. 'A bit mad, but why not?'

'You're right,' Sally said, studying her image in the mirror. 'Not too bad, after all. Your turn for a top.'

'Okay.' Jasmine giggled, feeling a surge of pure joy at seeing her mother like she used to be: frivolous and fun. She closed her eyes and quickly grabbed something from the left part of the wardrobe. As she opened her eyes she discovered the glittery top Sally had just been reminiscing about. 'Great. The top you wore for a date with that glamour boy. Not my style, but whatever.'

'You need to break out of that classic navy-and-black-only look. I know it's chic but it's rather boring, you know.'

'Hmm…' Jasmine held the top against herself. 'Maybe. Just for tonight.'

'You have to, or you break the rules of the game.' Sally closed her eyes again and pulled a black miniskirt out of the wardrobe. 'God, that's short,' she said, horrified. 'I'm too old for this.' She thrust the skirt at Jasmine. 'You wear it. Perfect with the top.'

'No, it's yours, Sally. You'll look gorgeous.' Jasmine closed her eyes and took something out of the wardrobe, collapsing on the bed laughing as she opened her eyes and discovered what she had ended up with. 'Brilliant.' She held up a pair of white culottes. 'We'll be such a hit at the party.'

'They'll think we've been drinking,' Sally said, looking suddenly worried. 'What will Kamal think?'

'Who cares?' Jasmine got up from the bed, gathering the clothes in her arms. 'Let's change and slap on a bit of make-up and get going. I'm looking forward to the Guinness and the oysters now. And maybe if we beg, Aiden will grill us a steak or two.'

'Steak,' Sally mumbled. 'Not allowed in my diet. But maybe I can have a bit when nobody's looking…'

'I'm sure you can break the diet for once, can't you? It wouldn't be the end of the world as we know it.'

'You naughty little devil,' Sally said affectionally. 'You make me feel young again.'

'You *are* young, Mam,' Jasmine argued. 'I mean, you're about to turn sixty, not ninety-five. And you look amazing. Why not celebrate that instead of moping about it? Throw a party on the day and show everyone you really don't care.'

Sally sank down on the bed, the clothes in her lap. 'A party?' she said. 'I don't think I want to do that. Then everyone will know.'

'And why shouldn't they?' Jasmine sat down beside Sally and put her hand on her shoulder. 'I think it'd be fun for everyone. You'd be an inspiration to other women who're trying to come to terms with growing older if you threw a fab party and invited all your friends.'

Sally sighed. 'I'm not sure I want to do that.'

'Why not? I think it would be fantastic to see you all glammed up and staring old age in the face without fear.'

Sally sighed. 'While I'm terrified inside?'

'Yes,' Jasmine urged. 'Maybe if you laugh it off and own it, you will come to accept it. Fake it till you make it, you know?'

Sally's eyes brightened. 'You might be on to something there.' She looked thoughtfully at Jasmine. 'Yes, I'm beginning to like the idea. Why fight what you can't change?'

'Exactly.' Jasmine got up and walked to the door. 'Think about it. But it's time to get ready or we'll be late.'

*

Later, alone in her room, having applied a smoky eye, Jasmine studied herself in the mirror. Her hair had settled back into its sleek bob and her face had a glow she didn't recognise. Must be the long walk yesterday and the happy moments with her mother. She didn't look bad even with the strange mix of clothes. The sequined top clashed with the white culottes, but it was a fun look. The only shoes she had were the pink Prada trainers and a pair of black ballerina flats. On a whim, she slipped on the ballerinas and smiled at herself in the mirror. She looked good, she thought, despite the clothes, relaxed and happier than she had felt for weeks. She wondered idly if Connor would like it, too.

Chapter Eleven

They settled Milou on Sally's bed, telling him to 'mind the house'. He lay down and gave them a sad look, as if to say he would have loved to come to the party.

'Dogs are not allowed in restaurants,' Sally told him. 'But we'll take you for a nice walk when we get home.'

'He shouldn't even be on the bed,' Jasmine scolded. 'He'll be impossible when we get back to Paris.'

'Oh well, that's then, this is now,' Sally said and patted Milou before they turned off the light and left. 'Didn't you say we should live in the present?'

'That wasn't about spoiling a dog,' Jasmine said with a laugh as she closed the door and went down the steps to the front gate. 'But I'm glad you're cheering up.'

Sally put her arm through Jasmine's as they walked down the street towards the restaurant. 'I'm cheering up because you're here and we're finally getting to be friends again. It's been too long, sweetheart.'

'I know,' Jasmine said, feeling that old dart of guilt again. 'I've been too stubborn and stupid, ever since your divorce.'

'We just drifted apart, Jasmine, as the saying goes. Each one doing their own thing and not wanting to give up our independence. Your father wanted a wife who was devoted to him, the house and the family. He resented my job and the fact that I had to work late and go away from time to time. He didn't want to stay at home and hold the baby while I worked. I have a feeling he wanted it to be the other way around.'

'Oh,' Jasmine said, beginning to understand the problem. 'And you were both too stubborn to give in?'

'Something like that. But there were other things, too. Do we have to do this now?' Sally looked up at the sky where the crescent of the new moon was rising over the rooftops of the village and the stars glimmered as it grew darker still. 'It's such a beautiful evening.'

Jasmine had to agree that it was too nice an evening to talk about sad things. The light breeze was soft against her face, turf smoke mingled with the smell of cooking and the lights glowed through the windows of the houses. A dog barked outside a door and was let into a small cottage where Jasmine could glimpse the warm glow of the fire and a man sitting in an armchair reading a book to a small child. Then the door closed and she could imagine the family sitting around the table having dinner. This was such a contrast to the busy streets of Paris, where people were constantly running to work or out to restaurants or parties. A hectic, exciting life, but right now it didn't appeal to her the way it had before. A small village in the west of Ireland – who'd have thought it would feel so good? But it did, and Jasmine felt a calm come over her as they walked along the street, while Sally stopped to say hello to whoever she met. 'My daughter,' she said proudly, as she introduced Jasmine. The brief, friendly greetings made Jasmine feel welcome and oddly part of this small community, even though she had just arrived.

When they reached the restaurant, they joined the small gathering outside waiting to be let in. Nuala, dressed in black trousers and a white angora top, rattled the handle and peered in through the window. 'Is there someone in there?' she called.

Aiden opened the door. 'Sorry. Didn't know it was locked. Come in and take a seat. We've pushed all the tables together and you can sit where you want.'

They all walked inside and were soon joined by the rest of the party, all except Kamal, who hadn't arrived yet. A long table had been made by pushing the smaller tables together and it was laid with a blue and white tablecloth and white paper napkins. There were tealights set into seashells that had been found on the beach and a turf fire blazed in the fireplace. The whole effect was charming and inviting, like the inside of a beach hut, Jasmine thought.

In the light of the many candles and tealights, Nuala looked at Sally in surprise. 'I like the gear. Nice change from the kaftans. Would look like a dog's dinner on me, but then most things do.'

'Don't be silly,' Jasmine said. 'You look *très chic*, Nuala.'

'Ooh,' Nuala said, looking pleased. '*Très chic*, eh? Woohoo, Paris has come to Sandy Cove at last.'

Sally laughed and hugged Nuala. 'You have a style nobody could copy.'

'Is that good or bad?' Nuala asked, looking doubtful.

'Hi, Jasmine,' Cordelia said behind them. She had just walked in with a tall, attractive man by her side. 'This is Declan, my fiancé,' she said and stepped back to let him shake hands with Jasmine.

Jasmine immediately liked Declan, who smiled as he shook her hand. 'Hi,' he said. 'Welcome to Sandy Cove. Looks like another blow-in has joined the club.'

'Ah sure, she isn't a real blow-in,' Aiden cut in. 'She's an O'Rourke and we don't mess with them.'

Declan stepped back and held up his hands. 'Another O'Rourke? Goodness. The old rogues had a lot of descendants.'

'The old rogues?' Jasmine asked, laughing.

'Yeah, you know. The O'Rourkes were a scary lot on the old days.'

'We're very civilised now,' Sally interjected. 'We were tamed long ago.'

Declan winked. 'Yes, but there's still a wild streak waiting to break out, I bet.'

'It won't come out as long as you behave,' Sally said. 'But... did I hear the word fiancé? Are you two engaged at last?'

'Yes.' Cordelia beamed and held out her left hand where a solitaire diamond gleamed on a platinum band. 'We finally did it. He got down on one knee and everything.'

'And then she had to help me up,' Declan joked. He put his arm around Cordelia. 'But now we're a proper couple.'

'Congratulations,' Jasmine said, smiling at the couple so obviously in love. But it reminded her of her own engagement and that diamond ring shoved into a drawer in her bedroom. She had been just as happy as Cordelia before it all went so horribly wrong. 'When's the wedding?' she asked to distract herself from the painful memories.

Declan rolled his eyes. 'Sometime in the next century, I suspect. It took me two years to get her to come this far. It's going to take a long time to get her to agree to be my missus.'

Cordelia gave him a shove with her elbow. 'Oh, come on, it was the two of us dragging our heels. We're too comfortable, your mom said. But then there was this diamond in the window of Weirs in Dublin… Couldn't resist it.'

'She likes me to spend my royalties on her,' Declan filled in.

'How's the book going?' Sally asked.

'Great, thanks,' Declan replied. 'In fact, my publisher wants me to write another one. I got an advance and a very tight deadline. So you won't see much of me for the next six months.'

'So there'll be another detective story set in Kerry?' Nuala's husband asked. He was a tall man who didn't seem to say much, letting his wife do all the talking.

'Yes,' Declan replied with a wink. 'I'll be drawing on my life here for inspiration. You might be in it, Sean Óg, if you're not careful.'

Nuala laughed. 'Oh, please put him in your story. He would make a perfect Garda sergeant who tells everyone to stay at home until he has solved the case.'

'Not a bad idea,' Declan said with a laugh. He looked at Jasmine. 'And you could be the mysterious Frenchwoman who comes to town to hide from a jealous lover.'

Jasmine shivered suddenly. 'Uh, no, that wouldn't work,' she said with a weak smile.

'Nah, too clichéd,' Nuala cut in. 'Make me the good-looking housewife with murder on her mind.'

Aiden snorted a laugh. 'I knew you were dangerous, Nuala. Hey, folks, could we sit down and get a few pints going?'

'I'll give you a hand,' Sean Óg said and walked to the bar.

'Thanks, mate,' Aiden said. 'We'll have the pints ready for you in no time, lads. The food is on its way, too. Connor is cutting his hands to ribbons opening those oysters in the kitchen.'

'All ready,' Connor said as he emerged from the kitchen carrying two huge platters full of oysters. 'Sit down and dig in.' He put the platters at each end of the long table and then pulled out a chair. 'Jasmine, do you want to sit next to me?'

'And I'll sit on her other side,' Aiden shouted from the bar counter where he and Sean Óg were pulling pints as if their lives depended on it. 'We have a lot to catch up on.'

'I thought you had spent a whole day together out walking,' Connor countered.

'Ah sure, we only managed to gossip about half the class,' Aiden shouted back. 'And we were too busy trying not to fall down the cliffs to get into the dirty details.'

'Ooh, two men fighting about Jasmine,' Nuala squealed. 'Can I sit opposite to watch?'

'Oh, please,' Jasmine said with a giggle. 'This is ridiculous. Nobody's fighting.' She sat down on the chair Connor had pulled out for her and smiled at him. 'Thank you.'

The party was soon in full swing as the pints of Guinness were handed down the table and the platters with the oysters were passed around. Everyone proceeded to help themselves and enjoyed the oysters washed down with sips of Guinness, followed by sounds of 'ahhh' and 'mmm', which made Jasmine laugh. She took an oyster and sipped at the salty liquid before she slid one into her mouth, savouring the incredible taste of the sea and the moist flesh of the mollusc that slid down her throat, followed by a gulp of Guinness. The combination of the salty oyster and the deep, bittersweet taste of the Guinness was incredible, unlike anything she had ever tasted.

'Oh, *mon Dieu*,' she mumbled.

'You like it?' Connor asked beside her, wiping his mouth. 'It's an acquired taste, so if you prefer, I'll get you a glass of white wine.'

'No,' she protested, and picked up another oyster from her plate. 'It's delicious. Such a strange combination, but it works. And these oysters… Yummm,' she said before she tipped another into her mouth and grabbed her pint. 'Cheers,' she said and downed half of it.

'Steady,' Connor said, laughing. 'Guinness isn't strong, but a lot of it could make you sloshed in no time.'

'I know.' Jasmine wiped the foam from her upper lip. 'I'll slow down now and just sip it.'

'I never thought you'd become such a huge fan of Guinness,' Aiden said in her ear. 'I expected you to be one of those annoying wine snobs.'

'I like wine, too, of course,' Jasmine replied. 'But I'm not a heavy drinker or anything.' She pushed her pint away. 'In fact, I think I've had enough of the Guinness for now.'

Aiden nodded. 'Me, too. And the oysters have been devoured. We will serve a seafood chowder in a minute. Great party, don't you think?'

'Wonderful.' Jasmine looked down the table at everyone drinking and chatting. All except Sally, who was slowly sipping her Guinness and looking at the door. There was an empty seat beside her and Jasmine realised she was waiting for someone. 'Where is Kamal?' she asked. 'I think my mother is waiting for him.'

'He said he'd be late,' Aiden replied, looking at his watch. Then the door opened and a tall figure came inside. 'But talk of the devil. Here he is now.'

'Oh, yes. He just slid inside like a plume of smoke.' Jasmine watched as Kamal glided into the room and, spotting Sally, sat down beside her and whispered something in her ear, which made her smile and look into his eyes with something akin to worship. 'Mam looks like it's suddenly Christmas. I don't think I like it.'

'I'm sure she's just a little starstruck,' Aiden said. 'I mean look at what all the yoga has done for her. She looks amazing.'

'You should tell her,' Jasmine said. 'She needs reassuring right now. We had a long talk before the party and I think I managed to cheer her up. And we laughed like the old days and fooled around with clothes.' She squinted down at her top and shorts. 'That's why we're dressed like this tonight. It's a game we play sometimes. And it was so great to see the old Sally come out and make her laugh. But when she's around *him*, she's a different person.'

'She'll snap out of it,' Aiden said reassuringly. 'And I'm sure she'll snap out of the raw food diet, too. Nobody could keep that up for long.'

Jasmine sighed. 'I don't care about that. She can eat what she likes if only she were happy. She seems to have *le cafard* a lot.'

Aiden touched her arm. 'You'll be able to cheer her up. I don't know anyone better to do that.'

'What was that you said?' Connor asked on Jasmine's other side. '*Le cafard*? Doesn't that mean cockroach?' He glanced around the room and lowered his voice. 'The health inspectors gave us a clean bill of health the last time, you know,' he muttered in Jasmine's ear.

Jasmine giggled. '*Avoir le cafard* means to be sad and lonely, like having the blues, or being down in the dumps. But yes, it does directly translate as "having the cockroach". Silly, don't you think?' she said, smiling at him.

He smiled back, looking relieved. 'I see. You had me worried there for a while. I must brush up on my French if we're going to continue seeing each other.' He put his hand on hers briefly and looked at her with a glint of flirtation in his green eyes. 'Are we?'

'I don't know,' she stammered, unsure of how to reply. With his sun-streaked blonde hair, green eyes and that lovely smile, he was attractive in a sporty, outdoorsy way. Not smooth and polished like Damien, but even more so because of that. With his slight tan and the lines around his eyes, he looked like he had spent his life squinting against the sun on the deck of a sailing boat or skiing down a snow-covered mountain. She knew it was too soon and she should stay off men and try to recover from Damien's betrayal which had wrecked her life. But being with Connor had helped her forget for a while and he made her feel good. 'As you know I'm…'

He squeezed her hand. 'Me, too,' he murmured in her ear. 'I just thought it would be nice to see each other. No strings, no commitments, just for fun. And we can try to lick each other's wounds as we're both pretty bruised and battered right now.'

'Oh yes,' Jasmine heard herself say. 'Let's just have some fun.' She pulled her hand away, suddenly worried that everyone in the room had noticed them. But they were all chatting to each other and Aiden had disappeared into the kitchen with the empty platters, promising to come back with more food.

Connor smiled and let go of her hand. 'Great,' he said. 'I'm off to Kinsale early tomorrow but will be around here next week. I'll think of something fun to do in the meantime.'

'Great. I think I have your number. I should have bought a smartphone,' Jasmine grumbled as she looked up the contact list. 'This thing is a bit of a pain.'

'Yes, but much safer,' Connor argued. 'A smartphone can be traced. By the way,' he continued. 'You might consider parking your car somewhere more discreet than outside your mother's house. I know it's unlikely that your man will pop up around here, but you never know. The French number plates are a huge giveaway.'

'Oh.' Jasmine blinked and stared at him. 'I never thought of that. I'll put it in the garage tonight. And ask Mam if I can use hers.'

'Good idea.' Connor turned to Cordelia on his other side.

They didn't talk much during the rest of the evening as Aiden and Seán Óg kept the pints coming, and Connor brought a steaming pot of seafood chowder from the kitchen along with a raw food bowl for Kamal. The talking and laughing grew louder, making any intimate conversation impossible. With a warm glow inside, Jasmine chatted and laughed with the others, thoroughly enjoying the company and the food and drink. Paris and all the upset of the past weeks seemed suddenly so far away, as if it had happened on another planet. All except Damien, whose dark presence loomed in a corner of her mind. Would he find her here? And if he did, what would she do? She looked at Aiden, who was laughing at something Connor had just said, and her mother smiling at Kamal with a look of adoration; at Nuala, who was teasing her husband, at Cordelia and Declan so in love, and all the other people enjoying an evening out – and wondered if she would ever find the peace of mind they all seemed to have.

When they got up to leave, Kamal offered to walk Sally and Jasmine home which was met with a sigh of pleasure from Sally. Jasmine followed behind them as they walked out, waving goodbye to everyone, trying not to blush as Connor winked at her and blew her a kiss behind Aiden's back. She knew he was flirting just for fun but it stirred something deep inside that worried her. She couldn't get involved with another man so soon, she told herself. But there was no denying the spark of attraction between them.

Chapter Twelve

Later that evening, Jasmine drove her car into the garage and parked it beside Sally's Ford Focus. Feeling more at ease and a little less nervous, she banged the door shut and went inside, where she found her mother and Kamal enjoying a pot of camomile tea in front of the fire, Milou curled up at their feet. It was a cosy scene, but Jasmine felt a rising irritation as she joined them, determined to break up any romantic atmosphere.

'Camomile tea?' she asked, lifting the lid of the teapot. 'Is there enough for me?'

'Of course,' Sally said with a bright smile. 'Get a cup from the kitchen and help yourself.'

Jasmine did as she was told and returned with a cup and saucer and sat down beside Kamal on the sofa. 'Nice party, wasn't it?' she said as she poured tea into her cup.

'Wonderful,' Kamal said. 'It's a nice group of people. They have all been so kind to me, which I didn't expect.'

'Why not?' Jasmine asked.

Kamal shrugged and sipped his tea. 'Oh, you know. Racism and so on. Not that it affects me much. You can't change people's points of view if they're determined to stick to their prejudices.'

Jasmine studied him with interest. He seemed so aloof and cool, able to deal with negative reactions from others. 'I suppose your yoga teaching and all that is a help, though. I mean, a yoga teacher from India with your learning and experience is bound to attract a lot of people now that it's such a big part of a lot of people's lives. It's become more than a trend, hasn't it?'

'Indeed it has,' Kamal replied. 'Many people see it as some kind of sport at first, but then when they discover what a calming, healing effect it has, they begin to understand that it's a lot more than just exercising the body.' His dark eyes focused on her with an intensity that made her shiver. 'How did you feel, Jasmine, when you tried yoga for the first time?'

'Exhausted,' Jasmine said with a giggle, feeling a need to trivialise what he was trying to make into something life-changing.

'Oh, but you were so much calmer afterwards,' Sally argued. 'I could see how the tension had left your body as we walked home.'

'I think she knows deep in her heart what it does to her,' Kamal said and put his hand on Jasmine's. 'But maybe she doesn't want to share it with anyone, but keep it inside. That's fine. Yoga isn't about other people, it's about you and what you find out about yourself while you're practising. It's about learning to love yourself and your body and about being proud of what you can do.' He drew breath and continued. 'The basis of yoga philosophy is how to handle life as a human being, a guideline for how to interact with yourself and the world around you. It takes me back to the most important question: how do I want to put my own imprint? I'll never claim life to be easy, but sometimes we over-complicate things unnecessarily. We get shocked, react with fear and lose contact with our intentions. Yoga can help us get back on track again. And again, and again.'

'I see,' Jasmine said, beginning to understand the passion in his eyes. 'That sounds great.'

He hadn't finished. 'Practising yoga is supposed to be joyful so what I'm reaching for is sweetness, sukham, within every posture. The essence of yoga and the essence of life.'

The touch of his hand was as soft as silk and his eyes burned into hers with a look of conviction, but Jasmine still wasn't ready to fall under the spell. What he said sounded so perfect, as if practising yoga would bring you into a whole new world and a whole new way of thinking. She began to understand why Sally, at this watershed moment in her life, might have been drawn into her new lifestyle by this man who exuded such otherworldly wisdom. 'Uh, yeah, maybe,' she stammered.

'So I hope you will keep going and discover for yourself what a wonderful journey is waiting for you.'

Jasmine nodded. 'I'll certainly come to the classes. I like how it made me feel physically. But all the rest...'

He patted her hand. 'It will come. Don't rush it. Just let your body and mind take it all in.'

She pulled her hand away and stood up, feeling slightly dizzy. 'I should really take Milou out for his evening walk.'

'We already let him have a wander in the garden,' Sally said. 'I think he'll be fine until tomorrow morning.'

Jasmine glanced at Milou, who looked as if he had no intention of budging from his place on the rug and nodded. 'Oh, great. Thanks.'

'But you should go to bed,' Sally continued. 'You look tired, darling.'

'A good night's sleep would do you good,' Kamal agreed.

'I know. I'm off to bed,' Jasmine said with a feeling she was being dismissed. She hovered in the doorway, starting to say good night, but nobody heard her.

Sally and Kamal had started talking softly to each other, oblivious of whatever Jasmine was saying. She gave up and went to her room, knowing she couldn't draw her mother's attention away from Kamal's nearly hypnotic presence. She knew she shouldn't interfere, but she felt instinctively that Sally's obsession with Kamal wouldn't give her a lasting peace of mind and happiness. Yoga was all very well and good for body and mind, but believing it was going to solve everything in life seemed so wrong. In any case, Jasmine had plans for her mother and they didn't include falling in love with a yoga guru who might disappear whenever it suited him.

Her phone ringing as she went into her room pulled her thoughts away from Sally and Kamal. It was Aiden.

'Hi,' he said. 'Sorry for calling so late, but I meant to talk to you about that hike we were planning. The weather forecast is good for Saturday, so I thought we'd start early and see if we can get down to the hidden bay then. Winds will be slack so windsurfing is out of the question. What do you say?'

'Oh, Aiden, that would be lovely,' Jasmine exclaimed. 'I'm dying to explore further down the slope. And now that I've got boots and a proper jacket, it'll be much better than last time.'

'Couldn't be worse in any case,' Aiden remarked with a laugh. 'I've got walking sticks, too, which are a great help going down steep slopes.'

'Sounds perfect,' Jasmine said, her excitement growing. 'Can't wait.'

'You're just humouring me, aren't you?'

'No, I'm serious. I'm dying to get down there and discover more.'

'Me, too. Great party wasn't it?' Aiden continued.

'Brilliant.'

'You got on well with Connor, I take it?'

'Very well,' Jasmine said, smiling as she remembered their flirtatious conversation.

'He's a great guy to work for.'

'I can imagine,' Jasmine replied, wondering if the attraction between her and Connor had been obvious to others. 'He's very… nice,' she ended lamely.

'I thought you might come up with a better adjective than "nice," the way you looked at him,' Aiden remarked dryly.

'What way was that?' Jasmine asked.

'Oh, you know. You were positively swooning.'

'That's ridiculous. I don't swoon.' Jasmine cringed at the thought of Connor listening to their conversation.

'Don't worry. He's asleep on the living room couch,' Aiden cut in, eerily reading her thoughts. 'Probably exhausted after trying to fight you off when you flirted like mad at him.'

'I wasn't flirting!'

'Oh yes, you were. Loved your outfit by the way, even if I found it a little mismatched.'

'That's because you know nothing about fashion,' Jasmine countered, beginning to enjoy their repartee.

'Neither do you, judging by that mix of clothing.'

'You're just trying to annoy me.'

'Trying? I think I'm succeeding with flying colours.'

'Okay, you win. I'm officially annoyed. Three cheers for you, hang out the flags,' Jasmine said, trying not to laugh. 'Happy now?' she asked, with a pretend little sob.

'Very. Oh, come on, Jazz, I was just teasing you. Nobody could have guessed in their wildest dreams you found Connor remotely attractive. I just threw it out there for a laugh.'

'Just like you always used to tease me. And I fell for it again.'

'You enjoyed it,' Aiden said.

'The highlight of my day, of course. But you know what? You're right. I found Connor very attractive. At least he's mature. And considerate, and—'

'Yeah, well, I'd better sign off now,' Aiden interrupted with a noisy yawn. 'It's late and I'm exhausted. Good night, Jazz. Sleep tight.' He hung up before she had a chance to say good night.

Jasmine smiled and hung up. They were teasing each other like they used to in their teens, and she had enjoyed it, but there had been a more grown-up tone to it tonight, something quite flirty alongside that same affection they had before. She felt she could say whatever came into her head to Aiden because she knew he always understood her. Behind it all, they were just themselves and trusted each other.

She put her phone on the bedside table and got ready for bed. Once she had finished in the bathroom and put on her pyjamas, she settled into bed with her laptop. There were no further emails from Damien, but a new one from her confidant in Paris: a short message thanking her for her earlier email and asking her to keep in touch.

Jasmine smiled, and she was about to reply, when a thought struck her. She had occasionally used Damien's laptop to check her emails and he could probably get into her account if the details were still there. He might be able to read her messages. The thought sent a shiver through her as she tried to remember if she had revealed her whereabouts in any of her messages. She had only mentioned Kerry as far as she could remember, and never said anything about Sandy Cove. The best thing to do was to create a new email address. She nodded to herself, and quickly set up a new email account through Gmail, calling herself 'jorourke'. Her contact would know who she was. That done, she quickly tapped in a message in French explaining what she was doing.

Jasmine smiled and sent the message, knowing her friend would be looking for it over there in his cosy apartment in Paris. Cosy but lonely, she thought, feeling a little sad for him. Hopefully he was considering what they'd discussed… But that was wishful thinking. She sighed and put away the laptop. Time for bed and for sleep. She left the curtains open so she could look at the stars and the new moon. She was slowly settling into life in this small village. So much to see and do still, and so many people to get to know. And the hidden bay that beckoned her, its turbulent past waiting to be discovered.

Chapter Thirteen

The next day, Jasmine woke up late and spent a leisurely morning finally getting settled in, sorting her meagre wardrobe and going through her mother's clothes in search of things she could use. Sally had told her to take anything she wanted as she was planning to slim down her wardrobe and get rid of 'the relics from the past'. It would be cleansing, she said, and prepare her for her new life and the new venture she was planning.

'New venture?' Jasmine asked, taken aback by the gleam in Sally's eyes.

Sally smiled and put her finger to her lips. 'Shh, it's a secret. To be announced as soon as it's all in place. Forget I said anything.' She waved and left for the shop, leaving Jasmine standing in the middle of the bedroom, frowning.

'What did she mean?' Jasmine asked Milou at her feet. But he wagged his tail and jumped up on the bed, looking smug, as if he knew but wasn't going to tell.

'I'm going to forget about it,' Jasmine said out loud, but no matter how hard she tried to distract herself, it was niggling at her all morning as she went through the clothes. *New venture?* she asked herself. Could it have anything to do with Kamal? Were the two of them planning to move in together? *No, that can't be true*, she told herself sternly and turned her attention to the array of outfits, some of them so off-the-wall it made her laugh. Sally sure had eclectic tastes before she came here. Hopefully she wouldn't lose that part of herself. Jasmine was determined to remind her mother of the fabulous life she used to lead.

Jasmine held up a minidress with splashes of red, gold and blue and wondered if it had been worn at a fancy-dress party. It didn't suit Jasmine, but on Sally it would have been spectacular. *Probably for some fashion do*, she thought and put it back in the wardrobe. After sifting through the whole collection, she had a small pile of trousers, tops and shirts that were not too outrageous, and a handknitted Aran sweater for cold days. She decided to go and look in Sally's shop for more sweaters, some scarves and maybe some fun jewellery in case she had to dress up for anything.

With a feeling of satisfaction she carried her loot back to her room and put it all away, deciding to take a trip to Sally's shop and invite Cordelia for a coffee if she could get away. As the name popped into Jasmine's mind, she remembered Cordelia's happy face and her beautiful engagement ring with a pang of envy. Then she remembered her own ring and took it out of the drawer she had shoved it into so carelessly the evening of her arrival. She put it on her finger and looked at it, admiring the huge diamond and the beautiful setting. How nice it looked on her slim finger. Then she sighed and pulled it off, looking at it thoughtfully. It was a four-carat diamond from Cartier and it must have cost at least fifty thousand euros, she calculated. But it was bought with money from gambling, of course. She didn't want to keep it, or even give it back. In any case, it was too valuable to be left lying around, even in a safe place like Sandy Cove.

She looked around for a place to hide it. There was nowhere really safe, except perhaps in the hem of the curtain? Jasmine nodded to herself. Yes, why not? She found a pair of nail scissors in the bag with her toiletries and snipped off the threads of the hem to form a tiny hole into which she pushed the ring, easing it further along the bottom. She let the curtain fall back into place and stepped back. It dipped slightly at the end, but nobody would notice. As safe as could be, she decided and got ready to go to the shop.

Milou was already sitting at the door, his ears pricked up, as if he knew where they were going. Jasmine laughed and clipped the lead on him.

'You're getting to be a real Irish dog,' she told him. 'Walks are more interesting here. You never know who you're going to meet. Old friends and new, who knows what will happen?' Jasmine said with a feeling that every day in this part of the world was an adventure.

Jasmine didn't have to walk far to come across someone interesting. As Milou stopped to lift his leg against a lamp post, Jasmine spotted an old man sitting on a bench outside a tiny white cottage where a donkey stuck his head over the white picket fence. He was dressed in a tweed jacket and baggy trousers and wore a flat cap on his woolly white hair. With his long beard and the clothes, he looked like the epitome of the Irish peasant sitting outside his quaint cottage taking in the sun. He looked at Jasmine and winked.

'Hello there, pretty girl. You light up the whole street with your beauty. And that little dog is the cutest animal I've seen in a long while.'

Jasmine stopped and smiled at him. 'Hello there. You must be M— I mean, Brendan.'

He lifted his cap. 'Mad Brendan, they call me. I'm not mad at all. That was a name I was called when I was a boy because of some shenanigans I'd been up to. I don't remember what it was exactly, but the name stuck.' He peered at her. 'You're that O'Rourke girl's daughter, isn't that right?'

'Yes, I am. My name's Jasmine.'

He shifted on the bench. 'I've heard you were around. Come, sit beside me and we'll have a bit of a chat.'

'Why not?' Jasmine said, laughing, and sat down beside him.

He peered down the street. 'Any of them tourists around?'

'I can't see anyone,' Jasmine replied.

'That's grand, so. It's not high season yet. But you never know when those folks take into their heads to go up the Wild Atlantic Way. The tourist season seems to happen all the year around these days. I made twenty euros yesterday just sitting here minding my own business.'

'The Wild Atlantic Way is very popular,' Jasmine remarked. 'Because it's so beautiful.'

'Ha,' he exclaimed. 'Wild Atlantic Way, huh? We used to call it the west coast, but them tourist board people think that a fancy name will lure foreigners to come here in droves and spend their money.'

'It seems to work, though,' Jasmine remarked.

'You think?' He shrugged and pulled a pair of Ray-Bans out of his top pocket and put them on. 'I suppose you're right. Great way to make a few bucks just sitting her looking interesting.'

'You look very Irish,' Jasmine said, studying him. 'Like something out of a tourist brochure.'

'That's the idea, girl,' he said, grunting.

'I like your cute little cottage.'

'Not my cottage. It belongs to an old woman called Maura. She doesn't mind me sitting here and the donkeys keep the grass down in her front garden. I live in the little bungalow at the end of the street. Central heating and all mod cons, ya know,' he said proudly.

Jasmine giggled. 'You're a great actor.'

'Who's acting?' He gestured down his body. 'This is all me and no faking. I just added a few bits and keep sitting here and let them take their pictures. Then they give me a tip and say thanks and go on their way. Money for old rope, m'dear.'

'I suppose. But you have the old Irishman look perfectly. Nobody else could do that.'

He shrugged. 'Of course not. Why would they? Anyhow,' he continued. 'Enough about me. Before you go on your way, tell me how come you're here.'

'I'm here staying with my mother for a bit.'

He patted her knee. 'That's good. Your mother needs you. She's a little confused and lost right now.'

Jasmine stared at him. 'How do you know?'

He touched his nose, looking mysterious. 'I know such things. I can read people.' He turned to her. 'And you are also a little lost, aren't you? At a crossroads? Looking for a new beginning? Having left something precious behind, I think. And now,' he continued, without waiting for an answer, 'you want to explore. You want to know the history of this village where your ancestors were the rebel kings of the day and ruled the roost.'

His Kerry accent was so strong she found she had to listen intently to decipher what he said. 'Tell me,' she urged him. 'Tell me about the O'Rourkes and Wild Rose Bay.'

He nodded. 'That's what I meant about them O'Rourkes. They were wild in the old days down there in the bay. Hundreds of years ago it was. When the village was built down the slopes. Later, they came up here as it was safer and easier to get to and the houses above the bay were abandoned. But the legends lived on, and the stories of pirates, smugglers and shipwreckers were told around the fire long after the houses had been abandoned. The O'Rourkes became respectable and started a sheep farm up in the hills, and some of them moved here and set up shops. But that wild spirit is still in them, and in *you*, my dear.'

'Maybe,' Jasmine whispered, feeling a little shiver. 'I just have to find it.'

'You will,' he said with great certainty. 'And you will find the man you are meant to love, too. Just like Siobhan did.'

'Who was Siobhan?' Jasmine asked, intrigued.

'A young woman who lived a long time ago,' Brendan replied. 'In the early nineteenth century. She loved a fisherman named Oisin but she was an O'Rourke and he was a Donnelly.'

'What happened to them?' Jasmine asked.

He shrugged. 'Nobody knows, really. They had become engaged despite their families trying to stop them. Then he was lost at sea and never heard of again. He probably drowned. Some say it was the O'Rourkes who made it happen. But nobody knows. Siobhan went mad with grief, they say, and her soul is now wandering over the slopes of the mountains. You can hear her wail on dark, windy nights.'

Jasmine laughed. 'That has to be the wind howling.'

'Who knows?' Brendan said. 'Could be the wind or – a lost soul. People around here don't want to go down there anyway. That's why the path stops just above it.'

'It's a sad story.'

He sighed. 'Yes. Very sad. But not unusual. They say that anyone who finds the ring will be lucky in love.'

'Her engagement ring?'

Brendan nodded. 'Yes, the one Oisin gave her before he went out to sea.'

'It's just a legend, though, isn't it?'

'A legend, yes. But maybe based on truth?' He pushed off the bench and got up. 'But now I must take the critters to the field where they have a little more grass. Nice to talk to you, darlin'. See you around, I'm sure.'

Jasmine jumped off the bench and pulled Milou with her. 'I'm off to the shop. Thanks for the chat, Brendan. It was nice to meet you.'

He waved and opened the gate to the front garden of the cottage. 'Maura,' he yelled so loudly Jasmine gave a start. 'I'm taking the donkeys home now. Give us a shout if you need anything.'

There was no reply. 'Deaf as a post,' Brendan muttered and grabbed one of the donkey's neck straps. 'Come on then, ya fool.'

Jasmine bubbled with laughter all the way to the shop. What a character, and what a story he had told. It made her even more anxious to get down to the hidden bay. The ghost story didn't frighten her in the slightest. It made the place seem even more interesting. It related to her family and its history and it suddenly seemed to her that finding out more would anchor her to this part of Ireland and the O'Rourkes. Their history was part of her and learning about it would not only make her feel more grounded here, it would bring her closer to her mother. She had been feeling rootless and a little lost when she arrived, but now there was a purpose to her coming here and she was determined to further explore Wild Rose Bay and find what it might reveal.

Chapter Fourteen

The rest of the week flew by, even though Jasmine had thought she'd have nothing much to do. But the days had been full of little things like walking Milou, helping Sally in the garden now that spring had arrived with mild winds and sunny days. They put out pots of geraniums, tended to the rose bushes, mowed the lawn, clipped the hedge, used the strimmer around the shrubs, weeded the herb garden and tidied up the small shed at the back.

Stiff and sore, Jasmine found yoga a great help to loosen her up after the back-breaking work. Kamal was his usual serene self, but she had to admit he was an excellent teacher. Even at her second ever yoga class she found herself managing the poses, even if she found it quite challenging. She was also getting to know the other women in the class, who were very interested in her life in Paris and gave her helpful tips of things to do and see in the neighbourhood. In fact, she found herself the centre of attention as they all came back to Sally's house for tea on the Friday night.

After a fun evening spent laughing and chatting, Jasmine went to bed with a smile on her face, relaxed and happy, looking forward to the morning, when she would meet Aiden for their hike down to Wild Rose Bay. She had asked her mother about Siobhan and the legend of the ring when they were working in the garden earlier that day, but Sally shrugged it off, saying it was just a fairy tale and not to listen to Mad Brendan.

'He was probably just having you on, as you're new here,' she said. 'He likes telling tales to people who might be gullible enough the swallow them. I'm sure he enjoyed seeing you taking it all in.'

'So there's no ghost down there, then?' Jasmine asked, disappointed by Sally's disinterest. She had hoped exploring the history together might bring them closer, but it didn't seem as if this was going to happen.

Sally let out a snort. 'Ghost? Don't be silly. It's just that it's a sad place with an eerie feel. I've walked a bit of the path along the cliffs a few times but never gone that close. Those ruined houses are a lonely sight. But ghosts? Not at all. Brendan was pulling your leg and having great fun while he was at it.'

'So there were no lovers called Siobhan and Oisin?'

'I think there was a Siobhan O'Rourke sometime in the early eighteen hundreds. There's a headstone in the graveyard with that name. But nobody really knows who she was. I don't know about Oisin. I've got no idea if he really existed as it was all so long ago.'

With that the subject was closed and they continued weeding, talking about other things. But Siobhan and Oisin and their story was still vivid in Jasmine's mind and she refused to believe it was just some silly tale Mad Brendan had told her for fun. It had to be true and she felt even more compelled to go down there and see the bay for herself, ghost or no ghost.

*

The next morning Jasmine woke up to a beautiful spring day with white fluffy clouds scudding across the blue sky and a fresh breeze. It didn't take her long to get ready and run down to the main beach where Aiden was waiting for her. He looked approvingly at Jasmine's dark green anorak and sturdy hiking boots. 'That's a great improvement on the other day.'

'Couldn't be worse in any case,' Jasmine said, remembering her silly designer trainers and flimsy jacket. 'Lucky I fit into my mam's clothes, or I'd have to buy a lot more.'

Aiden looked her up and down with a glint in his eyes. 'You fit into those jeans very well, I have to say.'

'Thanks. Let's go and buy sandwiches and get going,' Jasmine urged, eager to start the adventure. That look Aiden gave her from time to time when he thought she wasn't watching made her feel a little strange. Although she found him attractive, she wasn't sure she wanted their friendship to be ruined by any kind of romance. Aiden had matured into a very handsome man and she could imagine women falling for his charm and warmth, but she wanted a friendship that would last forever and she didn't want to do anything to ruin that.

'Okay,' Aiden replied with an expression that told her he had read her thoughts. 'We shouldn't hang around. In any case I have to get back by early afternoon. Saturday nights are usually busy and as it's a nice weekend, I already have bookings from some people coming from Cork.' He handed her a walking stick. 'Here. Take this to help you when we go down that steep slope.'

They hurried into The Two Marys' and collected the sandwiches Aiden had already ordered. After a quick cup of coffee, they were on their way out the door and down the path that led to the trail along the cliffs, Jasmine in front and Aiden behind, the picnic in his rucksack.

Jasmine found the walking stick a great help even on the flat as the path was rough and uneven. Proper hiking boots were also an improvement. Feeling a lot more secure than during their first outing, she began to enjoy the walk, looking out over the glittering sea where she could see birds swooping down to catch fish and a seal poke its head up through the waves only to disappear just as quickly. With the wind in her hair and the sun warming her back, she felt a surge of joy at being here in this beautiful place with someone she was so fond of.

She glanced up at the majestic mountains towering over them, casting a shadow over the slopes below and thought that this was exactly the same landscape the people who lived here hundreds of years ago had walked through. They had not been hiking for pleasure, but struggled to survive in this rugged land, where only sheep could manage to find something to eat. She glanced down at the dark water below and imagined fishing boats swaying on the waves, and women on the shore waiting for them to return. Had Siobhan been standing down there waiting for Oisin? Or was that story just a legend? She would never know, but felt, as they approached the ruined houses, that even if that story wasn't true, similar tragedies might have happened to young lovers like those two.

They reached the ruins after an hour of walking and sat down for a brief rest before tackling the steep slope that led down to the shore below. Aiden leaned on his walking stick and looked down at the beach.

'Incredible to think that people lived here in these little houses and walked down these dangerous slopes to get down there. I think there must have been some kind of pier in those days so they could unload the boats more easily, but the rest of the time the vessels must have been at anchor in the bay.'

Jasmine climbed over a wall to stand in the middle of what would have been a cottage. She put her hand on the stones and pointed at the gable end that was blackened with soot. 'Look, that must have been the fireplace. The chimney is gone but the soot marks are still visible.'

Aiden nodded and walked around the house to an arch made of stones in the side of the hill. 'I think this is an opening to something. Maybe there was a passage under the ground down to the beach?' He peered inside. 'It's hard to see. I'd need a torch. But even so, it'd be dangerous. If it's a tunnel it'll have caved in.'

'We'd better just try the slope,' Jasmine replied and climbed back over the ruined wall. 'I don't want to go down any tunnels. We're already a lot further than we got last time, even if we don't get right down to the beach.'

'You're right. Let's see how far we get, then.' Aiden walked around another ruined wall and poked his stick through the bushes. 'I can see something here that looks like stone steps, and more cut into the rock. Must have been the way down. Let's try that. Follow me, Jasmine, but be careful.'

'Okay.' Jasmine followed Aiden down what looked like jagged steps cut into the steep slope, holding onto bushes and branches as she went. She sat down twice when she felt herself about to slip, and the second time she looked down and wondered if this was really wise. She gazed up behind her and saw how steep the incline was. How on earth were they going to get back up? Lucky it hadn't rained for a while and the ground was dry, otherwise they would have slithered down all the way to the beach.

Aiden was a lot further down and stopped, looking up at her. 'You okay?' he shouted.

'Fine,' she shouted back. 'Is it much further?'

'Don't think so,' his muffled voice replied. 'I can hear the waves. Be careful coming down and hang on to the little bushes. I nearly slipped and bruised my backside.'

Jasmine carefully picked her way down, stepping sideways, planting her stick into the ground for support, and could finally hear the waves before she crawled under dense vegetation and could push through to drop down onto the white sand. Amazed, she looked around and discovered that they were standing on a curved beach where the waves lapped gently onto the shore and the crystal-clear water was nearly turquoise.

'How beautiful,' she said, nearly breathless with wonder at the view across the small bay and the green slopes of the mountains plunging into the sea.

'Heavenly,' Aiden agreed. 'But it'll be even more beautiful when the roses are in bloom. The slopes here will be covered in them.'

'Wow,' Jasmine said, nearly breathless at the thought. 'I'll fly back from Paris to see that.'

'Of course you will,' Aiden agreed.

'She would have stood here,' Jasmine said dreamily. 'And waited for him to come back.'

'Who?' Aiden asked, looking intrigued.

'Siobhan. The girl whose lover was lost at sea. The only thing she had left was the ring he gave her.'

Aiden laughed and shook his head. 'You've been talking to Mad Brendan. He loves to tell that old story. It's just a legend, you know. One of those stories that get better and better through the years.'

'You don't believe it?'

Aiden shrugged. 'Not really. But I'm sure there were loads of women mourning their men who drowned out there in bad weather. So in a way it's true.'

'It's a sad story,' Jasmine said, feeling a strange connection with Siobhan, an O'Rourke like her.

'I think the Famine was a sadder story. That's when the village up there was abandoned. Everyone must have starved to death.'

'Horrible.' Jasmine shivered as a cold wind swept over the beach. 'That's probably why there's such a lonely feel up there.'

'It's much nicer down here.' He pointed at the far side of the beach, where the waves washed over the rocks. 'I can see the Sandy Cove lighthouse from here. Nice to see it from this angle.' Aiden sat down on the sand and started to open the rucksack. 'This is the perfect place for lunch.'

'Oh yes.' Jasmine sank down beside him, her knees like jelly after the long hike. 'Can't think of anywhere better.'

Aiden took a waterproof sheet out of the rucksack and spread it on the sand. 'Here, sit on this. The sand is cold.'

'You are the perfect companion on a hike like this,' Jasmine said as she sat down on the sheet, grateful to be protected from the damp sand. 'What else do you have in that magic rucksack?'

'It's a surprise,' Aiden said with a wink. 'This is like Mary Poppins' carpetbag. Whatever you need is in here. But only when you need it.'

Jasmine laughed and took the sandwich and bottle of water Aiden handed her. Leaning against a boulder, she started on the sandwich and drank some water, staring out at the view. 'What a magical place this is. Like something from a fairy tale.'

Aiden, sitting on a rock a little further away, looked at her and smiled. 'And you're the lost princess.'

'Without a prince,' Jasmine said with a sigh.

'Did you lose him?' Aiden asked softly.

Jasmine shrugged and swallowed her bite. 'He turned out not to be a prince at all, just a frog I kissed who pretended to be a prince for a while.'

'Then what happened?' Aiden asked. 'Do you feel like telling me?'

Jasmine finished her sandwich and looked at Aiden's kind face, feeling a sudden urge to unburden her heart. 'I want to tell you. It's not very nice and you'll think I was stupid to have fallen for…' She stopped, suddenly not sure she wanted Aiden to know the truth about what had happened. It seemed so naïve to have believed all the lies.

'Let me hear it,' Aiden said, getting up and sitting beside her on the sheet. 'I won't think anything at all until I know what happened.'

Jasmine nodded. 'Sorry. I tend to jump to conclusions about what people will think about me.'

'That's because you're beating yourself up and believe other people will, too.'

'I suppose,' Jasmine said bleakly. She stared out across the bay for a while, and then launched into her story, not leaving out any detail, telling Aiden everything from the moment she met Damien to when she had left Paris. She drew breath and stared at Aiden. 'So there it is: the ugly, horrible story about a gullible woman who gave her all to a con-man. Now do you see why I feel so ashamed?'

'No.'

'What?' Jasmine stared at Aiden. 'Can't you see how he fooled me and how I believed anything he said? He wrecked my life and I never saw it coming, not for a second.' She buried her face in her hands and burst into tears. 'I loved him so much,' she sobbed. 'More than I have loved anyone apart from my parents. And I thought he loved me, too. How could I be so stupid?'

Aiden pulled Jasmine into his arms and hugged her close. 'Don't punish yourself, Jazz. Of course you loved him, why wouldn't you? He seemed like the perfect man for you and he was probably very good at fooling people.'

Jasmine turned up her tearstained face to look at him. 'And women like me, of course. Looking for love and—'

'Okay, I get it,' Aiden interrupted. 'Maybe you were stupid, but I bet any woman would have fallen for him. Even the smartest, most powerful woman in the world. He played to all your feelings, but most of all your self-esteem.'

'I suppose.' Jasmine sighed and leaned her head against Aiden's chest. 'I couldn't believe he wanted me, when he could have had anyone. I felt so proud to be seen with him. You have no idea how handsome he is.'

'I can imagine,' Aiden muttered, and she felt his chin against the top of her head.

'Sorry. I shouldn't go on like that. I don't know why I can't just move on and stick my life back together. But I feel so hurt.'

'It's about being rejected, isn't it? You told me years ago about your dad leaving and how you never got over it. I guess this felt like something similar and it tore all those old wounds open again.'

Jasmine pulled away from Aiden and nodded. 'Yes. I think that's what made it worse. A man I loved leaving me again.' She leaned her head back against his chest and stayed there for a moment, comforted by his arms around her. He knew her so well and understood her completely. Then Jasmine sat up and tried to wipe her face with her sleeve. 'I shouldn't blame myself, should I?'

'No, you shouldn't.'

'Do you have a hanky in that magic bag of yours?'

Aiden dug in his rucksack and found a packet of tissues. 'Here. I bring these in case I cut myself or something. I have Band-Aids and some Vaseline too.'

Jasmine took the tissues. 'I don't think there's any Band-Aid big enough to cover my stupidity,' she said and blew her nose.

'There you go again, beating yourself up. Could you stop the self-pity?'

'No,' Jasmine sniffed.

'Not even for a bar of chocolate?' he asked with a cheeky expression.

'What kind?'

'Salted caramel. Your favourite.' He pulled a bar out of his pocket and held it over his head. 'But you can only have it if you stop the self-pity.'

'You monster,' Jasmine said with a weak laugh. 'Okay, I'll stop. Hand it over.'

He broke off half and gave her the rest and they ate the chocolate in silence for a while. Then Aiden sat back and looked at Jasmine. 'And now he's following you?'

'Did Connor tell you?'

'Yes. He said your ex-boyfriend was stalking you. Is he?'

'I wouldn't say he's stalking me exactly. But I think he's trying to find me. I'm not even sure it was him I saw. It looked like him anyway. I have a feeling he wants to try to get me back or something. He's so self-centred that he can't accept that anyone wants to leave him.'

Aiden nodded. 'Sounds like a correct diagnosis. Hard to know what goes on in the mind of someone like that.'

'A narcissist, you mean?' Jasmine said, feeling suddenly cold. 'That's what Connor said. But isn't that going a bit too far?'

'It sounds a bit dramatic. But in any case, it's best to be careful with someone who behaves like that.'

'I suppose.' Jasmine sighed. 'I shouldn't have run off like that. Maybe I should go back and sort things out, get another job and…'

'Don't do anything for the moment,' Aiden said and patted her head. 'Chill for a bit. Reconnect with your mother. Hang out with me and Connor. Have a bit of fun.'

'You're right.' As the sun warmed her, Jasmine took off her jacket and got up, looking out at the view of the rocks and the lighthouse in the distance. 'I'm just going to walk for a bit and then we'll get back, if we can make it up that slope.'

'We'll fly up it, darlin',' Aiden quipped.

'Yeah, sure we will,' Jasmine replied, smiling at him. It was such a comfort to have a friend like him, who truly understood her and never judged.

She walked along the beach, thinking about Siobhan and Oisin, the wild roses, fishing boats, and a long-forgotten village overlooking the ocean. As she stood there, she was momentarily transported to that village and the people who had lived there, walking along the same beach but with a different purpose. She blinked as the cry of a seagull pulled her out of her daydream, squinting into the sun, slightly disoriented for a moment. Turning around, she looked for Aiden, but the beach was deserted.

'Aiden?' she called, her voice echoing across the water. Where had he gone? Suddenly chilled, she put on her jacket and called his name again.

'Here,' his muffled voice replied. 'In the tunnel.'

'What tunnel?' she asked, annoyed. 'Stop playing games.' She gave a start when Aiden's head emerged from between two boulders further down the beach.

'I found the end of that passage we saw up above. I thought it was a small cave, but there's some kind of entrance at the back. I went inside and then I saw that it had caved in completely, so the tunnel is no more, I'm afraid. But isn't it amazing that they would have dug their way down to here? Must have been handy in bad weather. I saw a few steps when the tunnel went up the hill and then there is a wall of debris that would be impossible to get through.' He brushed dried mud off his shoulders and hair and walked out onto the beach. 'Time to get back, I think.'

'You're right.'

They put everything back into the rucksack and pushed through the shrubs to start climbing up again, but were interrupted by Jasmine's phone ringing in her pocket. She pulled it out. 'My mother.' She put the phone to her ear. 'Hi, Mam, what's up?'

'Can you come home?' Sally said, sounding slightly flustered.

'Uh, right now?'

'Yes.'

'But I'm—' Jasmine started.

'Please, Jasmine. I need you.' Then the signal died and Jasmine couldn't hear Sally's voice any more.

'What did she want?' Aiden asked.

'I don't know. She asked me to come home and then the connection broke.'

'The signal is hopeless here. Did she sound upset?'

'Not really. Maybe a little nervous or something. But we'd better hurry all the same. Something's up and she needs me.'

'Okay. It'll be a bit of a climb, but the path is dry. You'd better go ahead so I can catch you if you fall.'

Jasmine nodded, thinking Aiden had caught her many times in the past when she'd fallen in one way or the other. She felt secure knowing he was there behind her and the climb back up wasn't as bad as she had feared, even though it was tiring and her mind was on Sally and whatever her phone call was about. Was it something to do with Kamal? Or had she been taken ill? The climb seemed suddenly endless and her heartbeat increased, not because of the strenuous effort but because of what she imagined her mother might be going through. After twenty minutes of hard work, they were finally back up in the ruined little village and starting up the path to the main beach, Jasmine running ahead.

As she ran, Jasmine wondered why Sally wanted her to come home at once. She hadn't sounded frightened, but nervous. Maybe she was just reaching out? Wanting Jasmine to come home because she felt lonely? Jasmine calmed down and said a quick goodbye to Aiden as they reached the main street. She walked swiftly the rest of the way, wanting to find out what was troubling her mother. She finally reached the front gate and ran up the hill, pulling the front door open as she heard Milou bark.

Chapter Fifteen

Jasmine ran into the living room and stopped dead, breathing hard, staring at her mother standing in the middle of the floor, Milou at her feet barking frantically. 'What's going on?' she asked, trying to catch her breath. She looked around but saw no sign of anything wrong or different to what it had been early that morning. She peered at Sally. 'Are you ill? Do you want me to call a doctor?'

'No, of course not,' Sally protested. 'There's nothing wrong with me.'

Jasmine calmed down. 'Thank God. But why did you call me and ask me to come home?'

Sally gave Milou a shove with her foot. 'Stop barking, you're making me deaf.' The dog stopped barking and immediately trotted to Jasmine's bedroom door and ran inside, whining.

'So?' Jasmine asked. 'What's going on? Why did you panic like that?'

Sally sank down on the edge of the sofa. 'Panic? Not really. I just had the uneasy feeling someone's been in the house.'

Startled, Jasmine looked around then stared at her mother. 'What? Who? Did you see someone?'

'No. But I think someone's been here.'

Jasmine looked wildly around. 'Someone broke in to the house? Are you sure?'

'No, but…'

'Through the front door?'

'No. That was locked. He – or she – came in through the kitchen door. It was wide open when I came home.'

'And you had locked it?'

'Of course not,' Sally replied. 'I always leave that unlocked in case I forget my key.'

'Oh noo,' Jasmine groaned. 'What's the point of that? If anyone's been here, did they take anything?'

'No, but my bedroom's in a mess and some of my clothes are missing. I think I might call the Guards.'

'Oh.' Jasmine started to laugh. 'I see. Don't call the Guards, though. That was me. You said to take anything I wanted, so I did. I raided your wardrobe big time. Must have forgotten to tidy up afterwards. Sorry about that.'

'Oh, God.' Sally let out a long sigh of relief. 'I should have known it was you. I forgot how untidy you used to be. I see that hasn't changed.'

'Will do better, promise,' Jasmine declared. Feeling calmer, she took off her jacket and sat down on a stool, unlacing her walking boots. 'But you shouldn't have left the back door unlocked. Do you realise how stupid that is? What's the point of locking the front door, if the back door is open?'

Sally shrugged. 'We don't lock anything here, really.'

Jasmine pulled her foot out of the boot and wiggled her toes. 'I know. You told me. The door must have been blown open by the wind.'

'But maybe it wasn't the wind?' Sally suggested. 'Maybe someone was here after all? Milou started barking and growling the minute we got inside.' She sniffed the air. 'And I can smell something… like a scent I don't recognise.'

Jasmine sniffed. 'I don't know what you mean. I can only smell a bit of turf smoke.' She got up and went to her room, where Milou was sniffing around, still whining. Jasmine looked all about her. Everything was the same as it had been when she left that morning: her laptop on her desk, her handbag hanging on the back of the chair and the window… She stiffened.

The window that she was sure she had closed when she left was off the latch. She went across and opened it, leaning out to look at the ground. Nothing to see. The ground under the window was dry and there were no footprints of any kind, not even on the grass. She must have forgotten to close the window properly. She turned from the window and looked at Milou, who was still running around, sniffing and whining. Then she felt it, like a tiny whiff of something exotic, something that didn't belong here. It was gone before she could identify it properly, but she knew what it reminded her of. Damien's aftershave.

Could it be? she asked herself then dismissed the idea. No, it was just a whiff of turf smoke mixed with Sally's lavender oil. She was being hypersensitive and imagining things. Damien might be looking for her, but he would never find her here, in Sandy Cove, which was well off the beaten track. In any case, he might not have followed her at all. Just a trick of her imagination. She was on edge after what had happened and seeing that man in Killarney. She told herself to calm down. She was safe here.

*

'I thought he was here,' Jasmine said to Aiden when he phoned her a little later. 'I nearly thought I could smell his aftershave, but then I realised it was just lavender oil mixed with smoke. Milou was acting strange, but I guess he just doesn't like the smell of lavender. It's quite similar to the aftershave Damien used. He never really took to Damien and I had to put him in another room when we were together. Damien hated him. He pretended to like him but then he said he was allergic to dogs and that I'd have to get rid of Milou when we were married. I was going to ask my dad to take him.'

'How could you fall for someone who doesn't like dogs?' Aiden asked incredulously. 'Wouldn't that be a real deal breaker?'

'It should have been,' Jasmine said, knowing he was right. 'But I was blinded by all the things he said to me. All that love and attention during a time when I was feeling lost and lonely.'

'I know,' Aiden said, his voice gentle. 'And then he stole your money and took off.'

'Yes,' Jasmine whispered.

'What a total—' Aiden stopped, sounding angry. 'If I ever meet him, I'll—'

'You won't,' Jasmine cut in, touched by Aiden's anger on her behalf. 'He'll never find me here. And if he were to turn up, he won't get to me again or cajole me into believing him. I'll never let myself get drawn in to his lies and empty promises.'

'You're sure about that?' Aiden said, sounding happier.

'Yes, absolutely,' Jasmine declared with feeling. 'And I don't think he was here at all. I just imagined that smell because I'm so jumpy.'

She sniffed the air. 'Can't smell it now.' She looked at Milou, who had leaped up on her bed, wagging his tail. 'Milou has stopped whining, too.'

'He probably smelled something else. Like a mouse or a bat hanging somewhere in the house?'

'I hope not,' Jasmine said with a shiver. 'I hate bats.'

'Have a look around. If nothing has been moved or touched, it was probably your imagination. It's natural for you to be on edge after all you've been through.'

'I suppose,' Jasmine said, beginning to calm down. 'You're probably right.' Then she started to laugh. 'My mother was going to call the police because some of her clothes were missing and her room was in a mess. But that was me. I was in there to take a few things as I hadn't brought much from Paris. I forgot to tell her and of course didn't tidy up afterwards, so there was a bit of a mess. Imagine if she had called the Guards and told them her wardrobe had been raided by thieves.'

Aiden chuckled. 'I can see the headlines. "The police are looking for someone dressed in a T-shirt with the design of a peacock and shocking pink harem pants with a Dior handbag dangling from their wrist."'

'I know,' Jasmine said, still giggling. 'How ridiculous.'

'Typical of you, though, Miss Messy,' Aiden remarked. 'I remember your locker at school. You used to have to pull everything out to find anything. I see you haven't changed.'

'No,' Jasmine said, sighing. 'That will probably never change. Would that be a deal breaker for anyone, do you think?'

'I have no idea. But I'm sure all your other talents make up for that little flaw.'

'I hope you're right,' Jasmine said.

'I'm sure I am. Hey, listen, I have to go. It's nearly opening time. Bye for now. See you after the weekend.'

Jasmine said goodbye to Aiden and looked thoughtfully at Milou. 'What were you barking at? A mouse? Or a bat?'

Milou wagged his tail and put his head on his paws, looking at her with soulful eyes. Jasmine shrugged and went back into the living room. Everything seemed in order and the sun shining in through the windows, casting a pool of light on the rug, made her feel all peaceful inside.

Jasmine found Sally in the kitchen and did her best to reassure her. 'Nothing there but Milou smelling something he didn't like,' she said. 'No need to panic any more.'

'Are you sure?' Sally asked, still looking a little shaken.

'Positive,' Jasmine said. 'Relax, Mam. Nothing but butterflies in your stomach and a lively imagination.'

Sally let out a long sigh. 'Oh yes. I think you're right. Just Milou getting excited and scaring me.'

'Exactly. Let's have some tea and forget about it.'

The usual calm had been restored. Nothing had really happened except in her imagination. She was just jumpy after all she had been through. Better to try to forget it and calm down. Damien would never find her here anyway. And she had her date with Connor to look forward to. All was well in her world. All except that hint of a scent that still lingered in her mind.

Chapter Sixteen

Connor's warm voice on the phone the next morning swept all thoughts of Damien from Jasmine's mind.

'Morning,' he said. 'Sorry to call so early and give you such short notice, but would you like to come with me to Kinsale today? I'm driving there from Killarney, but I can take a detour and pick you up. Then we'll have lunch at a great pub and walk around Kinsale. It's a nice little sailing town well worth a visit. Especially on a nice spring day like today. Then I'll drive you back along the coast. That way you'll see a bit of west Cork, which is just as beautiful as Kerry but in a different way.' He drew breath and laughed. 'That was a long speech.'

'It was a good speech,' Jasmine said, wondering why he sounded so nervous. Maybe he wasn't used to dating after having been married for a long time. 'That sounds like a lovely day to me.'

'Good. But feel free to say no if you have better things to do.'

'Not really,' Jasmine replied, smiling. What could be better than spending the day with such a gorgeous man? 'I was going to sort my sock drawer, but I can put that on hold.'

'If you're sure,' Connor said with a chuckle. 'I wouldn't want to upset your plans.'

'I haven't really got any,' Jasmine confessed. 'My mother is doing yoga on the beach, but I decided to give it a miss. Two yoga classes in a week is enough for me. So, yes, please,' she continued, unable to keep her excitement out of her voice. 'I'd love to come with you.'

'Terrific. I'll pick you up at around eleven.'

Jasmine smiled when he had hung up. 'He likes me,' she said softly to herself. 'And I like him.' Then she lay there for a while wondering why she liked him and felt she could trust him. Probably because Aiden knew him and that meant that he hadn't hidden anything from her. With his broad smile and twinkly green eyes, Connor was the complete opposite of Damien. He was honest.

She dressed casually in jeans, a white shirt and one of Sally's old sweaters, brushed her hair and applied just a little mascara, and blusher to her already rosy cheeks. After a light breakfast of yoghurt, fruit and a slice of sourdough bread, she was ready to go. Milou trotted across the floor from his cushion by the fire and looked mournfully at her.

'You want to come?' Jasmine asked and picked him up. 'Okay, then. You can come with us. I hope Connor likes dogs and doesn't mind a hairy fella like you in his car.'

She was about to leave when Sally appeared at the door, her yoga mat under her arm.

'Hi, Mam. Nice morning.'

'Divine,' Sally said with a blissful smile.

'Looks like you had a good morning,' Jasmine remarked, wondering if yoga was all she had been doing. 'I'm going for a drive with Connor and I'm taking Milou with me.'

'Oh.' Sally looked at Jasmine as if she had just noticed her. 'That's fine. I have a meeting at the yoga studio with Kamal later.'

'What kind of meeting?' Jasmine asked. 'I mean, didn't you just do yoga together?'

Sally's cheeks turned pink. 'This is more like a… business meeting. It's about… Well, a new venture we're planning together. I'll tell you when I'm ready. And it's not what you seem to think,' she added hotly.

'I don't think anything, Mam. Just be careful, okay? Take things slowly?'

Sally nodded. 'I'll lock both doors this time. And hide the key in the shed.'

'That's not what I…' Jasmine sighed. 'Fine. Whatever works for you.'

She had intended to warn her mother not to get too involved with Kamal, but the right moment hadn't occurred. Sally was too breezy and bright to Jasmine's liking, too ready to skirt all the issues they should be discussing. And far too distracted by her new lifestyle and her new friendship to spend any time researching their family history that seemed so fascinating. She hoped Sally wouldn't make any big life-changing decisions before her birthday party. She glanced out the door as Connor's car drew up at the gate. 'He's here. Got to go.'

'In all the excitement yesterday, I forgot to tell you there's a letter for you on the hall table,' Sally said.

'Okay. I'll take it with me.' Jasmine kissed her mother, picked up the letter, shoved it into her handbag, and with Milou under her arm, ran down the hill to the car.

'You be careful, too,' she heard Sally shout as she reached the car and Connor jumped out.

'Hi, there,' he said and kissed her on both cheeks. 'I believe this is the way you do it in France.'

'That's right,' she said, laughing. 'The French hello. But you don't have to kiss Milou. Is it okay if he comes with us? He's as good as gold, I promise.'

Connor shook Milou's paw. 'Good morning, Milou. Delighted to meet you. Of course he can come. I love dogs.'

'That's a point in your favour,' Jasmine said and deposited Milou on the back seat.

'And you looking so fresh and happy is a point in yours,' Connor said and beamed his thousand-watt smile at her. 'Off we go, then. Next stop Kinsale. Or… we might stop for coffee on the way, if we feel like it.'

'Yes,' Jasmine stated. 'I'm a coffee addict, just so you know.'

'So am I, actually,' Connor said and started the engine.

Jasmine looked at his profile as they drove through the village and continued down the main road. His clean-cut cheekbones and straight nose were as if hewn out of the granite rocks that lined the coast. Honest and true, she thought, someone she could trust. But right now she would just enjoy the day and have fun. Flirt, yes, but not give her heart away like she had done in the past, not believe anything a handsome man told her just because he said he loved her. *Never again*, she thought, *will I let a man own my heart and soul and hurt me so deeply part of me is lost.*

*

They reached Clonakilty, a small town nestled between green hills, an hour later. Connor pulled up outside a cute café called The Copper Kettle, where they sat down at a window table that overlooked the town square.

'I hope Milou doesn't get lonely in the car,' Connor said. 'I'm afraid Irish restaurants don't allow dogs on their premises.'

Jasmine laughed. 'Unlike in France where dogs are welcome in restaurants but babies are not. How weird is that?'

'So French, though. They love their pooches.'

'That's very true.' Jasmine smiled at the waitress who brought their coffees to the table. 'I'll get this,' she said and groped in her handbag for her wallet.

'Thanks,' Connor said. 'I'll get lunch, then.'

'That was the idea,' Jasmine said with a cheeky smile.

'Clever,' Connor said, laughing as he stirred sugar into his coffee.

Jasmine didn't reply as her fingers met something in her bag. The letter addressed to her she had found on the hall table and forgot to open in her haste to meet Connor. She pulled it out. It was a small envelope with a card inside. She opened it and stared at the image of a dove with an olive branch in its beak reading the words '*pardonnes moi*'.

'What is it?' Connor asked, looking concerned. 'You're as white as a sheet.'

Jasmine didn't reply but brought the card to her nose. 'My God,' she whispered. 'I can smell his aftershave.'

'Whose?' Connor said, looking around.

'His. My ex's. He sent this to me. And that was what I could smell in the house. It was in the envelope on the hall table. My mother said someone had been in the house, that she could feel it. I thought she was being hysterical, but still… I thought I could smell his aftershave. Dune by Dior. But it was so faint I decided it was just my imagination. I've been a bit jumpy ever since I thought I saw him in Killarney. But this was what it was.' She put the card on the table and looked at it. '"Forgive me," he says,' she mumbled, looking at Connor without really seeing him. 'How can I ever forgive him for wrecking my life? Could you forgive your wife?'

Connor clenched his jaw. 'Not at the moment, no. Maybe in about fifty years if we're both alive. And even then…' He turned his head and looked out the window. Then he looked at Jasmine again. 'Do you think he means it?'

'Means this?' She flicked the card. 'Not in a million years. He says he wants forgiveness, but he doesn't mean it. He could never admit he was wrong. I'm quite sure he just wants me back.'

'And how do you feel about that?'

Jasmine thought for a while, trying to explain how she felt. 'I never want to see him again,' she said hotly. 'Not that I'm afraid of him at all. He has a terrible temper, but so do a lot of French people, me included. We're temperamental and hot-headed.'

Connor let out a snort. 'You think the Irish are any different? The French are pussycats compared to an Irishman in a snot. Especially if he's had drink taken, as my granny used to say.'

Jasmine laughed. 'I know. I've seen it in pubs in Dublin.'

'So you're not afraid of this guy?'

Jasmine shook her head. 'His temper doesn't scare me at all. And I know for sure that I will never believe anything he says again. I don't want to meet him, though. But now that I think of it, I realise that the best thing to do is not to hide or run from him, but to confront him if he finds me, and make him realise we're finished for good.'

'And you're strong enough to do that?'

Jasmine smiled, suddenly feeling an odd kind of strength soar through her. 'Yes, I am. I'm not going to let Damien fool me any more. I'm not going to fall for his pretences. He'll probably try to make me believe he is truly sorry and that he has changed and that he loves me, which I know he doesn't. I fell for his fake image once and I'm not going to do that again.'

'You're scaring me now,' Connor said with mock horror in his eyes. 'That look in your eyes is terrifying. I don't think I'd like to cross you.'

'You'd better not,' Jasmine said sternly. Then she smiled and shook her head while their eyes locked. They looked at each other for a moment while they seemed to exchange a thousand unspoken words. She felt there was a new understanding between them that neither of them could say out loud.

Connor nodded and reached across to touch her cheek. 'You're amazing,' he said softly.

Kinsale was a delightful little town with a beautiful inlet. It also had a fort from which there was a beautiful view of the glittering ocean dotted with white sails as far as the eye could see.

'There are so many sailing boats,' Jasmine said.

'A typical Sunday in Cork. Do you know why a real Corkman doesn't play golf?' Connor asked in an exaggerated Cork accent.

'No?'

'Because if he did, everyone would think he doesn't have a boat.'

Jasmine laughed. 'I see why there are so many boats out there now.'

'Ah sure, it's a grand day for sailing.' Connor dangled his legs off the wall they were sitting on and shaded his eyes to look at the boats. 'I can see some amazing sailing out there. The wind is strong today.'

'Do you have a boat?'

'I'm a real Corkman, so of course I do. She's down there in the marina. We can go there after lunch if you want to see her.'

'I'd love to. What's her name?'

'*Sarah*. After my wife. My ex-wife, I mean,' he corrected himself.

'Oh.' Jasmine felt a strange little shiver go through her. The boat must be a constant reminder of the woman he had been married to. 'Must be hard,' she said, looking at him to gauge his mood.

He shrugged. 'Not really. The boat and the woman are not one and the same. We had only been dating a few months when I bought the boat. I moored her up in Dublin then, at the yacht club in Dun Laoghaire. We used to go out every Sunday, and those were wonderful days, when we were falling in love. Sarah loved it, and so did I. Then, when we broke up, I moved both myself and the boat here.'

'You must have been sad to leave in such circumstances,' Jasmine remarked, hoping she wasn't being too personal.

'Of course I was,' Connor replied with a sad little shrug. 'But at the same time I was coming home to Cork and I got back into sailing. Being out at sea in rough weather helps to take your mind off things. Sailing is not the same in Dublin Bay and up the east coast. Here it's a lot more interesting and more challenging.'

Jasmine nodded as she looked across the inlet to the open water beyond. The west coast would be wilder and more difficult to navigate with all the islands and rocks sticking up from the sea. Her thoughts drifted to Wild Rose Bay and the cliffs around it. 'Great place to be a shipwrecker in the old days,' she said.

'And a smuggler,' Connor filled in.

Jasmine turned to him. 'You know there's a little bay on the other side of the main beach in Sandy Cove?'

He nodded. 'Aiden said something about that. Can only be reached by a very steep path.'

'That's right. We were there yesterday. There are only ruins where the village used to be. I think some of the people in the old village were involved in stuff like that.'

'I'm sure they were. Not shipwrecking as much as smuggling. All the little villages along the coast were involved in that around two hundred years ago. Tobacco, tea, spirits, linen and silk and lots of other things, too. I'm sure your Irish ancestors participated in that.'

'Yes, they must have done,' Jasmine said, staring out to sea. 'I'm sure Oisin was a smuggler and not a fisherman,' she added as if to herself.

'Who?' Connor asked.

'Oh, just a man in a legend. He was supposed to be engaged to a girl called Siobhan and then he was lost at sea.'

'There are lots of legends and stories like that around these coasts. Lots of feuding among families, too.' Connor got off the wall and held out his hand. 'But let's have lunch.' He pointed down the steep hill. 'The pub is in the yellow building down there by the pier.

Oldest pub around here, built in the seventeenth century. Best fish and chips in the business. And they serve it with mushy peas, too.'

'Mushy peas?' Jasmine asked.

Connor laughed as they walked down the hill. 'I love it when you say that with a bit of a French lilt. Mushy peas are those marrowfat peas that have been soaked overnight and then cooked and mashed and spiced up. They look like a dog's dinner but they taste divine with fish and chips.'

'Sounds a little strange but I believe you,' Jasmine said, looking up at his handsome face and bright green eyes.

She was enjoying the day and the company of this attractive man who was so cheerful despite going through something as heartbreaking as a divorce. *He's been left as well*, she thought, *just like me. Maybe that's why I feel so happy to be with him?* He reminded her of Aiden, with the same openness and honesty. It felt good to be with such a man after Damien's betrayal and strange behaviour. She knew she could never forgive what he had done, but she was no longer afraid. She wouldn't be a victim no matter what he did. Something had to happen to give her that final closure.

Jasmine smiled into Connor's eyes as he opened the door for her and suddenly knew she might be ready to fall in love again.

Chapter Seventeen

The weather had turned breezy and chilly just before St Patrick's Day and while preparations for the celebrations were in full swing, Jasmine found herself helping out both at Sally's shop and Aiden's restaurant. It had happened by accident. Over coffee in The Two Marys', Aiden had said he was looking for an extra pair of hands during the weekend now that the season was already beginning.

'Can't believe how many customers we had yesterday,' he said one bright Saturday morning as they had coffee at The Two Marys' before he set off windsurfing. 'Don't know how I'm going to find a waitress in a hurry. Someone who is willing to only work Friday and Saturday.'

'I could help you out for a week or two,' Jasmine suggested. 'Until you get a real waitress. I don't have any experience but I'm willing to learn.'

Aiden blinked and stared at her. 'Oh. I never considered you at all. You're far too qualified.'

'But it'd be fun,' Jasmine argued. 'And I speak French and a bit of German. I promise not to spill on anyone or break the crockery. It'd be something for me to do. I miss working.' She tilted her head and batted her eyelashes at him. 'Oh, come on, Aiden, what do you have to lose?'

'Yeah, but you're dating the boss,' Aiden said. 'I'm not sure he'll like it.'

'We're just having fun,' Jasmine said, feeling her face flush. 'Nothing serious. We've only known each other a few weeks anyway. I'm sure he won't mind.'

Aiden nodded, looking thoughtful. 'Okay. I'll ask him. He's always busy at the weekend anyway.'

'That's right. We see each other during the week when he's coming this way to see to his restaurant. And we sometimes go sailing on a Monday if the weather permits.' She smiled at the memory of their dates during the past weeks, ever since that Sunday lunch in Kinsale. They had such fun together and nothing much had happened except a kiss on each cheek. It was an easy, sweet relationship without promises or demands, just as Connor had said when they first met. Jasmine felt like a soppy teenager when she thought about him, remembering his brilliant smile and the expression in those amazing green eyes whenever he looked at her. She wanted it to stay like this, even if she sometimes felt she wanted more.

But neither of them was willing to take the first step into something that would lead to romance, especially Connor. He was too raw and too hurt, and needed to heal. He needed more time and so did Jasmine. This light-hearted flirty friendship was just the remedy after her turbulent time in Paris. That and yoga, to which she was becoming increasingly addicted. She had to admit that Kamal was right, the yoga sessions helped her find herself again and her inner strength and confidence were beginning to return.

'Have you heard from your man? You know, your ex who was stalking you?' Aiden asked.

'No. I haven't heard or seen him since I spotted him in Killarney.' She shrugged. 'But you know what? It doesn't worry me. I'm not scared of him or anyone. Must be the yoga, or seeing Connor, but I feel kind of invincible. Like I suddenly have superpowers or something. I'm not going to let anyone walk over me. So watch out,' she added with a cheeky smile.

He put his hand on hers. 'I'm glad to see you smile like that again. Even if it's because of another man.'

'Thanks, Aiden. And it's because of you, too. I know I can trust you,' she replied.

He smiled slowly. 'There might be a wolf hiding under my wholesome exterior.'

'Oh really?' Jasmine said, laughing at his expression. 'All men are wolves deep down.'

'And you're all sugar and spice and all things nice?' He shook his head. 'Nah. You have another side to you.'

Jasmine winked. 'I only show that to you.'

He tightened his grip on her hand. 'I hope you keep it that way.'

'Of course I will,' she said, and laughed. 'But joking aside, you'll always be my friend no matter what, Aiden. And I'll always be yours. Nothing and nobody can change that.'

There was an odd look in Aiden's eyes as he slowly pulled his hand away. 'I know,' he said and lifted his cup to drink the last of his coffee. Then he got up. 'I'd better get going and get my board. Could you come to the restaurant tonight and we'll go through everything? Paddy's Day is on Sunday, so Saturday will be hectic. I'll have a word with Connor about you helping out.'

'Okay.'

'Great. See ya.' Jasmine stayed at the table watching Aiden walk down to the beach and join the group of windsurfers who were pulling on their wetsuits ready to take off into the wild waves. She sighed and picked up her cup, but it was empty.

As if reading her mind, the younger of the two Marys arrived at the table and took her cup. 'Another coffee? And maybe some of our fruitcake that Mary just took out of the oven?'

Jasmine laughed. 'Yes, please. I can smell it all the way here.'

Mary hovered at the table, the cup in her hand. 'So how are you getting on? Settling in okay?'

'Oh yes. Everyone is so nice and helpful.'

'Sure, you're one of us, aren't you? Must say your mum is looking so much happier since you came. She's positively blooming these days.'

'She's just happy with life in general, I think.'

'And that's terrific to see. I'll get you that coffee,' Mary said and walked off.

As she waited for the coffee and cake, Jasmine thought of Sally and her seemingly new-found happiness. Mary was right, Sally was blooming right now. But it wasn't because of Jasmine. There was someone else making her happy. Someone Sally kept secret. Jasmine had suspected Kamal, but she wondered if he really was the man who was making her mother's cheeks flush pink every time her mobile phone rang, or kept her chatting softly in her bedroom late at night. Sally had also announced that she was planning 'the mother of all parties' for her birthday in April and that she had decided to embrace her 'coming of age' and 'celebrate life and the joy of a new spring', and Jasmine was glad to see her happy like she used to be.

Sally had gone to a craft fair in Dublin, leaving Cordelia in charge of the shop and Jasmine had offered to help out. Sally had left that morning in her car, looking wonderful, as if she had just stepped out of a beauty parlour and Jasmine wondered if she was really just going to Dublin for work as she had discovered Sally packing lacy underwear and a black silk nightie into her small suitcase. She was about to tease Sally about it but stopped herself. If Sally was meeting someone, it was none of Jasmine's business. She only hoped it wasn't Kamal. She felt a dart of annoyance as she thought of that man – whoever he was. Jasmine had come here for comfort and to spend time with her mother, repairing any damage that had been done to their relationship in the past. This was beginning to be resolved and they now got on better than ever before. But she had also come to put a plan into action, and had invited a special someone to the birthday party. That could end in failure instead of the huge surprise she was hoping for.

Things in Sandy Cove were getting complicated; Jasmine may have felt cosy and safe walking through the village, waving at Mad Brendan on his bench and shouting hello to Nuala coming out of the grocery shop, but she would probably decide to return to Paris eventually. To work in a busy office, to meet friends at a noisy restaurant, to sit at a café and watch the world go by and feel the pulse of a big city was something she missed despite the cosy village life she had come to appreciate. She didn't quite know if she would go back. But if she did, what would happen to her and Connor? Was he really what she wanted? She really didn't know and decided to stop worrying about it and just enjoy the moment. What good would it do to agonise about the future? It only made her feel torn and confused. The here and now was lovely, Jasmine told herself, hurrying down the street when rain suddenly smattered against the pavement.

She arrived inside the shop, panting and laughing. 'Hi,' she said to Cordelia. 'The wind blew me in.'

Cordelia looked up from the old-fashioned cash machine. 'I can see that.'

'Does that thing really work?' Jasmine asked.

'Yes, but we have to register each transaction into the computer, too. But it looks great, doesn't it? I love ringing in each sale.'

'It's wonderful. Like a relic from the nineteen twenties.'

'That's exactly what it is.'

'Fabulous.' Jasmine's gaze homed in on Cordelia. 'And you look pretty fabulous today, too. Being engaged suits you.'

Cordelia smiled and looked at her engagement ring. 'Thank you. I love being engaged. Makes me feel special and loved.' She laughed. 'But enough about me. I just got a call from Maeve. She wants to meet you. I mean, not just being introduced in the street, but as in having dinner together. Nothing fancy, she says, but Paschal is in Cork for a few days and Kathleen, her nanny, is staying the night, so we'll have a little peace and quiet and can have dinner in the kitchen. Just us girls, she said.'

'In Willow House?' Jasmine asked. 'That lovely old house at the other end of the village?'

'That's the one. And I'd love you to come and have a drink beforehand at my house. It's the cottage on the edge of the beach beside Willow House. You haven't seen it.'

'I'd love to,' Jasmine said, excited at the thought of seeing both houses. She had glimpsed Willow House through the trees and longed to see the inside. 'Mam's away in Dublin for a few days for the craft fair, so Milou and I are on our own. It's okay to bring him?'

'Of course. The kids will be excited to meet him,' Cordelia replied just as the door opened to admit the first customers of the day.

They were kept busy all through opening hours, as many tourists had started to arrive in the area for St Patrick's Day to experience what they called the 'real feel' of Ireland's national day.

'Real feel,' Nuala said with a derisory snort when she popped in to say hello. 'This was usually just a day for Mass and a drink in the pub when I was a child. And a little parade with the kids, just like we still do around here. It was mainly a religious holiday in those days. The huge parades with floats and dancing in the streets is something that came from America, made up by the Irish over there. It's spread all over the world. There's even a parade in Moscow of all places. Don't get me wrong, it's great fun, but it's not authentic. Everyone wants to get dead drunk on green beer, which is a little ridiculous but fun all the same. We're having traditional music and dancing, too, on Saturday. Everyone will be there swinging their hairy legs. Hope to see you there, girls.'

'We wouldn't miss it for the world,' Cordelia replied. 'It's always a fab evening.'

'I'll come when the restaurant has closed,' Jasmine promised. 'I'll be helping out there at weekends now.'

'The real fun won't start until ten or so. And then we have the parade on Sunday after Mass,' Nuala said as she opened the door to leave. 'You must come to both. That's the real family feel of St Patrick's Day.'

'It's always a beautiful Mass,' Cordelia said. 'And the parade will be a bit of a hoot.'

'Of course it will with Mad Brendan and his donkeys leading the way. See you then, lads.'

Cordelia laughed as Nuala rushed up the street. 'She's a real powerhouse. Always happy to chat and works so hard, with three kids, a husband and the pub. Don't know how she does it.'

'I think she's amazing,' Jasmine agreed, folding an array of scarves a customer had pulled from the shelf.

'When is Sally coming back?' Cordelia asked as she straightened maps and books on a stand.

'She didn't say, but I think she'll be back for the weekend. I haven't heard from her since she went.'

'And Kamal is away, too. No yoga until Monday.' Cordelia sighed and stretched. 'Pity. I need to work on my back.'

'Where did he go?' Jasmine asked, alarmed. *Is Kamal with Sally in Dublin?* she wondered.

'No idea. Maybe he's gone to Galway for that international yoga workshop I saw advertised in the paper? He didn't say.'

'Oh, God,' Jasmine said. 'I hope he's not with…'

'Sally?' Cordelia filled in. 'Don't think so. She was talking to someone on the phone just before she left. Laughing and blushing and making plans. But it couldn't have been with Kamal.'

'Why not?'

'Because she was speaking French.'

Chapter Eighteen

Stop worrying, Jasmine told herself as she walked from Sally's house to Cordelia's cottage later that evening, Milou trotting beside her. *So Sally's in Dublin with some Frenchman? How did that happen?* She had been so busy worrying about Kamal she didn't realise that someone else could have been distracting Sally. Jasmine sighed and pulled her jacket tighter against the chilly breeze.

She knew she couldn't live her mother's life and try to manipulate her to suit the plan she had hoped to implement. You couldn't plan other people's lives, or even your own. All she could do was hope that Sally would be sensible and not end up in yet another brief, disastrous affair only to be on her own again. She was too old for that. She needed someone she could be happy with and who would stay with her for the rest of her life. Was her new partner such a man?

The only one who had fitted the bill was her father. But it hadn't worked out between them as they were both strong-willed, hot-tempered people who couldn't share the same space without arguing. But they had once been so in love, Jasmine thought as she remembered those early days, especially when they were on holiday together as a family. Then they had been far away from work and all the things that used to cause arguments. The three of them together, having fun, sunbathing, swimming, building sandcastles…

Jasmine smiled at the memories, wishing that Sally might have found some of that happiness with this new man and that it would last a long time. And once Sally had revealed his identity and introduced him to Jasmine, they would have a different, even better mother-daughter relationship. The conflict she felt about her own future was something she'd have to deal with herself. It would be unfair to expect anyone else to solve it. These thoughts didn't make her feel any more cheerful but facing reality was better than hoping for something that might never happen. She was still feeling lost and confused, both about her own future and her feelings about Connor. *One step at a time*, she thought as she walked along. *No need to rush into anything right now.*

Jasmine pushed all those thoughts away and looked up at the darkening sky, where stars were already glinting among the clouds. The silhouette of Willow House rose before her, but she went past the gate and down the side lane to Cordelia's cottage, taking the path along the edge of the cliffs, as there was just enough daylight to see where she was going. She stopped for a moment to look out across the bay, where the sun had just set behind the Skelligs, their dark shapes outlined against the sky streaked with gold and orange. The wind dropped suddenly and there was a stillness as night fell and the evening star glinted just above the peak of Skellig Michael. Jasmine took a deep breath of the sweet air and then continued on, eager to get to Cordelia's house before it became too dark to see where she was going.

The cottage gleamed white in the gloom and the warm lamplight shone through the windows as Jasmine walked up the garden path.

Before she could knock on the red door, it flew open and Cordelia smiled at her. 'Hi and welcome,' she said and stepped aside. 'Come in and have a drink before we go to Maeve's. I lit the fire and Declan's opening a bottle of Prosecco. We thought we should celebrate St Patrick a little ahead of time.'

Milou padded inside and Jasmine followed him into the cosy living room, where a turf fire blazed in the fireplace. Declan smiled at her as he opened a bottle with a large pop which made Milou bark.

'Oops, I think I scared your dog,' he said and poured the Prosecco into three glasses on the small table in front of the red velvet sofa. 'Welcome,' he said to Jasmine and handed her a glass. 'Let's drink a toast to Paddy and then I'll leave you girls to chat. I have a deadline for a feature that'll be in tomorrow's paper, so I have to go and finish the article. After that, it's back to editing my novel.'

Cordelia clinked glasses with Declan and Jasmine in turn. 'Cheers to St Patrick and all his good deeds, especially getting rid of the snakes.'

'*Lá Fhéile Pádraig sona duit*,' Declan said as he lifted his glass. 'Even if it's a few days early.'

'Cheers to that,' Cordelia said and took a sip. 'Whatever it means.'

'It means happy St Patrick's Day.' Declan downed his Prosecco in one go and coughed. 'And now I must love you and leave you and go back to the salt mills.' He kissed Cordelia on the cheek. 'Enjoy the evening, sweetheart. Great to see you again, Jasmine. And your nice dog.' He bent to pat Milou on the head before he disappeared into an adjoining room and closed the door.

'His study,' Cordelia explained. 'Used to be the nursery when Maeve lived here, and it will be again if we get lucky.'

'You're planning to have a family?' Jasmine asked.

'We're doing our best.' Cordelia smiled. 'But so far no sign of any baby. We've only just started so I'm sure something will happen soon. Keep trying, the doctor said. So that's what we're doing,' she added with a happy sigh. 'But sit down. Help yourself to olives and crackers. We'll head over to Maeve in a little while. She said she'd give us a shout when the kids are in bed. Before that, it's a bit of a battlefield over there.' She sat down on the sofa and lifted a delighted Milou onto her lap while he wagged his tail and tried to lick her face.

'He loves you,' Jasmine said as she sat down.

'Sure, we're old friends,' Cordelia replied and hugged Milou. Then she put him down on the floor. 'But no dogs on the sofa, please.'

'I wish Mam would stick to that,' Jasmine said with a sigh. 'But she treats him like a prince.'

'Ah, Sally is a law unto herself.' Cordelia popped an olive into her mouth. 'And right now she's very happy.'

'I know. When did that happen?' Jasmine asked.

'Very recently, I think. About two weeks ago. That's when she started getting these text messages that made her go all pink and giggly. Then she started going into the back of the shop, talking to someone in French. I don't speak the language but I do understand the words "*mon amour*" and "*chéri*" and stuff like that.'

'Hmm,' Jasmine mumbled through a mouthful of crackers. 'Who could it be? Someone she met at a craft fair or on one of her trips?'

'She hasn't been out of the country for over a year,' Cordelia remarked. 'Only around Ireland and not very far at that. Craft fairs, markets and one or two trips to Dublin, that's all.' Cordelia sipped her Prosecco. 'But why don't you just wait for her to tell you? If it's serious, she will.'

'What about Kamal?' Jasmine asked. 'Where does he come into this?'

Cordelia looked thoughtful. 'I'm not sure he has anything to do with her love life. They're working on some kind of project, she says. Could have something to do with selling yoga-related things in the shop. But as I said, wait for her to tell you.'

'Oh, maybe I should give her some more time,' Jasmine said feeling a dart of guilt. 'I haven't been a very good daughter, really, but I've been trying to make amends and get close to her but with her new lifestyle, she seems so distant, somehow.'

'The yoga and new diet and this romance are all so new to her still,' Cordelia said and sat back against the cushions in the sofa. 'I'm sure she'll want to spend time with you when it all settles down.'

'I know. But I'm not very patient,' Jasmine said with a sad little sigh. 'Sorry to burden you with this tale of woe.'

'It's no burden,' Cordelia said and leaned forward to touch Jasmine's hand. 'If it helps you to tell me, I'm happy to listen. Sally's a dear friend and that makes me feel close to you. I know that some memories can make you sad.'

'That's very kind of you.' Jasmine smiled at Cordelia. 'I didn't have an unhappy childhood, really. My mother did her very best, I had a lovely granny who helped me and my father was there in the background when he could be. In fact, later on, I used the situation to my advantage and made them all feel so guilty I could have everything I wanted.' Jasmine shook her head and laughed. 'You have no idea what a spoiled little madam I was.'

Cordelia smiled. 'I can imagine. But still, a divorce is always hard on a child.'

'If I ever have children, I'll never put them through that,' Jasmine declared with feeling.

'Neither will I,' Cordelia agreed.

'I'm dating a man who's just been through a divorce,' Jasmine said. 'But he has no children. If he did, I'd never go out with him.'

'Is it Connor? The man you sat beside at the oyster party?'

'That's him,' Jasmine said, her cheeks turning pink.

'I noticed that he seemed attracted to you,' Cordelia remarked. 'But so does Aiden, of course.'

'Aiden?' Jasmine asked, startled. 'Attracted to me? God, no. We're very close friends, that's all. We've known each other since we were teenagers. I'm very fond of him and he of me. We're great pals.'

'He seemed more than fond to me. The way he looked at you…' Cordelia stopped. 'Okay. None of my business.' She held up the bottle. 'More Prosecco?'

'Thanks, but I think I've had enough for now.'

Cordelia put the bottle back on the table. 'Very wise. We don't want to arrive drunk at Maeve's. She'll be serving wine as well, I'm sure.'

Right on cue, Cordelia's phone pinged on the table and she picked it up. 'All clear. Everyone's asleep and Maeve has dinner on the table. Let's go.'

They put on their jackets and headed to the door, shouting their goodbyes to Declan. Jasmine clipped Milou's lead onto his collar. As it was by now pitch black, they walked the long way around, down the lane that was partly lit by street lights around to the front door of Willow House, illuminated by the light over it. Cordelia ran to the door, opening it for Jasmine. She walked inside, carrying Milou, looking around the hall with its polished wooden floor, antique hallstand and old prints on the walls. A staircase with a beautifully carved bannister curved its way to the upper floor, and a pair of double doors led to a long corridor with Persian rugs and walls hung with an array of paintings and more prints. The inside of the house was even more beautiful than she had imagined.

Cordelia and Jasmine hung their jackets on the hallstand and walked down the corridor, Cordelia opening the door to a large dining room with a huge mahogany table in the middle and tall windows swathed in green velvet curtains.

'The dining room,' she said. 'We're usually here for Christmas dinner and family events. It's always great fun.' She closed the door and opened the one opposite, turning on the lights. 'The formal living room. Great place for parties.'

Jasmine peered into the beautiful room with a huge Donegal carpet on the floor, pale yellow velvet sofas flanking the fireplace and an oil painting of a woman in a white silk dress and three rows of pearls. 'Who's the lovely lady?' she asked.

'Maureen McKenna. The first lady of this house,' Cordelia replied. 'Not related to me, but to the other side of the family. Don't ask me to explain. The family tree is very complicated.'

'But you and Maeve are cousins?'

'Yes. A cousin I didn't know about until recently. There I was, all alone in the world after my mom died, and then... well, I met Phil when we were both living in Miami and discovered we were related. But it took a little while and some research to find all the family connections. It was a kind of miracle, really.'

'I'm sure it was.' Jasmine noticed a glint of joy in Cordelia's eyes. It must have been nice to discover a family in Ireland when she thought she was all alone.

'Hello?' a voice called from further down the corridor. 'Are you burglars or have you come to eat?'

'Burglars,' Cordelia called back. 'But we'd love some food when we've stolen the silver.'

'The soufflé will be ruined if you don't come soon,' the voice replied.

Cordelia laughed. 'She's getting impatient. Come on, let's go and meet Maeve.'

They walked out of the living room and further down the corridor where they could smell something delicious. Cordelia opened the door to a warm, bright kitchen, where a tall woman with auburn hair was standing by the cooker stirring something in a casserole. She turned and smiled at them.

'Hi there. The stew has been simmering for hours, and it smells wonderful.' She walked towards them and held out her hand. 'Hi, Jasmine. I'm Maeve. I don't think we've met since we were kids. I remember you on the beach with your mother when you were small. A chubby little girl in a red swimsuit. But you've grown into one of those gorgeous French women, I see.'

'Hi, Maeve.' Jasmine put Milou on the floor and shook Maeve's hand. 'Were you that girl with the skinny legs who played rounders on the beach with the boys?'

'That was me,' Maeve said with a laugh.

'Then you have grown into a true Irish beauty,' Jasmine said, admiring Maeve's shining hair and dark green eyes.

'Ah shucks, that's a tall order these days,' Maeve said, wiping her hands on a towel. 'Hey, why don't we sit down and eat? I'm starving. The kids are asleep so we have a window of calm until one of them wakes up again. The twins are teething,' she explained. 'And Aisling wakes up at the slightest sound and then she wants to sleep in our bed. It's total bedlam around here most of the time.'

'And you love it,' Cordelia said with a laugh. 'Can we give you a hand with anything?'

'Thanks, but I think it's all there.' Maeve pointed at the large table by the window that was laid with cutlery, glasses and napkins. There was a basket of fresh bread, a jug of water and a bottle of red wine. 'Please take your plates and help yourself to some stew and I'll pour the wine.'

They did as they were told and sat down at the table, Milou settling at their feet. Maeve lit the candles in the tall brass candlesticks and joined them, having helped herself from the pot of stew. 'Sorry about the plain food, but I wasn't up to gourmet cooking tonight.'

'This is delicious,' Cordelia said as she tucked in.

'Wonderful,' Jasmine agreed, as the full flavour of lamb, onions and herbs hit her taste buds. 'And this soda bread is the best I've ever eaten.'

'Phil's recipe,' Maeve said. 'I think that was her best legacy to us.'

'Not the best,' Cordelia argued. 'But certainly a lovely memento.'

'That's true. The best legacy was you,' Maeve said, smiling at her cousin. 'But the smell of the bread always reminds me of her.'

'I make it all the time,' Cordelia filled in. 'Declan loves it.'

'Irish food is underrated,' Jasmine remarked. 'I think Aiden is right. Someone should open an Irish restaurant in Paris. There are Irish pubs, but no real Irish restaurant. Then they could get Irish produce directly from Ireland and serve all these lovely fish dishes and soda bread, and stew and all kinds of other things.'

'Maybe he will?' Maeve said, helping herself to a slice of bread. 'I have a feeling he won't stay here forever. He's too young and talented not to go to somewhere bigger and more challenging.'

'He loves his windsurfing,' Jasmine said. 'And he loves this place. I'd say he'll settle here for good.'

'What about you?' Maeve asked. 'Do you want to stay here for good?'

Jasmine squirmed. 'Uh… not sure. I don't think so. It's a great place for a break and it seems to have so much to offer. But forever is a long time.'

'I thought so myself,' Cordelia said. 'I was about to leave and go back to the States. But then I found a family here and Declan…' She smiled and picked up her glass. 'When you find the love of your life, you could live anywhere, I think.'

'I suppose,' Jasmine said, her thoughts drifting to Connor. Would he turn out to be the love of her life? And if he did, would she settle for life in a small Irish village? She felt increasingly drawn to him and she knew she would have to decide where this was going. But Paris… could she leave her life there for good? Her friends, her father, her roots? Paris and the French way of living were in her blood, in her soul. Maybe they could compromise and have a long-distance relationship?

'God, yes,' Maeve said with feeling, pulling Jasmine out of her daydream. 'I had a great career in London, but when it came to the crunch, I didn't hesitate for long.'

'Well, this house would be a great incentive,' Cordelia remarked. 'And then Paschal…'

'And the village,' Maeve filled in. 'Now I can't imagine living anywhere else. I wouldn't go back to London even if the Queen herself asked me to remodel Buckingham Palace.'

Cordelia giggled. 'That'd be a job for life. That place could do with a revamp. I'm sure you wouldn't know where to start.'

'I'd say a stick of dynamite would make a huge improvement,' Maeve said, helping herself to wine. Then she froze and cocked her head. 'What was that sound?'

'Nothing,' Cordelia said. 'There is no sound at all from upstairs.'

'Exactly.' Maeve got to her feet. 'It's silent. That's unusual.'

'Isn't Kathleen on duty?' Cordelia asked.

'Yes, but…' Maeve ran out the door and down the corridor while Cordelia shrugged and topped up Jasmine's glass. 'Same old, same old,' she said.

'What?' Jasmine asked.

'She's a little jumpy when it come to the kids. But that's understandable. She never thought she'd have any at all, but here she is with three of them at the age of forty-four. Must be a little nerve-racking.'

'I bet it is,' Jasmine said as Maeve came back in, looking relieved. 'Everything okay?'

'Asleep. All of them. Including Kathleen, who seems to have nodded off reading Aisling a story. I found her on Aisling's bed with an open book and the two of them out for the count. The boys, too.'

'So now you can relax,' Cordelia said. 'Sit down, woman, drink some wine and enjoy yourself.'

'Yes, ma'am,' Maeve replied and sat down with a contented sigh.

The evening continued with friendly chatting, more wine and food, until Maeve yawned. 'I'm sorry,' she said with an apologetic laugh. 'I'm getting so sleepy, I can't stay up later than ten these days.'

Cordelia glanced at the clock on the wall over the sink. 'It's past eleven. I think it's time for us to wash up and let you go to bed.'

Maeve shook her head. 'No need to wash up. I'll just put everything into the dishwasher and go to bed. Kathleen will help me with the rest of it tomorrow.'

'Okay,' Cordelia said. 'If you're sure. We should get going, too, Jasmine. Tomorrow's Friday and it'll be busy.'

'That's true,' Jasmine agreed and stood up. 'Thank you so much for this evening, Maeve. It was so nice to meet you and to see this gorgeous house. Sorry to have missed the children, though.'

'You'll see them another time,' Maeve said. 'Drop in whenever you have a moment during the day. But we'll all be at the Patrick's Day parade on Sunday of course. Mostly consisting of the school-children and their parents who will march up the main street and down the lane to the beach, ending at The Two Marys'. Everyone dressed in green hats and all sorts of mad costumes, with Irish music played by the school band and everything.' She looked at Milou coming out from under the table and bent down to pat him. 'Now there's a good dog. He didn't beg for food once.'

'He wouldn't dare when he's with me,' Jasmine said and picked him up. 'But with Mam, it's another story.'

They said their goodbyes and left, Jasmine turning into the lane that led to the village, waving goodbye to Cordelia. Then they walked down the street towards home, Milou stopping now and then to sniff at lamp posts and trees. They had reached the front gate of the house and started up the hill when Milou suddenly stiffened and stood still, his hackles raised, growling.

'What's the matter, Milou?' Jasmine looked at the dark house. There was nothing to be seen or heard, but she still had the feeling someone was there, waiting. 'Who's there?' she called.

Nobody answered. Milou still growled softly. Then Jasmine froze as she saw a movement beside the door, and then someone stepped out of the shadows. 'Damien?' she whispered.

Chapter Nineteen

Jasmine picked Milou up and held him tight. 'Quiet, Milou,' she said and then switched to French. 'Okay. So you're here and didn't break in.'

'I'm not a burglar.' Damien held out his hand. 'Can we talk?'

'I don't believe anything you say,' Jasmine snapped, a surging anger giving her courage. 'And I don't want you in the house. Say what you came to say and then go.'

He let his hand drop and sighed. 'Please. Let me come in for a moment. It's a cold night.' He stepped even closer and touched her sleeve. 'Please, Jasmine. There is so much I want to tell you. I lied to you, and that was wrong. You didn't deserve all that happened to you. I should never have…' He stopped. 'I'm not leaving until you've let me talk.'

Jasmine gave in. She didn't want to stand there in the dark any longer and she felt a dart of pity as she looked at his sad face. 'Okay. I'll give you ten minutes.'

He let out a long sigh. '*Merci, chérie.*'

'Step away from the door so I can open it.'

'*D'accord.*' He moved sideways to let her pass and she flinched as he brushed her side with his body.

She felt her strength falter as she caught sight of him when she switched on the light over the front door. That dark wavy hair, those eyes, that little smile…

'Come in then,' she ordered, still holding a growling Milou. 'Stay in the living room while I put Milou in the kitchen.'

'He still hates me,' Damien said.

'He's a very good judge of character,' Jasmine retorted. She put Milou down, shooed him into the kitchen and closed the door.

'May I sit down?' Damien asked.

'If you must.'

Damien sat down on the edge of the sofa while Jasmine settled on the chair opposite him. She clasped her hands in her lap and stared at him. 'So go on. Talk.' She checked her watch. 'You have exactly ten minutes from now. Then I'm calling the police.'

He snorted. 'There's no police station in this village, so it would take them hours to get here from the nearest town.'

'I'll call some of the local men, then. There is an ex-rugby player in the pub by the harbour. He'll be here in no time if I ask him. He'd be delighted to help me out.'

'You're bluffing.'

Jasmine shot him a cold look. 'You're wasting time.'

Damien blinked and stared at her. 'You've changed a lot since the last time I saw you,' he said, then he sighed and sat up straight, looking at her with a sad expression in his velvet eyes. 'Okay. This is what I wanted to say: you have to believe me when I say how sorry I am about everything. I used you and I lied to you.'

'I know,' Jasmine said, steeling herself not to fall for his contrite tone, or the sad eyes. She had once been so in love with him, and the memory of that love still lingered in a strange way.

'I didn't mean it to happen.' He sighed and ran his hand through his hair. 'The first time we met, I meant everything I said to you. I thought you were so beautiful. I fell in love with you that night.'

She nodded. 'I'm glad to hear it. But then what happened? You lied to me when you said you were working for your uncle and you kept lying about what you did all day. I thought you were working when you were involved in gambling. Those business trips... were they to some casino?'

He nodded. 'Yes. Deauville. I had a run of luck there and thought it would keep going. But then I started losing big time. And I lost a lot of money gambling online, too.'

'Why didn't you stop then?'

He sighed. 'I couldn't. I became addicted to gambling. I was convinced my luck would turn, but I kept losing. But I still couldn't stop.'

'And then you had that huge debt and had to pay it all back?'

'Yes.' He looked suddenly ashamed.

'So you proposed to me and gave me a huge diamond ring and pretended to want to buy an apartment just to get me to open a joint account and put some money into it?'

He avoided her gaze. 'Yes. But that was before I lost all that money. I thought I could keep winning and we could get married. But the luck ran out and I needed the cash quickly. So I took it.'

'That was a truly terrible thing to do. Why didn't you tell me?'

'I was ashamed. And I knew you'd want me to stop gambling.'

'Of course I would. You could have got help with the addiction.'

'I didn't want to stop. I wanted the buzz and excitement of winning to go on.'

'And that was more important than me?'

'Yes,' he said, looking at her with such sadness it made her heart ache.

She looked at him long and hard for several minutes. 'I loved you,' she whispered. 'With all my heart and soul. I thought I was the luckiest woman in the world. I was looking forward to our wedding. To living in that apartment with you. To having children eventually. It was the happiest time of my life.'

'And then I broke your heart.'

'Yes.' Jasmine kept staring at him, no longer attracted to that handsome face or the deep voice. All she felt was pity and a searing, deep hurt that burned like a knife through her heart. 'I loved you so much that when you held me in your arms I felt like we were fused together. I thought we would be together for the rest of our lives. I thought you felt the same. How could you do that to me?'

He buried his head in his hands. 'I don't know,' he whispered. 'Gambling was like a drug. Nothing was more important.'

'Not even me?' she asked, her voice barely audible as tears streamed down her cheeks.

He shook his head. 'Not even you.'

She nodded. 'I see.'

'I am so sorry, my darling, beautiful Jasmine.' He lifted a tearstained face and looked pleadingly at her. 'Please forgive me.'

Jasmine stood up. 'I'm not sure I can listen at this moment. Maybe in time. I feel sorry for you, I really do. But you're not the man I thought you were, that you pretended to be. And now I just want you to go.'

He slowly got to his feet. 'I'll leave now. Just one thing.' He hesitated. 'I know it's a lot to ask, but…'

'The ring,' she said bitterly. 'Is that why you're here? Not for forgiveness but for that diamond ring.'

His shoulders slumped. 'Not only for that. I wanted to tell you – to ask you to forgive me. But I understand that you can't and I don't blame you. But the ring would be a great help. It's worth a lot of money. It could tide me over for a while.'

'A long while,' Jasmine remarked, trying to keep the anger out of her voice. 'I feel I'm entitled to keep it, as you owe me quite a lot of money.'

'I know,' Damien mumbled. 'And I'll pay you back when my luck turns, I swear.'

Jasmine sighed. 'Oh please. That's a promise you won't be able to keep. The ring should be enough to cover it. But okay. I'll give it to you. I don't want it anyway and I never want to see you again. It's in my room. Wait here.' She quickly walked to her room, extracted the ring from the hem of the curtain, marched back and thrust it into his hand. 'There. Now go.'

'Thank you.' Damien slowly got to his feet and walked to the door. 'And thank you for listening.'

'You're welcome,' she said, her voice cold. 'So… Where are you going?' she couldn't help asking, feeling yet another dart of pity for him.

He shrugged. 'Don't know. I hired a car that's parked near the beach. I'll drive to the ferry port in Rosslare and get back to France.'

She nodded. 'I see. Well, thank you for coming, Damien. I had hoped not to see you again, but I needed this closure. Now I can put it all behind me. I only wish…' She stopped. Telling him to get help would be no use. 'Well, you know.'

'Yes.' They looked at each other for a while before he nodded and left, closing the door quietly behind him.

Jasmine stood there, unable to move or think, her emotions in turmoil. The man who had just left her was far removed from the romantic hero she had thought Damien to be. The glossy façade had quickly crumbled to reveal a weak little man who couldn't manage his own life. She couldn't forgive him, but despite this, she felt deeply sorry for him. A lingering sadness about the love she had felt for him flickered through her mind before she turned away from all those memories. She finally had closure.

Jasmine walked to the kitchen and let Milou out, picking him up and hugging him close. As if sensing her distress, Milou whined and licked her face. 'My darling little dog,' she whispered into his soft fur. 'Always there for me when I'm sad.' With him still in her arms, she sank down on the sofa, holding him tight, her tears dropping onto his head. She cried softly for a while, not so much for herself but for the lost soul out there in the dark night, on the run with nowhere to go and no one to comfort him. Feeling the need to talk to another human, she picked up her phone and punched in a number.

Aiden picked up on the first ring. 'Hi. What's up?'

'It's late, I know,' Jasmine started. 'But I need to talk to someone. You, I mean.' She stopped and sniffed. 'I woke you up, didn't I?'

'I wasn't asleep. I was watching a stupid movie on Netflix. What's the matter?'

His warm voice made her tears well up again. 'He… he was here,' she stammered.

'Who? Your ex?'

'Yes.'

'What did he do to you?' Aiden nearly shouted. 'Are you hurt?'

'Not physically, no,' Jasmine said, sobbing. 'But I feel so sad.'

'Is your mam there?' Aiden asked.

'No. She's in Dublin. She'll be home tomorrow.'

'I'll come over,' Aiden said and hung up.

Aiden arrived only minutes later, walking into the living room where Jasmine was still sitting on the sofa with Milou in her lap. 'I'm here,' he said, looking at her face with concern. 'You don't have to be scared any more.'

'I'm not scared,' Jasmine said, wiping her face with her sleeve. 'I'm just desperately sad.'

Aiden sat down by her side, taking her into his arms and holding her tight. 'I'm here,' he soothed. 'Tell me what happened.'

'Okay.' Jasmine took a deep breath and then told Aiden everything Damien had said.

'That must have been painful,' Aiden remarked when she had finished.

'He never loved me at all,' Jasmine said bleakly. 'The strange thing is that as he left and I watched that lonely figure walking away in the dark night, I felt such enormous pity for him. I know he wrecked my life, but still…'

Aiden grasped her shoulder. 'Don't waste your pity on him, Jazz. Guys like that deserve everything that's coming to them. If he loved you, he wouldn't have done what he did to you.'

'I know.' Jasmine sighed and leaned her head back against the cushions. 'It's okay. I feel better now. And it was good that he came. It closed that chapter and now I can move on. I felt like such a loser when I came here, you know? My life seemed to be such a mess and I hadn't spoken to my mother for over a year. And then... I met you and we discovered Wild Rose Bay together and became friends again. And I made up with my mother and we understand each other much better in an adult way. I have figured out a lot of things on my own and met so many lovely people here in Sandy Cove. There are still a few things that need to be sorted out, but I'm confident it will all resolve itself in time.' She drew breath and smiled at him. 'Maybe I need a little bit of that O'Rourke spirit, too?'

'We all have strengths deep down,' Aiden said. 'And you will find yours when you really need it.' He touched her knee. 'You need to go to bed and sleep. I'll stay here, if you want. The couch looks comfortable.' He yawned. 'And right now I could sleep anywhere.'

'You don't have to stay,' Jasmine protested.

'I know, but you're a little lost and lonely right now.'

Jasmine smiled. 'I have Milou and Mam will be back tomorrow – today, really as it's after midnight.' She slowly got up. 'I'll go to bed now. Not that I'll be able to sleep. Milou is fast asleep, I see. On the sofa and all, even though that's not allowed. But I'll leave him there.'

'I'm staying here,' Aiden said in a tone that didn't allow argument. 'I'll curl up on the sofa with Milou.' He lay down, grabbed the throw on the armrest and put it over himself, ushering her out of the room.

'Good night, Aiden,' Jasmine whispered. She tiptoed into her room and collapsed on the bed. Then she undressed and crawled in under the duvet, the knowledge that Aiden was out there soothing her.

But everything that had happened was still going through her mind and Damien's pale, tortured face swam in front of her when she closed her eyes. A lost soul, a man who had gambled with his own life and hers, all for nothing. Watching him walk away into the dark night had broken her heart. But lying there, she suddenly knew she would rise again and get her life back. Not because of the so-called O'Rourke spirit, but because of that strength Aiden had talked about. Everyone has it, he said, and she would find hers and choose the right path when the time was right. The only trick was to find it.

Chapter Twenty

St Patrick's Day started with gusts of wind and rain showers. But just before the parade, the wind eased and the sky cleared, the sun shining on everyone coming out of the church after Mass. Jasmine blinked against the bright sunlight as she and Sally stepped out of the church, the beautiful music still in her ears. It had been a truly wonderful Mass, with the choir singing hymns in Irish and the children bringing flowers to the altar. The church itself was so lovely, with stained glass windows glowing like jewels, and the ancient statues of saints looking down on them. The church was one of the first that had been built after Catholic emancipation in 1829 and some of the artwork had been rescued from an earlier church from the fifteenth century. Everyone in the congregation wore something green, either an item of clothing or a scarf or tie. Jasmine had found a bright green jacket in Sally's wardrobe and Sally herself was wearing an ankle-length moss-green dress that suited her to perfection. And, of course, everyone had a small bunch of shamrocks in their buttonhole.

They all took turns shaking hands with the priest, who wished them a happy St Patrick's Day, and Jasmine and Sally walked to the graveyard to put flowers on the graves of Jasmine's grandparents, and also on Phil's grave a little further down. There they found Maeve and her sister Roisin, and they all gathered around, talking about Phil and sharing memories of her life. Not having known Phil, Jasmine stood quietly, listening to what they said, feeling she had somehow lost out, only having met this amazing woman when she was a very small child.

She slipped away and left them to chat about their memories, walking down the path, dappled with sunlight through the budding foliage of the trees. Further away, behind the church, an area of the graveyard was dotted with old tombstones, some of them leaning over, the lettering barely legible. Jasmine peered at faded letters spelling out names and dates all the way back to the seventeenth century. She recognised many of the names of families from the village, like O'Sullivan, Byrne, Murphy and McKenna. She also found a few O'Rourke family graves, but one in particular made her stop and stare. It was the family grave of someone called Cornelius O'Rourke and his wife Orla who had lived and died over two hundred years ago. They had had five children, one of whom was called Siobhan. Was this the Siobhan of the old legend? The girl whose lover had been lost at sea and whose ring was still down there, buried somewhere near Wild Rose Bay? Jasmine decided it had to be and ran her finger over the name.

'So you found her?' a gravelly voice said behind her.

Startled, Jasmine turned around to find Mad Brendan standing there, wearing a green sweater, his flat cap in his hand.

'Is that her?' Jasmine asked. 'That woman you told me about?'

'It is, the poor craythur.'

'How do you know?'

He shrugged. 'I just know. My da told me and his da before him and so on all the way back to those days. If your family has lived here since forever, and you never left yourself, you know the stories by heart.'

'I suppose,' Jasmine said, turning back to the gravestone. 'She was only twenty-three when she died.'

'Broken heart?' Mad Brendan mused. 'Or some illness. Or hunger. Who knows? Life was hard in them old days. No central heating or running water or medicine.'

'They had to struggle to survive,' Jasmine agreed.

'We still do, but in other ways.' Brendan put his cap on his head. 'Must go and see what's going on in the village. Everyone's in the pub getting tanked up before the parade. It got a bit wild in the Harbour pub last night, I heard, so it's the hair of the dog for some. And I have to get my donkeys spruced up. They love the parade.'

Jasmine laughed. 'I'm sure they do.'

'I'll see you there, girl,' Mad Brendan said and walked away down the path, his boots crunching on the gravel.

Jasmine stayed where she was, still looking at the gravestone, reading the names of Siobhan's parents' other children. So many years ago, yet it seemed so close, as if they would walk up the path at any time, talking to each other. Siobhan maybe lagging behind, sadness slowing her steps. Then Jasmine shook herself. This was silly, standing here trying to conjure up ghosts. Life was for the living after all, and her life was a lot better than what it would have been two hundred years ago, even with all her recent upsets.

She walked slowly down the path to join the others, her mind on the night before, when she had worked in the restaurant, and for the first time seen the professional side of Aiden in action. There was no small talk or friendly asides as he swiftly created beautifully crafted plates with food that both smelled and looked delicious. He checked every minute detail before he allowed an order to leave the kitchen. A young apprentice chef had come from Cork to help out, and a girl from the village waited at tables with Jasmine. They worked hard for several hours, until the last plate of flambéed figs with vanilla ice cream had been served. As the guests in the restaurant relaxed with coffee or brandy, they tidied up the kitchen, washed the floor and turned on the dishwasher. Aiden had finally nodded and said they could go home, and told Jasmine she had done very well on her first night.

'I bet you found out that waitressing isn't exactly a breeze,' he said with a cheeky smile.

'It's a lot harder and takes more skill than I had ever imagined,' Jasmine replied, leaning against the cooker. 'And I will be a lot more generous with tips in restaurants from now on.'

'You did well, though.'

'Thank you.'

'I'm just going to see the last guests out and then I'm off to the pub at the harbour. The party should just be starting by now. Are you going?'

But Jasmine, feeling too tired to party, shook her head and said she was going home to spend the evening with Sally, who would be arriving back from Dublin. In any case, Connor wouldn't be there as he was spending the weekend with his family in Cork, but had asked her to go on an outing with him on Monday. Aiden said he understood and they went their separate ways: Aiden to the pub for the party and Jasmine home to welcome Sally back. She didn't feel she was missing anything, still feeling low after Damien's visit and in no mood for a wild Irish party.

Staying at home had proven to be a good idea, as Sally had arrived later that night, tired but looking as if she had spent the few days with someone special, wearing a lovely necklace with tiny sapphires and emeralds set in gold. That someone special must be well off, Jasmine thought as she admired it. And then she had to tell her mother about Damien's visit and what he had said. Horrified, Sally had done her best to comfort Jasmine and they had stayed up late, talking. Once Sally was satisfied that Jasmine was putting it all behind her, the conversation had drifted to Sally's mystery new love interest. Jasmine had tried her best to make her mother tell her who he was but Sally refused to answer any questions and had promised to 'reveal all very soon' with a cheeky smile and a dreamy look in her eyes that gave Jasmine goose bumps of fear. What was Sally up to? Who was the man she seemed so smitten with? Time would tell of course, but Jasmine had an eerie feeling the big reveal would not fill her with joy.

The parade helped Jasmine forget her worries about her mother. It was a jolly affair with Mad Brendan in his green cap and jacket in the lead with the donkeys sporting leprechaun hats. Schoolchildren in various St Patrick's Day-themed outfits followed and then at the back a Ceilidh band playing jigs and reels that made everyone move with the music, laughing at each other and their various levels of skill at Irish dancing. Aiden grabbed Jasmine and whirled her around the street until she screamed for mercy, threatening to throw up on him. He stopped, let her go and grinned at her. 'Nothing like an Irish reel to clear the head.'

'It made me seasick,' Jasmine complained.

'You just need to practise. Hey, let's follow the parade to The Two Marys'. They're doing green buns and green tea and possibly green coffee today. All free for us locals.'

Jasmine stepped back onto the pavement, trying to smooth her hair. 'Great. I need something to eat after that mad dancing.'

She was about to follow Aiden, who was joining the stragglers at the end of the parade, when someone called her name. She turned around to find Maeve behind her pushing a buggy with two wriggling toddlers, her husband Paschal beside her holding a little girl with dark hair by the hand.

'Hi, Maeve,' Jasmine exclaimed and crouched in front of the little girl. 'Hello, there. You must be Aisling. Am I right?'

The little girl nodded, a shy smile hovering on her lips. 'Yes,' she said. 'That's my name. What's yours?'

'My name's Jasmine.'

'Jasmine,' Aisling repeated. 'You're pretty. I like your outfit.'

'This?' Jasmine laughed and touched her green jacket. 'It's my mother's. I'm wearing it for St Patrick.'

'It's very nice.' Aisling looked at her with solemn eyes. 'Is your mammy here?'

Jasmine looked around. 'She should be here somewhere. Her name is Sally. Do you know her?'

Aisling nodded. 'Yes. She has a shop and she gives me sweets. She's very nice.' Aisling paused and peered at Jasmine. 'Do you have a boyfriend?'

Jasmine blushed. 'Uh… yes. I mean, I'm seeing…' She stopped, wondering how she should explain her love life to a three-year-old. 'Not sure he's actually my boyfriend yet. But I like him.'

'Has he kissed you?' Aisling stared at Jasmine with her green eyes that demanded an honest answer.

'Uh, yes, he has. But only on the cheek.'

'Then he's your boyfriend,' Aisling stated in a tone that said the matter was settled.

'Aisling,' Maeve chided. 'Stop asking Jasmine personal questions.'

Aisling looked up at her mother. 'What's a personal question, Mammy? Can we have sweets? I want to follow the parade,' she said all in the same breath.

Paschal laughed and lifted his daughter onto his shoulders. 'Yes, let's follow the parade, my princess.'

'Quickly,' Aisling ordered, grabbing onto her father's curly hair.

'Ouch,' Paschal complained and started to walk, bouncing Aisling until she screamed with laughter.

'Come on, then.' Maeve pushed the buggy down the pavement and they all followed the parade down the main street where the bunting was fluttering in the wind, and marched all the way down to The Two Marys', where they served green cupcakes, green cordial and tea in mugs decorated with shamrocks. The band stayed outside and continued to play Irish music.

It was all so over the top that it made Jasmine laugh and she felt such a surge of affection for this village and its people she thought her heart would burst. She realised she had missed out on so much by not coming here for her holidays. She smiled at Aiden over her mug of tea and knew he understood how she felt.

'Ah sure, you're here now,' he said as if he could read her thoughts. 'And whatever happens, you can come back whenever you want. Just like me.'

'Like you?' she asked, startled. 'You're not staying here, then?'

'Oh, I am for now. But I'm not sure I want to stay here forever. This is a great start but I'd like to do more, to get stuck into something really challenging. Not sure what that is yet, but I'm keeping an eye out. I'm in no rush to leave, though. I love it here. So for now everything's fine.'

She looked into his sloping blue eyes and knew what he meant. Sandy Cove was a lovely, safe haven, but out there – on the stormy seas of the world – there were opportunities and challenges that were exciting and scary. He needed to go out there and try it. And maybe she did, too.

'I feel the same,' she said. 'I miss the buzz of Paris and I want to go back and try to find a job there, but at the same time I feel so connected to this village.'

'Don't sweat the small stuff,' Aiden said in her ear. 'Just go with the flow and let it happen. The right things usually come around when you least expect it.'

'I suppose you're right,' she said, thinking that the wrong things also had a habit of hitting you in the face when you weren't looking.

'Are you okay?' he asked, studying her face.

She nodded and finished her mug of coffee that had been topped with green marshmallows. 'I'm fine. I'm trying to put it all behind me.'

'Good. Forget about the past and move on.'

'I will,' she promised. 'And now I want to find out more about Wild Rose Bay.'

His eyes lit up. 'You're still intrigued by it?' he said, surprised.

'I found her grave.'

'Whose?' he asked. 'That young woman?'

Jasmine nodded. 'Yes. Siobhan. Not sure she was the same one as in the legend but she's there buried with her family. Only twenty-three when she died.'

'That's sad. But it was all so long ago and life was tough in those days.'

'Oh, I know. It's just that it feels kind of eerie that she was an O'Rourke and that I might be related to her.'

'Lots of people would be. Still, it's centuries ago.' He shrugged and dug into the carrot cake with green icing on his plate. 'Let's not think sad thoughts today. Paddy's Day is supposed to be happy. You're even allowed to drink even though it's Lent and we are supposed to stay sober until Easter. Not that anyone does these days.' He looked around at the families crowding the tables and the children running around, chasing each other. 'See? They are all having fun and not brooding, even though some of them might have huge sorrows in their lives. And tonight, they'll all be in the pub for a drink and a bit of craic as tomorrow is a day off. Then they'll pick up the struggles of the everyday and carry on.'

Jasmine laughed and shook her head. 'You're getting awfully philosophical in your old age.'

He smiled. 'Yeah, I know. But who are you calling old? Aren't you two months older than me?'

'That's true,' Jasmine had to admit. 'Not that it makes me any wiser.'

'Who wants to be wise?' He ate the last bit of cake. 'So what are you doing tomorrow? Fancy another hike down to the bay?'

'I'd love it, but I'm going on a drive with Connor. We're spending the day somewhere nice, he said. He's picking me up at eleven.'

Aiden's face fell. 'Oh. I see. So the two of you really are dating, then?'

'Sort of. Nothing serious,' Jasmine said, trying not to blush. 'Just having fun at the moment.'

'Loads of fun, I bet,' Aiden remarked with a strange look in his eyes. 'I'm glad to see Connor happy, though. He was gutted when his wife left him. Must still be very raw as the divorce went through only a few months ago. Go easy on him, Jazz.'

Jasmine bristled. 'What do you mean? What do you think I'd do to him?'

'I don't know. But if he falls for you big time, and you're just "having fun",' Aiden said making quotation marks, 'maybe it wouldn't…' He stopped, looking embarrassed. 'Sorry. Forget I said anything. None of my beeswax, is it?'

'No, it certainly isn't,' Jasmine said and got up. 'I'll go and join Mam and Cordelia over there at the window. See you at the restaurant tonight.'

He nodded. 'Yeah.'

Jasmine hesitated, feeling guilty about having snapped at him. 'It's okay. I understand. You're worried about Connor,' she said.

'Not only him,' he replied.

They looked at each other for a moment, until Jasmine turned and walked away. What she had seen in Aiden's eyes was more than worry about his friend. There was something deeper there that had to do with a lot more than friendship. It wasn't Connor's broken heart he was worried about, but his own.

Chapter Twenty-One

Connor was waiting for Jasmine outside Sally's house the next morning. Sally was still asleep, Milou dozing beside her. Jasmine left them both and made her way down the hill in the bright sunshine, carrying her jacket and walking boots.

Connor jumped out of the car as she approached and enveloped her in a bear hug. 'Good morning, lovely girl. So nice to see you after all this time.'

'It's only been a week,' she replied.

'Feels like a year to me.'

She pressed her nose into his chest and breathed in the fresh smell of clean laundry and soap with a surge of happy anticipation. His broad smile was so beguiling and the way he looked at her made her feel warm all over. It was as if the sun shone through his luminous green eyes.

'You look so happy,' she said, returning his smile.

'Of course I am. The sun is shining, Paddy's Day is over and I get to spend the day with a beautiful woman.' He let her go and opened the door to the passenger seat. 'Step into the carriage, my lady, and I will take you to a beautiful little village and show you a part of Kerry that you might not have seen before.'

She got into the car. 'I have been all over the Ring of Kerry, so I doubt it.'

'Ah, but we're going somewhere else entirely,' Connor said with a cheeky smile. 'Fasten your seatbelt and get ready for a mystery tour.'

They set off down the road that led to Cahersiveen and on to Killorglin, where they stopped at a petrol station for coffee and to admire the view of a mountain range called MacGillycuddy's Reeks, the highest peak of which was called Carrauntoohil. 'The highest mountain in Ireland,' Connor explained. 'And the toughest climb. If you make it up there, you're a pretty strong hiker. But there are other trails up there, too, of course. We could go up there for a hike someday, but it's best to do it in the summer, when we won't be surprised by bad weather.'

Jasmine looked up at the snow-covered peaks glimmering white against the blue sky. 'That would be fantastic. But I think I need to practise first.'

'Plenty of time,' Connor declared as they left the petrol station. 'Let's continue.' He drove across the bridge and stopped on the other side, showing Jasmine the bronze statue of a goat. 'That's the symbol of Puck Fair, known as *Aonach an Phoic*, the Fair of the Goat. It's one of Ireland's oldest fairs that takes place in August. Mainly a horse and cattle fair, but there's a market and the pubs stay open nearly all night. You can imagine the shenanigans. There are different theories of how and when the fair started: some think it's of pagan origins and some claim that it started during the time of Cromwell.' He shrugged. 'Nobody really knows. It's a lot of fun anyway.'

'I'm sure it is,' Jasmine agreed. She glanced at Connor as he drove on, hugely enjoying being in his company. They got on so well and there was no tension or embarrassment between them. *An uncomplicated man*, she thought. *Without any hidden agenda or secrets he wouldn't share.* She felt safe with him, she realised. Safe and protected and maybe even loved, despite it being too soon to voice such feelings. He glanced back at her and their eyes met. Jasmine felt a jolt of something that she couldn't quite explain.

'He came back,' she suddenly said, realising she hadn't told him about Damien's visit. 'My ex-boyfriend, I mean,' she added.

'So he found you?'

'Yes. He appeared late one night when I came home from dinner at Willow House.'

'What happened? Was he violent or anything?'

'No. He wanted to explain some stuff to me and…' Not in a mood to tell Connor the whole story, Jasmine cut it short. 'He left after a short conversation that I won't go into. I know I won't see him again. End of story and now I just want to move on.'

'Onwards and upwards,' Connor said. 'That's what my dad always says anyway. Very good advice, I think.'

'Absolutely.'

Connor glanced at her as he turned left onto a road that ran along the shoreline. 'Let's not go on about the past. There is a bright new future ahead, I feel. And now,' he continued in the same breath, 'we are on the Dingle Peninsula. Not as romantic as the Ring of Kerry, but just as fantastic in a different way. I love it and I want to show you my favourite spots.'

They continued on, past Inch Beach which stretched all the way across the bay and then, after a few more kilometres, arrived at Dingle town, which was lovely, with colourful houses around a sheltered harbour where boats of all sizes were moored. Connor found a spot to park in the crowded parking lot and they got out and walked up the street to a little restaurant with a blue awning and fishing nets and floaters in the window.

'I booked a table here,' Connor said. 'It gets a little bit crowded during the holidays, but it's the best fish restaurant in Dingle. Nearly as good as mine, but not quite.'

They walked in and were immediately shown to a table by the window with a view of the harbour and the bay.

'We'll have the chowder and the turbot,' Connor said to the waitress as they sat down. 'Okay with you, Jasmine?'

Jasmine smiled and nodded, her stomach rumbling. 'Sounds great.'

'And a glass of the Sauvignon each,' Connor continued the order. 'That's all the wine I'm allowed as I'm driving, but I'll order some more for you if you want.'

'No,' Jasmine replied. 'That's fine for me in the middle of the day.'

The chowder arrived with the glass of wine and a basket of crusty bread. They both fell on the food and ate without talking until both bowls were empty.

Connor broke off a piece of his bread and looked at Jasmine. 'What did you think of the chowder. As good as Aiden's?'

Jasmine thought for a while, the taste of succulent salmon and mussels still in her mouth. 'I'm not sure. This was chowder and the one Aiden served was bouillabaisse. So even though the fish was roughly the same, the tastes are different. Chowder is made with bacon and cooked in milk, and…'

He nodded. 'You're right. And Aiden's bouillabaisse is far superior to any kind of fish soup. In fact, I'm thinking of having his made on a mass scale and selling a frozen version. I'm considering getting into that kind of food market.' He paused. 'Sorry for talking business on our date.'

'No,' Jasmine protested. 'I love business. I'm an economist after all. Have you studied this market? Does it have a future do you think?'

He nodded and smiled at the waitress when she came to clear the plates. 'The chowder was excellent,' he said to her.

'I'll tell the chef,' she said and walked away with the plates.

Connor turned back to Jasmine. 'Does it have a future? Yes, I think so. Now that the economy has taken off again and there are so many professionals out there who want to throw dinner parties but don't have time to shop and cook, ready-made gourmet dinners they can just heat up will be very popular. There isn't much out there right now, but if I can get it off the ground quickly, I think it'd do very well.'

'I think you're right. But there is so much to consider. You'll need a warehouse, staff and a distribution system. And of course money to invest before you make a profit.'

He laughed. 'Oh yes, I know all that. And I'm working on it. I'll need recipes and chefs, too, and some reliable office staff. I am going to base it in Cork and then maybe Dublin if it works out. It's a big project and a bit risky, but I like a challenge and the brand is already there. It'll be recipes from all my restaurants. They're all doing very well and have got great reviews nationwide.'

'Organic ingredients, and as much Irish produce as you can get, I'd say would be a big selling point,' Jasmine said, feeling excited. 'Gosh, if I had some money to spare I'd invest in your new venture.'

He laughed. 'I'm sorry you don't. I'd love to have you as a business partner. Wouldn't that be fun?'

'Oh yes,' Jasmine agreed.

They were interrupted by the waitress bringing the main course. They smiled at each other while she put a plate of turbot served with hollandaise sauce, buttered baby potatoes and spinach in front of each of them.

Jasmine breathed in the heavenly smell of fresh fish and hollandaise. 'Oh, God, this smells incredible.' She picked up her fork. '*Bon appetit*, Connor. I'm diving in.'

'Me, too.' He grabbed his fork and took a bite of the turbot. 'This is divine,' he mumbled as he drank some of the chilled white wine. 'And sadly not a dish that would freeze well.'

'Too expensive,' Jasmine said and sipped her wine between bites. 'Great choice of wine.'

'That's a fine compliment coming from a Frenchwoman.'

They ate in silence for a while, smiling at each other as they both enjoyed the excellent food. And when they had finished, Jasmine pushed her plate away and declared she couldn't eat another bite despite the tempting dessert menu. They had coffee and left, walking through the town, looking at the view of the sea from many vantage points. Then Connor suggested they take a trip further up the hills across the peninsula to the village of Annascaul.

The afternoon proved to be great fun, especially the visit to the South Pole Inn that was a little like a museum with mementoes of Scott's expedition to the Antarctic that Tom Crean had taken part in, turning out to be a hero who had saved the life of a fellow member of the expedition.

'What a great man,' Jasmine declared as she studied the handsome, craggy face of Tom Crean in a photo hanging on the wall along with many other pictures of the expedition.

'*Tom Crean first went south in 1901 with Scott's ground-breaking Discovery Expedition, on which he served his polar apprenticeship and learned the skills to survive in the most inhospitable place on earth,*' Jasmine read out loud from a framed newspaper article on the wall. '*He returned a decade later when Scott made his ill-fated bid to reach the South Pole in 1911. Crean was a key figure on the expedition, dragging a sledge to within 150 miles of the South Pole before being ordered to return to base camp. He was among the last three men to see Scott alive within reach of his goal, and only a few months later he went back to the ice to bury Scott's frozen body,*' Jasmine continued. 'My goodness.'

'It gets better,' Connor said and pointed at the rest of the text. 'Read this.'

'Okay,' Jasmine said and continued reading. '*It was during the return to base camp that Crean performed the greatest single-handed act of bravery in the history of Antarctic exploration. When one of his companions, Lt Evans, collapsed thirty-five miles from safety, the courageous Crean volunteered to go for help. It was a hazardous journey across treacherous terrain in sub-zero temperatures, and his only food consisted of two sticks of chocolate and three biscuits. He had no sleeping bag or tent and was already physically exhausted, having been on the march for three months and having covered around 1,500 miles. His solitary trek lasted eighteen hours and earned him the Albert Medal,*' *then the highest award for gallantry.*' Jasmine stopped and stared at Connor. 'I never knew he even existed. They must be so proud of him around here.'

'One of the local heroes of the day,' Connor agreed. 'And then he came home and built this pub.'

'And lived happily with his family,' Jasmine added with a sigh. 'What a lovely real-life story. Tom Crean must have been an incredibly strong man, both mentally and physically.'

'Yes, I think he was,' Connor agreed. 'But people were hardier in those days.'

'They were,' Jasmine agreed, mesmerised by the photo of the man.

'But come on,' Connor urged, pulling her away from the photos. 'Let's walk up the hill. I want to show you the view from above the lake. It's stunning.'

They went back to the car to put on their jackets and walking boots and set off up the steep street lined with little cottages and on up a path that took them to a gate and a trail up the mountainside. Jasmine stopped for a moment to catch her breath, while Connor kept walking ahead, realising he was a lot fitter than her.

He turned around and looked down. 'Are you okay?' he shouted. 'We can stop here if you feel too tired to do the climb.'

'No,' Jasmine replied. 'If Tom Crean can walk thirty-five miles in sub-zero temperatures to save his friend, I can walk a bit up the mountain.' She started walking again despite feeling exhausted, her heart beating like a hammer in her chest. Connor sprinted ahead of her and didn't turn around until he was nearly at the top.

'The view is amazing up here,' he called. 'But take your time and don't push yourself too hard. Only a little bit left.'

'That's easy for you to say,' Jasmine panted, sweat running into her eyes as she forced herself to walk up the last few metres to where Connor was standing. 'Finally,' she gasped as she arrived beside him, gratefully accepting a drink from his water bottle. Then she looked down and nearly stopped breathing as she saw the view. The mountain sloped all the way to the sea on the other side, and she could see Dingle Bay and the whole of the Iveragh Peninsula all the way to Valentia Island. She gazed at the outlines of the MacGillycuddy Reeks mountain range in the distance, misty and blue in the late afternoon light. Her legs suddenly weak, Jasmine sat down on a boulder, overwhelmed by the beauty around her. 'Stunning,' she said after a while.

'Worth the pain?' Connor asked, smiling at her.

'Oh yes. Thank you for taking me up here. And for the lunch and everything. It's been a beautiful day.'

He sat down beside her and took her hand. 'For me, too. I wanted it to be a special day for us. I'll be going away for a week or two, you see.'

'Oh?' she asked, startled by the look in his eyes. 'Where are you going?'

'To Dublin. I have to meet my… ex-wife and oversee the sale of the house. And we have to sort out the contents. It'll be a bit… difficult.'

'Of course,' Jasmine said, wishing she could wipe away the sadness from his face.

'So I'll be away for a week or so, maybe more,' Connor said, playing with her hand. 'I need to be on my own for a bit after all that, I think.'

'Of course.' Jasmine nodded. 'It's very hard for you. Selling the house will be a huge wrench. I want to give you some space. I'll be here when you feel like seeing me again. Not here on this mountain, of course,' she added with a laugh. 'But in Sandy Cove. I'll be busy with my mother's birthday party preparations and waitressing at your restaurant. And maybe I need a little space, too.'

'You do.' He kissed her cheek. 'It's been a wonderful few weeks. It's strange how close I feel to you already. But it's not a good idea to rush into a new relationship so soon. Not for me anyway.'

'Or me,' Jasmine said with a sad little smile. 'I'll miss you, of course.'

'Me, too,' Connor said, looking into her eyes. 'I'll miss your lovely brown eyes and your sweet smile and the French lilt in your voice. And your cheeky laugh.' He got up and looked out at the view for a moment. 'I think we should go,' he said. 'It's getting cold and it'll be dark soon. I'll take you back home and then we'll say goodbye for now.'

'You're right.' Jasmine stood up and took a last look at the view. 'I'd like to come back here with you when we pick up again.'

'That's a date,' Connor said as he started to walk back down the path. 'Then we'll be in a better place and can make a few plans.'

His blonde hair fluttered in the wind and when he turned to smile at Jasmine, she smiled back, trying to look both supportive and cheerful. But in her heart something didn't feel quite right. She knew he was devastated about the divorce and needed that space he had talked about, but after that, how would he feel? Would he be ready to commit to someone else?

The question nagged at her all through the trip back home, so much that she couldn't manage more than a quick goodbye when they got to Sally's house. They looked at each other as he pulled up, an awkward silence threatening to ruin the happy memories of the day.

'Well,' Connor said. 'This is goodbye for now, I suppose.'

Jasmine nodded, feeling miserable. 'Yes.'

Connor stared straight ahead, his hands on the steering wheel.

'Good luck with… everything. I'll be thinking about you,' she told him.

'Thank you,' he replied.

She turned her head to hide the tears welling up. 'Bye, then,' she whispered.

'Bye, Jasmine,' he said and reached out to touch her. But she avoided his hand, slid out of the passenger seat and got out, gently closing the door. They looked at each other through the window and then he drove off, leaving Jasmine standing on the dark pavement watching his taillights disappear up the street, feeling more alone than ever.

Chapter Twenty-Two

'He's gone to Dublin,' Jasmine said on the phone to Aiden later that evening. She was in bed but unable to sleep and had phoned Aiden like she often did, just for a chat.

'I know. He told me he'd be there for a couple of weeks.'

'To sort out the sale of his house.'

'He didn't tell me that.'

Jasmine sighed. 'No, but he told me. And then he needs some space so we won't be seeing each other for a few weeks.'

'I suppose that's a good thing,' Aiden stated. 'I mean it's a tough time for him.'

'I know.' Jasmine pushed another pillow under her head. 'But we had such a magical day together. We went to Dingle where we had a fabulous meal and then to Annascaul and the South Pole Inn and then up the mountain past the lake.'

'That's a hefty climb.'

'You're telling me,' Jasmine said with a groan as she moved her legs. 'I'm as stiff as a board. I have to do some more hiking to get fitter.'

'No problem. I'd be happy to be your personal trainer,' Aiden offered.

'Thank you. I'm sure you'll love making me suffer. But oh, it was such a romantic day.'

'You seem a little sad,' Aiden remarked. 'Is it the situation with Connor? You have only known him a month or so, though. Maybe you jumped in a bit too fast?'

'I don't know.' Jasmine paused. 'Maybe. But we haven't… You know…'

'You haven't kissed him? Is that what you're trying to say?' Aiden asked, sounding more cheerful.

'Well, yes. We have both been very careful not to get too close.'

'Nobody can help their feelings. It's what you do about them that matters.' Aiden cleared this throat. 'But I have to say I think it's a bit rough on you to have had a great day with him showing you all the fabulous sights and then him telling you he doesn't want to see you for a while. Seems a bit selfish to me.'

'He's just been through a divorce,' Jasmine protested. 'That's a huge thing to have to deal with. But I have an odd feeling that…' She stopped, unable to say it out loud.

'That what?' Aiden asked. 'Come on, Jazz. You can say it to me.'

'That he still loves his wife,' Jasmine said.

'Oh.' Aiden was quiet for a long time. 'I see. Maybe it's just your imagination? I don't have that feeling about him at all. I'm sure the divorce was rough on him. But he seems to want to move on. You're probably just a little raw after what happened to you. I can imagine it would be hard for you to trust anyone after that.'

'I suppose you're right. I find it hard to believe I could be happy with anyone again. So tell me what I can do about that,' Jasmine said. 'As you're such a wise old man.'

'I really don't know. But right now, try to go to sleep. And try not to think too much about all of this until you see him again.'

'How?' she whispered.

He sighed. 'I don't know, Jazz. But I'm here and I'll do my best to keep you busy. I'll need you most evenings at the restaurant. And I'm sure your mam will need help with her birthday party bash, which I hear is going to be the mother of all parties. And we can go down to Wild Rose Bay or up the mountains whenever you want. Don't worry. You'll be so wrecked you won't have the energy to think. And if you do, you can call me whenever you need a shoulder.' He drew breath.

'Oh, Aiden,' Jasmine said. 'What would I do without you?'

'I have no idea. Now sleep,' Aiden ordered.

'I'll try,' Jasmine replied. She said goodbye to him and hung up, staring into the darkness feeling that even if her love life was a bit of a mess, she still had Aiden.

Aiden kept her busy during the following week. And Sally, without knowing it, filled in the rest of the time by asking Jasmine to help out in the shop and to plan the party, which was going to be held in Willow House.

'Maeve very kindly offered to host it, but we have to organise the food,' she announced one afternoon as they were sitting at the kitchen table making lists. 'It's big enough to take a lot of people,' she declared. 'And we plan to be in the garden, weather permitting.'

'And if it doesn't permit?'

Then we'll have to move everyone into the dining room, which will be a bit of a crush. But we have to get some kind of catering for those who are not on the raw food diet.'

'Which would be most people,' Jasmine teased.

Sally laughed. 'Yes. Even those who were so keen in the beginning have fallen off the wagon. I've even sinned myself a few times. Kamal does not approve. But he can be a little strict at times, to tell you the truth.'

'That's the understatement of the year,' Jasmine remarked, laughing at Sally's expression, secretly enjoying the derogatory remark about Kamal. Could there be a tiny crack in the shiny, happy new lifestyle? 'I love his yoga classes,' she continued. 'But I don't think his lifestyle is that enticing. Who wants to live in a monastery?'

'I know,' Sally agreed, looking a little sheepish. 'I'm beginning to feel just a tiny bit fed up with all the rules.'

'That's good to hear,' Jasmine said. 'I was afraid you were getting hooked on it.'

Sally sighed. 'It seemed so fabulous for a while. But then… When something, I mean *someone* happened, I realised there is a lot more to life than eating salads and focusing on your body. I know health is important but it shouldn't take over your whole life.' Sally started to laugh. 'Oh, God, what must you have thought when you arrived? Your mother had turned into some kind of carrot-munching yoga fanatic. That had to be a shock.'

Jasmine nodded, relieved to hear Sally had finally come to her senses. Her fun-loving, slightly risqué mother was beginning to come back. She grinned.

'I was a little startled, I have to say. There I was, all bruised and battered having run off from everything, needing comfort in the form of some home cooking and then there you were, sitting on a cushion *chanting*, for God's sake!'

Sally looked suddenly guilty. 'And all you got was raw food and some sourdough bread. You poor darling.'

'I thought you had turned into Gwyneth Paltrow.'

Sally burst out laughing. 'That's scary. Especially when you had just arrived.'

'Aiden saved me that evening.'

'Thank God for Aiden,' Sally declared with feeling.

'In so many ways,' Jasmine said thinking of how Aiden was always there for her, especially now.

Sally got up and put her arms around Jasmine. 'I'm so sorry, sweetheart. I was so selfish, only thinking of myself and my hang-up abut growing old, when I should have helped you get over what you had been through.'

Jasmine kissed Sally on the cheek. 'It's okay, Mam. I understand. It's wonderful to see you so happy and that you've found someone special. I have to confess I wasn't too keen on that raw food diet and I was worried you were getting a little obsessed with yoga and all that mindfulness stuff. I'm glad you've put it into proportion instead of letting it control your whole life.'

'I still like the feeling of being fit and healthy,' Sally said. 'But I've realised I was getting a little obsessed.'

'That's true,' Jasmine agreed. She looked at her mother's glowing face and felt suddenly that the plan she had hoped to put into action was no longer possible. Sally had raced ahead and found solace on her own. And Jasmine realised right there and then that her own need for support from Sally no longer existed. She had managed to sort out her problems on her own, and that had made her a lot stronger than if she had been able to lean on her mother. She smiled and hugged Sally back. 'I'm so happy to see the old you back again,' she said.

'Not so much of the "old", please,' Sally ordered and went back to her seat. 'But yeah, I'm back. Only with a healthier body and a happier soul. I'm not giving it up completely, but there is a happy medium in everything. Yoga is fabulous, as you know, and eating healthy is great. But I'm not going to make it a new religion or anything.'

'That's brilliant, Mam,' Jasmine said, smiling at Sally.

'But back to the party,' Sally said. 'We have to send out invitations and get cards for that. There's a printing shop in Killarney who do invitation cards. The catering firms there will deliver, too. We have to look them up and see what kind of food they do and then pick one.'

By 'we', Jasmine knew Sally meant her. 'I'll get on it,' she promised.

'Maybe we should have a band?' Sally said. 'Or a disc jockey to do the music for dancing after the dinner. Maeve is very keen to have us dance in the dining room of Willow House like in the old days. Apparently, they used to throw a lot of parties. Or on the terrace if it's fine. I want to play eighties music with an English-French mix. ABBA mixed with Sardou and Hallyday, that kind of thing.'

'I'd say Nuala's son could manage the music,' Jasmine suggested, feeling Sally was getting a little carried away. 'We'll find the songs on

Spotify and do a mix. We could rig up a sound system or something. How many people are you going to invite?'

'Lots,' Sally said. 'At least fifty. It's going to be a very special occasion, you know.'

'Of course. You only turn sixty once in your life.'

'It's not only about that. It's also a celebration of… well, starting a new life with someone…'

'Really?' Jasmine studied Sally, who pretended to look at her list. The question had been gnawing at her ever since she had found out that there was a new man in Sally's life. Who was this mystery man? 'And you're not going to tell me who this new man in your life is? Or what you were up to in Dublin?'

'Uh… no,' Sally replied and looked back at Jasmine with a sigh. 'I will tell you, but not yet. It's too new and too fragile to be revealed yet. I'm a little frightened to talk about it. It might bring bad karma and wreck everything.' She sighed and pushed away her list. 'You know how it feels when you're falling in love but have been hurt before, so you're scared to death it will happen again? And if you tell anyone about it, you'll jinx it?'

'Yes, I think I do.'

Sally reached out to touch Jasmine's cheek. 'Of course you do, sweetheart. And you have been through so much lately. But now it's over and you can relax. That man won't bother you again.'

'Oh, I'm not worried about him,' Jasmine protested. 'I've put it out of my mind already.'

'But there is something worrying you,' Sally insisted. 'I can tell. I know you've been seeing Aiden's boss, but I thought it was just a bit of fun. Isn't that what you said?'

Jasmine sighed. 'It's a bit more serious than that. But he's just been through a painful divorce, so we've decided not to see each other while he's sorting out his house and putting it on the market.'

'But it's worrying you, isn't it?'

Jasmine nodded. 'Yes. A bit. But at the same time, I'm not sure about my own feelings for him. It's as if something has shifted between us. Something feels wrong in a strange way. As if we're not really as compatible as I thought. I need to see him again to find out how I really feel. But I suppose I have to be patient and wait for him to come back whenever he's ready.'

Sally nodded. 'That's not easy, I'm sure.'

'No, but Aiden said I should keep busy and he's being such a great help. We've been on hikes and all kinds of outings and we've hung out with his windsurfing gang at The Two Marys', which has been fun. It has helped me not to think too much. I don't know how I'd manage without him.'

'He's a wonderful friend,' Sally said and got up. 'Okay, so that's all sorted for now. We have yoga tonight, so maybe we should get changed. Or are you working at the restaurant?'

'No. It's the middle of the week and not too busy. Aiden said he could manage without me tonight.'

'Good. So then yoga and after that...' Sally paused.

Jasmine looked up. 'Yes?'

'How about a pizza and a beer at Nuala's?'

Jasmine gasped. 'Pizza and beer? Are you serious?' She gestured at the bowl of grated carrots, beetroot and nuts. 'I thought this was dinner for tonight.'

Sally shrugged. 'Nah. I'm getting bored with it. And I need to get back to cooking the old way. I'd like a bit more balance so I have time for the new man in my life.'

'So who is he? Your mystery man?' Jasmine asked, knowing she was nagging, but she couldn't help herself. 'I'm dying to know.'

'I can't tell you yet.'

'This is driving me crazy,' Jasmine complained. 'Are you afraid I won't like him?'

'Oh,' Sally said with a little smile playing on her lips. 'You'll like him. In fact, I think you'll adore him.'

Chapter Twenty-Three

Sally refused to reveal any more and stayed away from the subject of her love life during the following weeks. Jasmine stopped asking questions, even if it was frustrating to hear her mother giggle on the phone, or FaceTime in her bedroom late at night. She gave up trying to figure it out and concentrated on organising the party and spending nearly all her waking hours with Aiden. There was still no word from Connor, but as March turned into April and the weather improved, Jasmine felt a little more hopeful. It had been two weeks since their day in the mountains and she was sure she'd hear from him soon. He had said he needed a little time to reflect, so she figured he'd be in touch in another week or two.

Yoga helped her a lot, and when Kamal started each class with 'if stressful or negative thoughts should try to enter your mind during this class, concentrate on your breathing and they will disappear,' Jasmine felt the usual calm come over her as she pushed all bad thoughts away. She found herself doing that at other times, too, especially before going to sleep and the fears and doubts seemed to float away as she attempted slow, steady breaths before she drifted off. *A week*, she thought, *in a week, we'll figure things out.*

But she had to wait another ten days before Connor came back. Then he called her early one morning, saying he wanted to see her.

'Things have changed,' he said. 'In ways I could never have imagined. But I have to tell you in person. I'm in Killarney right now but I'll be at the Sandy Cove beach at eleven. Can you be there then?'

'Of course,' Jasmine said, her heart beating faster.

'See you then, Jasmine,' he said and hung up.

Jasmine felt as if a hand was squeezing her heart and her stomach churned. His voice had been so shaky and troubled. What had happened? Was he ill? Or… was he regretting the divorce? She had had a niggling doubt about his feelings for his ex-wife all along, but dismissed it. And she had been wondering about her own feelings for him. She had started to feel that something didn't quite work between them – a lack of chemistry perhaps – and maybe he felt those vibes, too? As they said goodbye that time, he had looked at her without his usual cheery smile that she found so attractive. Whatever he wanted to tell her, she feared the news would not be good. But if he needed her, she would help him through it.

She showered and dressed, trying to figure out what she would say to him. She even managed to swallow some tea and toast before she went out.

'What's up?' Sally asked as she came into the kitchen with Milou at her heels. 'You look upset.'

'Connor called earlier. He's back and wants to see me.'

Sally brightened. 'But that's good news, isn't it?'

Jasmine patted Milou absentmindedly. 'I'm not sure. He sounded so strange. As if he's about to tell me something important. Something that might affect me, too.'

Sally sat down on a chair opposite Jasmine. 'Oh. You think it's bad news?'

'I'm not sure. He might want to talk about our relationship. And I think we do need to talk about it, actually. We've had a lot of fun, and he's a lovely man. But I'm not sure he's right for me. I mean, I do enjoy his company, but if he wants it to be something more, then—'

'Stop it,' Sally interrupted. 'Don't sit there second-guessing. Go down there and find out and then deal with whatever it is.'

'I will.' Jasmine checked her watch. 'He'll be there in half an hour. But I'll go for a walk while I'm waiting. I can't just sit here and worry.'

'Good idea. It's a lovely day.'

'Is it? I haven't noticed.'

'Go out there and see for yourself. I've just done a little yoga session in the garden with Milou.'

'Oh, good,' Jasmine said, her mind on other things than her dog. 'I'm off now,' she said, getting up from the table.

'All right, pet. Let me know what he says.'

Jasmine nodded. 'I will. I'll pop into the shop later today and tell you.'

Sally smiled. 'Great. Don't worry, I'm sure it can't be that serious.'

'Maybe not,' Jasmine said, feeling a little more cheerful.

She walked down the main street and continued down the lane to the beach, her spirits lifting as she looked across the bay to the open sea. It was a glorious spring day with clear blue skies and a warm breeze that felt as if it was already summer. Jasmine was glad she hadn't bothered with a jacket as the hot sun warmed her back through her T-shirt. She had brought a bottle of water and a bar of chocolate in her bag, along with her phone and a light cardigan in case it got colder later on.

Apart from two people walking their dogs, the beach was deserted, as the winds were slack – windsurfing, or even surfing, was not an option. Jasmine settled on the grassy verge and gazed out to sea, too shaky to attempt a walk. She settled down, crossed her legs and put her hands on her knees. She tried to breathe slowly and evenly, chasing away her fears, seeking strength and confidence from deep within her to cope with what might come.

Good karma, she thought, *that's what I need.* Her breathing slowed, and after a few minutes she felt a calm come over her and she knew whatever Connor would tell her, good or bad, she would cope with it.

'Jasmine?'

She opened her eyes and gazed at him, standing there on the sand, looking like the same Connor she had last seen over three weeks ago, except for the expression in his eyes. 'Hi,' she said, shading her eyes against the sun. 'I was doing a little meditation while I was waiting. Isn't it a lovely day?'

'Grand,' he said, sitting down beside her. 'Very nice. And you look lovely, too.'

'Thanks.' She paused, waiting for him to speak. But he didn't say a word, just sat there looking at the sea and the coastline, blinking against the bright light, his body tense. 'You don't look too bad yourself,' she said after a while. Then she couldn't stand it any more. 'Tell me,' she said. 'Is it the divorce?'

'Yes.' He let his arms fall and looked helplessly at Jasmine. 'We're going to have a baby. Sarah's pregnant.'

'What?' Jasmine felt her knees shake. 'She's pregnant? But... I mean...'

'Is it mine?' He sighed, looking embarrassed. 'Yes, it's mine. We... we had sex three months ago, just after the divorce was final.'

'After—?' Jasmine asked, confused. 'Why?'

He shrugged. 'Don't know. It just happened. Hormones, sadness, a spark of love that wasn't quite over. Then there were more rows and bitterness and then I left for Cork and moved into my apartment and she stayed in the house and started sorting out her stuff. She didn't know she was pregnant until a few weeks ago. She told me just before we were about to go to the estate agent to put the house on the market. She was confused, didn't know what she wanted, really. She said if still I wanted to sell the house she would go along with it and we'd share custody of the child. I'll have to move to back to Dublin whatever we decide. I can't share custody of my child if I'm not living in the same town. But of course, there is the other option. Of getting back together and bringing the baby up like real parents. That's where we are now. Trying to decide what to do.'

'Oh.' Jasmine sat down on the grass again, her legs too weak to hold her upright. 'Trying to decide? Why?'

'Because of you.' Connor sat down beside her and took her hand. 'When I left you, we were so close. It felt so good, somehow. I was leaving all the misery in Dublin behind and starting again.'

'I see,' Jasmine said, the touch of his hand making feel warm all over. 'But we didn't know each other that long, did we? I mean, I'll be going back to Paris one day, when the dust has settled over there. Had you thought about that?'

He nodded. 'Yes. Of course. But I thought we'd solve it somehow.'

'We could have, if we were really falling in love.' Jasmine eased her hand out of his grip. She turned to face him. 'Look, I think you had a more romantic idea about our… friendship or whatever it is than I did. We got on so well and had so much fun. And of course there is a certain attraction there, too. But it never got any further than that. And I think the reason is that we're not quite right for each other. That's what I feel, anyway.'

He looked at her for a while. Then he nodded. 'I suppose you're right. Maybe it's my fault. I wasn't ready to jump into another relationship so soon.'

'No, you weren't. And neither was I. We just grabbed onto each other like two drowning people, trying to get comfort after a lot of pain. And then it didn't get any further because the right ingredients just aren't there.'

'What are those?'

Jasmine sighed. 'I don't know. Chemistry? A spark of something more than that? When it's right, you just know. You feel it deep down. And I didn't.' She put her hand on his chest. 'Connor, you have no choice. You have to go back to your wife and be a full-time dad to that baby. You have no idea how sad it is to grow up with a father who doesn't live with you. Who takes you to the zoo and the cinema and the park to play, but is never there to read you a story or tuck you in at night or to yell at you when you come home too late. That's too sad for everyone. Don't do that to a child because of me or anyone.' Jasmine drew breath. 'I have always felt that you still love Sarah. That's why you were so upset about it. And that's why we – us – didn't work. I think I knew it all along, actually.'

Still sitting on the grass, Connor looked up at her. 'Maybe you're right. About everything.' He scrambled to his feet. 'Deep down, I was hoping you'd say just that. I needed a push in some direction.'

'No, you didn't. You'd have chosen the right path without being pushed,' Jasmine said with a sad little smile. 'But hey, we had fun and I think it helped us both to be together for a while. It would never have worked in the long run, especially with the baby on the way. We'd both feel guilty and that's not a good thing to build a relationship on.'

'No.' He looked at her for a while. 'So this is goodbye, then?'

'It has to be.'

'I know.' Connor leaned forward as if to kiss her, but Jasmine stepped back.

'Please. No hugs or kisses. We're friends, but that's all it can ever be.'

He sighed and nodded. 'Of course. Sorry.' They looked at each other while the soft breeze played with their hair. 'Goodbye, Jasmine,' Connor said. 'Good luck.'

'You too,' she whispered, tears welling up in her eyes. 'Have a good life. You'll be a great dad.'

'Thank you.' He touched her cheek and then turned around and jumped down on the sand, walking away, his hands in his pockets and his shoulders square.

Jasmine watched him, her heart breaking into tiny pieces. She didn't quite understand why she felt so sad as their relationship had never been that close and never moved beyond a light-hearted, flirty friendship. And there had been that feeling deep down that they weren't that compatible anyway. She had never felt as close to him as she did with Aiden for some reason. But as she watched Connor walk away, she felt a sense of failure, of having yet again been rejected. There was no logic to it as there had been no other solution to his dilemma. But she still felt so utterly lost and lonely.

Connor disappeared from view and she heard his car start and drive off. Then she turned away and walked in the other direction, up past The Two Marys' and onto the path that led to the only place she knew she'd find solace. Wild Rose Bay.

Chapter Twenty-Four

Jasmine stumbled along the path, tears blurring her vision. She groped in her shoulder bag for her sunglasses but couldn't find them. They must still be in the bowl on the hall table with keys and other paraphernalia. But she found a crumpled cotton sun hat and put that on to shield her eyes from the bright sunlight, which helped a little bit. She kept walking at a steady pace, determined to get where she was going without anyone following her. But why would they? She hadn't told anyone where she was headed and only her mother knew about her meeting with Connor on the beach.

When she reached the ruined houses, she sat down on a boulder, found her water bottle and took a swig, catching her breath. The beautiful view and the soft winds made everything more painful. It was as if the gods were mocking her, giving her a heavenly day, laughing at her while her heart was breaking.

Oh, Connor, she thought, *why did you have to come into my life just when I was so vulnerable? I thought you'd save me from my misery, but that was just a foolish dream.*

Jasmine sighed as she stared out at the view, trying to sort out her feelings. It wasn't Connor that made her feel so sad, it was the feeling that everyone was moving on and she was still stuck, trying to work out what to do with her life. Even though she had become closer to her mother and they now had a much better relationship, and she had got the closure she needed with Damien, there was something important missing: her own future. She had no idea what to do; move back to Paris or stay here, in Sandy Cove? She couldn't decide and that made her more lost and confused than ever. She felt she had no roots anywhere.

No job, no future and no idea how to move on.

Jasmine started to cry again, sobbing loudly, giving out a sound that echoed down the hill and over the water. Then she stopped and sat there, empty of emotion, unable to move. After a while, she tried to come to her senses and pull herself together.

She looked around at the ruined houses and thought of the people who had lived here a long time ago. They had endured hardship and poverty but had still carried on, falling in love, getting married, having children. Her thoughts turned to Siobhan and her tragic love story that now felt all the more real because of her own sorrow. Siobhan's lover had perished at sea and they had never seen each other again. Of course it was just a legend, but at that moment Jasmine truly believed it had happened. She could nearly feel Siobhan's sadness in the whisper of the wind over the grass.

Trying to shake off the eerie feeling, Jasmine got up and walked around the houses, touching the stones warmed by the sun. She wandered in under the low archway beside one of the houses and peeked through it to discover a kind of cave inside. It must have been an entrance to a tunnel, or maybe a place where food was stored. She ducked under the arch and went inside, where she discovered rough steps leading down into the darkness. They must have dug into the ground to make a cool space to store meat and other foods. She stepped further in and stood on the top step, bending down to look into the space below.

All she could see was darkness and she was about to take another step when the ground seemed to disappear beneath her feet and she fell down what felt like a tunnel spiralling downwards, getting steeper and steeper. She tried to grab onto the sides of the tunnel but her fingers only found earth that crumbled at her touch. Terrified, she tried to scream but no sound came out while she continued to slide down the narrow space and finally landed with a hard thump at the bottom.

Dazed by the force of the fall, Jasmine tried to sit up. All was black around her, and looking up she saw nothing but darkness. She felt as if she had fallen several hundred feet. She blinked and managed to heave herself into a half-sitting position, but as she turned her head, she saw a chink of light in front of her and crawled towards it, feeling the sides of the dim space with her hands. Then she reached forward towards the place where the light was coming in and felt a wall of earth and stones, the light coming from a wide crack at the top. She heard a sound and sat still, listening. It sounded like waves lapping onto the shore and she realised where she was. The beach at Wild Rose Bay.

So this must be the tunnel Aiden was talking about, a tunnel from the tiny village above to the beach. They must have used it for getting to and from the beach and the little pier in bad weather, or even when they were involved in smuggling, hiding the goods inside… She imagined torches would have lined the walls and that the steps would have been cut into the rocks. She had felt them when she had bumped down the hill and her back and buttocks ached as a result.

She shivered and rubbed her arms, feeling the cold seep through her light T-shirt. Then she remembered her bag and felt around to see if she had by some miracle managed to hang onto it. She remembered it on her shoulder as she went in under the archway and it must have been still there as she fell. Jasmine got on her hands and knees and crawled around the dark space, feeling the earth for the strap of the bag, but she couldn't find it. She thought with longing of the bottle of water, the bar of chocolate and the cardigan she had put there when she left the house. And the phone… If she could only find her phone, she could call Aiden. But there was no sign of the bag or the phone. She'd just have to try to dig herself out, which, as she looked at the hole in the wall of mud, seemed quite possible, even if it would be hard work.

She stared at the small opening in the solid wall of dried mud and stones. *Right, time to get stuck in.* Jasmine got up on her knees and started clawing at the wall, just under the crack that let in that bit of light. She managed to make the crack slightly wider and tore at it with her nails until they broke, which made her swear loudly. Then she lay on the ground and kicked at the wall with her feet, hoping some of it would give way. Some of the mud and stones rained down on her and she got back on her knees and started on the crack again, and managed to dig out a lot more.

Then, suddenly, Jasmine heard a sound that was different from the waves, a kind of heavy breathing and panting. Then another sound started, like someone scratching and whining and then – barking. Jasmine stuck her head out of the hole and laughed as she saw the little dog running towards her.

'Milou,' she called. 'Milou, come here!'

Milou barked even more and started to frantically scratch at the wall.

'Oh Milou,' Jasmine exclaimed, 'keep digging. Get me out of here. You know you can do it!' She listened to his barking and whining while the dog dug with his little paws, then she saw a pair of legs and heard a familiar voice that said, 'What's up, boy? Have you found something?'

'Aiden,' Jasmine called, sticking out her head again. 'How happy I am to see you. Gimme a hand to get out of here, will you?'

'Jazz,' Aiden said and fell on his knees. 'Don't worry, we'll get you out. Keep digging, Milou!'

'I'll have a go at it from the inside if you work at it from your end.'

'Will do,' Aiden shouted back. 'Milou, work away there, pal. We have to get her out.'

After what seemed like hours, there was finally a hole big enough for Jasmine's head and shoulders to stick out. Milou kept digging and Aiden tore at the sides of the hole until it was big enough for Jasmine to try to get out. She pushed from the inside while Aiden reached in and got his hands under her arms. 'If I pull, do you think you could kind of kick off in there and get your hips through? I'll count to three.'

Jasmine stood on her tiptoes and as Aiden counted to three, managed a kind of jump as he pulled with all his might. The edges of the hole scraped painfully against her hips as Aiden pulled and then, suddenly, like a cork out of a champagne bottle, Jasmine catapulted through the hole in the wall of dried mud and landed on top of Aiden, who fell onto the sand. They lay there for a while, panting, laughing and crying while Milou scrambled on top of them, frantically licking Jasmine's face.

'Oh Aiden, I love you,' Jasmine exclaimed and planted a kiss on his mouth. 'You saved my life.'

'Steady,' Aiden said, looking shy. But he wrapped his arms around her and held her tight for a moment before he tried to move. 'Uh… could you get off me, hun? I don't seem to be able to breathe.'

'Oh my God,' Jasmine panted as she eased herself off Aiden. 'I think I flattened you. Are you okay?'

Aiden lay there, smiling at her. 'I'm fine, darlin'. How about you?'

Jasmine rolled onto her back and closed her eyes, hugging Milou. 'I feel wonderful. I thought I'd have to dig for another hour before I got out and I broke all my nails. I lost my phone so I couldn't call anyone, and nobody knew where I was. How did you find me?'

'Connor,' Aiden said. 'He stopped by the restaurant to tell me he's moving back to Dublin and getting back with his wife. Said he'd told you when you met at the beach and that you might be upset. So I legged it down there but you were gone. I asked the Marys if they'd seen you and they said they'd spotted you through the window heading in the direction of the cliff path. I knew you were going here, as you love it so much.'

'And Milou?' Jasmine asked, hugging her dog.

'He was running around the main beach. Must have escaped from the house, I thought. So I decided to bring him with me and it didn't take him long to find your scent. He was like a bloodhound following it. But it stopped at the ruined houses, where we found your bag, so he was a little confused up there. And then he stood at the edge and cocked his head as if he had heard something. He barked and whined and then he disappeared down the track to the beach. So I followed him.'

'Oh,' Jasmine said with a happy sigh. 'He might have heard when I was swearing as I tried to get out. Didn't manage more than a loud croak but he has fantastic hearing.' She put her cheek to Milou's head. 'My darling little doggie.'

'The slope is very slippery after the rain yesterday. But I thought I'd risk it and get down here in case you had climbed down the slope.'

'But I didn't,' Jasmine said with a little sob. 'I fell down the rabbit hole, like Alice. Only it was a tunnel, not a rabbit hole.'

'I knew it,' Aiden said. 'I knew there had to be some kind of passage down to the beach from the houses. But it must be dangerous. Why did you go into it?'

'I didn't. I just peeked in and took a few steps inside. Then the ground just disappeared from under me. I was terrified. I thought I'd break my neck.'

'But you didn't, thank God.'

'And thank God you came to rescue me, or I'd be still digging.' Jasmine let Milou go and turned to Aiden. 'When I saw your face, I thought I was dreaming.'

'I'm sure Milou was a prettier sight than my ugly mug.'

'No.' Jasmine touched his cheek. 'At that moment it was the most beautiful face in the whole world.' She ran her hand over her hair. 'I must look a mess.'

Aiden got up on his elbow and leaned over, looking at her, laughing. 'You're covered in mud and your hair looks like a rat's nest, but you have never looked cuter.' He touched her arm. 'But you're freezing.'

'It was like a fridge in there.' Jasmine closed her eyes and turned her face to the sun that was now low in the sky. 'I was hoping the sun would warm me. But I'm still cold.' Then a thought hit her. 'My bag. Did you bring it with you? There's a cardigan in it and a bar of chocolate.'

'Yes. It's here somewhere.' Aiden sat up and looked around. 'Here.' He handed her the bag.

'Fabulous.' Jasmine took the bag and found her cardigan. 'Thanks,' she said, putting it on, groping for the bar of chocolate and the bottle of water. She glanced at Aiden as she devoured the chocolate and gulped down the water. 'You must be cold in just that thin shirt.'

'Nah, it's okay. It's warm today, over twenty degrees. And in any case, I called my friends who were at the Sandy Cove beach earlier with their rib and asked if they could pick us up. They'll be here soon and we can get you home fairly quickly.'

'Home,' Jasmine said and thought dreamily of a hot shower, and a cup of tea in front of the fire. 'I wonder if Mam is worried. What time is it?'

Aiden checked his watch. 'Just gone five.' He pulled his phone out of his pocket. 'Do you want to call her?'

'I don't want to worry her. Maybe I could just send her a text? Just to let her know I'm with you and I'll tell her everything later. She knew I was meeting Connor. She might have thought I went somewhere with him.'

Aiden nodded. 'Yeah. I have her number here. How about I say something like, "Hi Sally, Jasmine is out walking with me and Milou. Will be back in an hour or so." Is that okay?'

'Perfect. Then I'll tell her what happened when I get home.'

'Okay.' Aiden tapped the message into his phone. 'Done.'

'She'll get a fright when she sees me.' Jasmine touched her hair again. 'I don't know how I'll get all the clumps of mud out.'

Aiden pulled at one of the clumps. 'This one is big.'

'Ouch,' Jasmine complained as he pulled it out.

'Sorry.' Aiden looked at the clump of mud. 'It's like concrete, But there's something...' He rubbed at it. 'Something's in here. Looks like...' He stared at it and then handed it to Jasmine. 'Look. Is it gold?'

Jasmine took the small mud-encrusted object. 'It's gold and – it's a ring.' Jasmine stared at Aiden. 'A ring?' she whispered and got up. She walked to the water's edge and dipped the clump in the waves. Then she studied it while Aiden looked over her shoulder, and dipped it in the water again to get it even cleaner.

'It's a Claddagh ring,' Aiden said when Jasmine had managed to wash all the mud off.

'Oh yes.' She looked at the hands clasping a heart and the crown above it on the ring. 'That's what it is. A Claddagh ring. But they're quite common, aren't they?'

'Yes, but I think this one is old,' Aiden said. 'Look at how rough the design is.'

'You're right. It's very basic. Not quite like the ones you see for sale these days.' Jasmine peered inside the ring. 'There's a stamp, but I can't see it clearly.'

'We'll look it up on the Internet. It will give us an idea of when it was made.'

'Could it be *that* ring, do you think?' Jasmine asked, as the thought of holding Siobhan's ring made her forget how cold and sore she was. 'It could be. I mean the first Claddagh rings were made in the seventeenth century. I saw something about the history behind it on the Internet recently. Such a sweet story.'

'There are several stories,' Aiden remarked. 'But it's true that the ring originated in the early seventeen hundreds in Galway and came to symbolise love, loyalty and friendship. It was often used as an engagement ring.'

'Love, loyalty and friendship,' Jasmine repeated, looking up at Aiden. 'Isn't that beautiful?'

'Oh yes, it is.' He put his arm around her. 'The most important things in life, really.'

Jasmine was about to reply but was interrupted by the sound of an engine followed by a rubber dinghy rounding the headland at full speed.

'Here are the lads now.' Aiden raised both his arms and waved them in the air. 'Here we are, guys,' he shouted. 'Here, let's get Milou. Put that ring in your pocket and we'll look at it later.'

The spell was broken, and as the rubber dinghy came into shore and they got in, Jasmine lifted Milou as she scrambled aboard. She touched the ring in her pocket and looked at Aiden as the dinghy took off, but he was looking ahead and she couldn't see his face. She sat back, hugging her dog, happy to be safe and thankful for her brave little dog and for Aiden and his true-blue heart.

Love, loyalty and friendship, she thought as the dinghy bounced on the waves, *that's him in a nutshell. Why didn't I see that before?*

Chapter Twenty-Five

Life settled down to a pleasant routine after the drama of Jasmine's adventure at Wild Rose Bay. She still felt sad about her break-up with Connor, but as the weeks rolled by and she was busy with the birthday preparations, the sadness faded and all that was left was a fleeting feeling of something that should never have happened. She knew getting involved with a man who was going through a divorce was bound to cause problems and she should have known better than to think that it would be plain sailing. The memory of Connor's handsome face and gorgeous smile sometimes popped into her mind but the image was growing steadily more faint as she began to realise that it had simply been a brief flirtation.

Sally had been wonderful and her empathy and concern were a great comfort. She was blooming, Jasmine thought, and she often felt like she was finally blooming, too. Was there a whiff of romance in the air that had both of them feeling like this? Or just the warm spring weather? She smiled as her mother, dressed in one of her beloved kaftans, floated through the house humming a little tune.

'I can't wait for the big reveal,' Jasmine said with a laugh as Sally bounced into the kitchen one morning. 'That man must be something else.'

'He is,' Sally said with a dreamy look in her eyes. 'The most wonderful man I have ever met in my entire life.'

Jasmine was about to ask Sally to explain, to finally tell her about this new man in her life, but stopped herself, knowing that it was better to wait and not try to poke into her mother's love life when she so obviously wasn't ready to talk about it. 'It's lovely to see you so happy,' she said instead.

'Oh yes, I am,' Sally said and kissed Jasmine on the cheek before she skipped out of the kitchen again.

'She's like a teenager,' Jasmine said to Milou, who was sitting at her feet. 'But she'll have to tell us very soon who this superman is. Only a week to go now.'

She got up and started to tidy up the breakfast things, glancing out the window to see if it had stopped raining. The forecast for the day of the birthday party was promising, Aiden had told her, and she hoped he was right. If they got a warm evening, they would be able to have the party in the garden of Willow House, which would be easier than cramming fifty hungry guests into the dining room and cooking the meal in the kitchen instead of barbecuing in the garden as they planned.

Everything was in place, the crockery, tables and chairs they had hired were arriving later that day, and they had decided on a menu for the hors d'oeuvres from the catering firm. Nuala and Sean Óg's son Turlough was putting together a playlist of French and English hit songs from the eighties as a surprise for Sally. He would connect his Spotify app to the sound system with loudspeakers that would be placed in the garden, he told Jasmine when they met in Nuala's kitchen for tea and to plan the party music.

'If it doesn't rain,' he added. 'In that case, we'll have to rethink the equipment a little.'

'We'll have to rethink the whole thing,' Jasmine said with a sigh, wondering how she could convince Mother Nature not to rain on their parade.

'Just bury a statue of the Child of Prague in the garden,' Nuala suggested, putting a plate of muffins fresh from the oven on the table. 'That's what we did for our wedding and it turned out to be the warmest February day for decades.'

'The Child of Prague?' Jasmine asked. 'What's that?'

'It's a statue of the infant Jesus in robes holding a globe with a cross on it,' Nuala explained. 'Comes from a legend from medieval times about a Spanish duchess who married some nobleman in Prague and brought this statue with her. It was supposed to bring luck and good fortune or something. No idea how it all came to Ireland, but this statue is supposed to protect you from bad weather at a wedding.'

'This isn't a wedding,' Jasmine argued.

'But Sally is supposed to reveal the identity of the mystery man,' Nuala remarked. 'And I wouldn't put it past her to actually do a wedding right there and then, having hidden the parish priest under the table.'

Jasmine burst out laughing. 'You're right. Anything could happen. But where on earth will I get a statue of the Child of Prague? I have never seen one around here.'

'You can borrow ours,' Nuala offered. 'I still keep it in the bedroom. Sean Óg will be delighted to have it gone from there. He doesn't like it staring at us when we… uh, you know,' she said, glancing at Turlough.

'Euuuwww,' Turlough groaned.

'Sorry,' Nuala said, laughing. 'The idea of your parents doing anything remotely romantic is cringe-worthy, right, Turlough?'

'Totally,' Turlough said and got up from the kitchen table. 'I'm off. I'll have it all set up the day of the party, Jasmine. And I'll have a plan B for the living room if the Child of Prague doesn't deliver.'

'He's a genius,' Nuala said proudly when Turlough had left.

'Very mature for fourteen,' Jasmine had agreed.

She smiled as she thought of their conversation the day before while she walked to the restaurant.

True to her promise, Nuala had buried the statue in the garden, just under the hedge the day before. 'Because you never know,' she had said. Jasmine hoped fervently that it would work, as the garden party would be beautiful and just what Sally would love, Mother Nature delivering and good karma all around. Jasmine sighed and wished a little of that karma would spread to her. Despite being a little homesick for Paris and the buzz of the big city, she was more and more drawn to Sandy Cove, the beautiful countryside and the friendly, safe atmosphere of knowing everyone. Delving into her family history had made her feel even more at home. Waitressing wasn't as bad as she had thought and she enjoyed working with Aiden at the restaurant on Friday and Saturday evenings. They would clean up together and then have bite to eat at the kitchen table, talking late into the night. Jasmine was surprised that they always found so much to talk about.

They often talked about Wild Rose Bay and the stories Mad Brendan told them. Jasmine kept the ring in her room, not knowing quite what to do with it. They had looked up the hallmark on the Internet and discovered it was indeed very old, from the late eighteenth century. But was it really the ring Siobhan had been given by the man she loved? There was no way of knowing and Jasmine didn't feel like burying it in that grave she had found in the graveyard. It felt wrong, somehow, as if something was telling her the ring should not be buried, but worn and loved.

'What should I do with the ring?' she asked Aiden over their supper later that evening.

'Wear it?' he suggested.

'It's too small.'

'Keep it, then,' he said, smiling at her with a look in his eyes that made her heart beat faster. 'Wear it on a chain around your neck. As a memento of when I saved you.'

She looked back at him with a tender smile. 'I don't need a memento to remind me. I'll never forget that moment when I saw your face through that hole in the wall of mud.'

He reached across the table and touched her cheek. 'And I'll never forget what you said.'

'That I love you?'

'Yes.' He cleared his throat, looking embarrassed. 'I know it was just relief at being saved. You'd have said the same thing to Mad Brendan if he'd been the one to save you.'

'No, I wouldn't,' Jasmine protested. She looked back at him and realised how she felt about him. 'I'm so fond of you, Aiden. I think I always have been. I know you're always going to be there for me. Like the stars,' she tried to explain. 'You can't always see them, but you know they're there. And I knew you were out there, somewhere, waiting for me.'

He sat back and looked at her thoughtfully with his kind blue eyes. 'I know what you mean. And I did, too. Because you were my best friend. But it's not the same any more for me. My feelings are different. I'm in love with you, you see.'

'Oh.' Jasmine didn't quite know what to say. It was her own feelings as he said those words that gave her a sudden jolt. Like a bolt of lightning from a clear blue sky. But it was too soon, too new and fragile. She didn't want to be pulled into something she couldn't handle. Damien's betrayal and Connor's sudden departure had made her afraid of any new commitments. What if this one failed, too?

'Are you sure?' she finally said.

'Yeah.' Aiden suddenly looked angry. 'Of course I'm sure. I know how I feel, and I also know you're not in love with me. I'll have to try to cope with that somehow. But something just came up that'll help take my mind off all of this. A great opportunity I haven't told you about. And that's why I'm leaving.'

'What? You're leaving?' Jasmine asked, alarmed. 'What happened? Where are you going?'

'Strangely enough, I'm going to Paris. How's that for irony?'

Jasmine's jaw dropped. 'What? You're going where?'

'Paris,' he repeated. 'I've been offered a job at one of the top restaurants there. This talent scout, or whatever he was, arrived here a few weeks ago; he wanted to sample the menu of this little fish restaurant that got a mention in *The Michelin Guide*, so I served him a few samples. I thought he was a restaurant critic from a magazine or something. But then he came back for some more samples and then, shortly afterwards, he offered me a job. I wasn't going to accept, but the salary is great and to tell you the truth, I do love Paris and always wanted to go back.'

Jasmine stared at him, feeling shell-shocked. 'So you're going to Paris?' she said, just to make sure she had understood.

'Yup,' Aiden said and stood up to clear their plates. 'Not immediately, but I'll be starting in September. So I'll have the summer here, which is great.'

She sat there, looking at him while he tidied up. 'I don't know what to say,' she mumbled.

'About what?' He closed the dishwasher with a bang and pressed the start button.

'About everything. About you going to Paris and being in love with me.' She got up and crossed the floor to stand in front of him. 'I'm still trying to decide what to do, you know. I was thinking of staying here and doing some work online. How do you feel about that?'

He looked down at her without speaking, his arms folded. 'How do I feel?' he finally said. 'That might be a good thing. If you were in Paris, too, we'd have to try to avoid each other.'

She put her hands on his arms and leaned closer. 'What if I don't want to avoid you? What if I'm in love with you, too?' she blurted out despite her resolve not to say it. 'How do you feel about that?'

His eyes softened. 'If that were true, I'd be over the moon,' he replied hoarsely. 'Is it?'

She nodded. 'I think so. Either that or I'm coming down with something.'

Aiden looked suddenly shell-shocked. 'You mean it? You're really in love with me?'

She laughed. 'No, I'm probably just sick.' Her knees wobbled as she looked into his dear face and knew that what she felt right now was a love so overwhelming it took her breath away. She had never felt like this about anyone.

He put his arms around her, looking into her face. 'What are the symptoms?'

She closed her eyes and leaned her cheek against his chest, breathing in the scent of garlic and herbs. 'I'm all shivery and hot at the same time. My pulse is racing and my knees feel weak.'

'Could be flu,' he murmured in her ear. 'Or just temporary insanity.'

'It's love,' she said, laughing. 'I just know it.' She hugged him tight and let out a long sigh. 'Oh, God, how stupid I've been. I was so blind and silly, falling for the wrong men, wasting time, when you were here, waiting for me.'

He put his cheek against her hair. 'Not your fault. I've fallen for a few weird women at times. All completely wrong. But let's not worry about whatever stupid things we've done.'

'You're right.'

She took his face in her hands and stood on tiptoe to kiss him on the mouth, which turned into a very long kiss, only ending when they had to come up for air. It felt so strange to kiss Aiden like this, her friend and soulmate. The physical attraction had always been there, she realised, but now it came to a head making her dizzy with love.

'Wow,' Aiden said. 'You're very good at that.'

'So are you, my friend,' Jasmine said with a laugh. She stepped back, suddenly shocked at what had happened between them. 'Oh, God, I can't believe this. It's far too crazy to be true.'

'I know.' Aiden's smile widened. 'Crazy and fantastic and totally awesome.'

'When exactly did you fall in love with me?' Jasmine asked.

'When you walked into the restaurant that night looking so beautiful and polished but lost and lonely at the same time. I wanted to wipe the sadness away from your face and comfort you.' He stopped. 'And then I loved you more when I watched you settling into life here and beginning to find yourself. I saw you beginning to bloom and come to terms with all the things that had happened to you. And then, when I found you in the tunnel and you had been so brave and came out all cold and covered in mud, I thought you were so adorable.'

Jasmine laughed. 'I must cover myself in mud again to turn you on.' She kissed him once more. 'I think my love for you was something that was always there, like a tiny bud waiting to unfurl. I felt so close to you all through this time, knowing you were there for me, always ready to talk when I was feeling lonely.'

He grimaced. 'I have to confess that you going on about Connor was a little hard to take.'

Jasmine cringed. 'Ugh, I'm sorry. Such a mistake. Not Connor's fault, but I think I grabbed onto him hoping he'd help me get over what happened with Damien. And he grabbed onto me for the same reason. I kind of felt he wasn't right for me all along, but I didn't realise that until later. You were such a help to me and just listened.'

'I didn't want to let you go. I loved hearing your voice.'

She smiled. 'I loved talking to you when I was feeling low. I had a feeling from time to time that there was something going on between us. And then... discovering Wild Rose Bay with you feels like it was meant to be, especially learning about Siobhan and Oisin. A love story that ended badly. But ours will be a happy one. I just know it.'

'Me, too. Whatever you do, wherever you are, I could never stop loving you,' Aiden declared, his eyes serious.

Jasmine kissed him. 'You make me so happy.'

'My flat's a mess,' he confessed, as if he had read her thoughts. 'I need to muck it out before I can invite anyone up there.'

'I don't care.'

'But I do,' Aiden said in way that did not allow argument.

'And my mother's at home,' Jasmine said with a giggle, moving away from him. 'We have nowhere to do anything more than kiss.'

'Come here,' he ordered.

She fell into his arms again and they kissed long and hard, until Aiden drew back, saying that was enough for tonight. He got her jacket and put it on her and then he walked her home through the dark night, the stars twinkling above them in the velvet sky.

Chapter Twenty-Six

Rain smattering against the window woke Jasmine up. She blinked and turned in the bed, looking around, wondering for a split second where she was. Then she saw the shape in the bed beside her, smelled the lavender scent of the sheets and knew she was in Aiden's flat, where she had slept for the past three nights, ever since they had told Sally that she was moving in with him. It didn't take long before the news spread through the village and everyone knew they were a couple. Nobody seemed a bit surprised, and everyone smiled at them wherever they went. The Two Marys even baked cupcakes decorated with red hearts to celebrate that they had finally realised what everyone else had known for weeks.

'Sure who else would you fall in love with but your best boyfriend,' Mary O said, beaming as she served them coffee and heart cupcakes on the house on the morning following their announcement.

The flat above the restaurant was surprisingly spacious, and now clean and tidy after several days of 'mucking out', as Aiden called it. It had a bedroom and a large living room furnished with an attractive mix of new and old: a sofa from IKEA, two large armchairs from a second-hand furniture shop in Waterville and a coffee table and bookcase painted a distressed white from his parents' house in

Dublin. The wooden floor was covered with a Donegal carpet in various shades of blue and the walls had posters from Paris, and a large photo of the view from Mount Brandon. An eclectic mix that felt cosy and inviting. He had even bought a new bed, and sheets from a fancy shop in Dublin so that his 'princess' would be happy staying there. Jasmine had thought it an unnecessary purchase, but Aiden had insisted. The bed was a four-poster that nearly filled the small bedroom but Jasmine had to admit it was amazing and she loved sleeping in it. She thought, as she lay in Aiden's arms, gazing into his lovely blue eyes, that she had finally come home.

But the rain alarmed her and she ran to the window, looking out at dark clouds and raindrops on the window. 'The Child of Prague is a hoax,' she muttered.

'Come back to bed,' Aiden grunted. 'It's only seven o'clock. The weather will improve later today. That's what they said on the news last night anyway.'

'I have to walk Milou.'

'He's probably still asleep,' Aiden remarked. He patted the empty space beside him. 'Come back to bed, woman. Let's have a cuddle before the storm hits.'

'What storm?' Jasmine exclaimed, rubbing her cold arms.

'The storm of the party, of course. The flurry of excitement of you organising everything and getting it all ready like five hours before the guests arrive.'

Jasmine laughed and got back into bed, snuggling into his arms. 'You know me too well.'

'I could never know you too well, darlin'.' He squeezed her tight and she closed her eyes and dozed for a while, half-dreaming of their new life in Paris and the little flat they were going to find that wouldn't cost them the earth. Money would be tight for a while, until Jasmine found a job, but that didn't worry her. They had each other and didn't need much more than a bed to sleep in and a small kitchen to cook their food.

She sighed happily, her head against Aiden's shoulder, trying not to worry about the party or Sally's new man or Matthieu standing there watching while his heart was probably breaking. Jasmine knew he had hoped to somehow reconnect with Sally again, and had thought that she had also through the years never stopped loving him. Her plan – that masterplan she had thought was so clever – was to bring her parents together and watch them fall in love again. But that was before Sally had met this new man, the man she was going to introduce at the party, the man she had said Jasmine would love. Jasmine lay there, trying her best to be happy for her mother and nearly succeeded. But how was she going to console her father?

Another problem niggled at Jasmine as she lay there beside Aiden, who had dropped off to sleep again. She hadn't quite come to terms that she was leaving Sandy Cove, the village she had come to love. She felt at home here and her Irish roots had become so important during her quest to find out about Wild Rose Bay and Siobhan O'Rourke. She wanted to go to Paris with Aiden, but she also wanted to stay here, where she felt so safe and loved. Would it be possible to do both? But Aiden was so excited about his new job. Would he understand how she felt, or would it create a rift between them? She sighed and crawled out of bed. Would her restless mind ever find peace?

*

By lunchtime, it had stopped raining and the wind dropped. Jasmine felt more hopeful and when the sun appeared behind the clouds, she began to make arrangements for the party to be held in the garden.

'I know I'm probably jinxing it, but I have a feeling we'll be outside the whole evening,' she said to Maeve as they put tablecloths on the round tables on the back lawn and hanging strings of light in the branches of the trees.

Maeve laughed. 'Jinx away. But I think you're right. It's only the end of April but it feels like summer today. A pet of a day, as they say.' She stood on a ladder hanging the last of the lights and watched as Aisling ran to the edge of the garden, chased by Kathleen carrying one of the twins. 'Aisling, darling, don't go down to the beach,' she called. 'Kathleen has to look after the boys and there is nobody to mind you.'

'But I want to swim,' Aisling protested. 'I'm hot.'

'The water will be freezing,' Maeve argued. 'It's only the end of April.'

'But it *looks* warm,' Aisling said. 'And there are fishes there and I want to see them.'

'Daddy will take you down there later,' Maeve said in a firm voice. 'Come and help us make the tables look pretty.'

Aisling sighed and walked slowly across the grass to her mother. 'Okay, Mammy. But if I work, I need to be paid. That's what Kathleen does. She works here minding us and then she gets a sala… salad… she gets money.'

'Of course,' Jasmine said, smiling at the little girl. 'I'll give you five euros if you help us.'

Aisling looked thoughtful. 'Is that paper money?'

'Yes.'

'I'll take it,' Aisling said, looking satisfied.

'Good,' Jasmine replied. 'Then go and get the baskets of bread in the kitchen and bring them out here and put them on the tables. One at a time.'

'Okey-dokey,' Aisling chanted and ran to the kitchen, her hair flying.

'She'll go far,' Kathleen said, laughing as she followed. 'I'll let her help me negotiate my next raise.'

'I'd say she'd be very good at that,' Jasmine said.

'You're spoiling her,' Maeve chided. 'She'll be expecting to be paid for every little thing she does from now on.'

'She reminds me of me when I was that age,' Jasmine remarked as she flicked a tablecloth open from the stack on one of the tables. 'I was such a precious little thing but I had a will of iron and could negotiate deals about practically everything. Especially with my father. I knew if I looked sweet enough, he'd buy me anything.'

Maeve tied the last string of lights to the branch. 'Did you say he's coming to the party?'

'Yes, he is. Please don't tell her. I want it to be a surprise.'

'I swear. Is he here already?'

'He came in on the mid-morning flight from Paris to Cork, and planned to rent a car and drive straight here. So he should be arriving sometime during the afternoon.' Jasmine sighed. 'I don't know how he'll take being introduced to my mother's new man. She's been keeping him secret from anyone, which I find quite irritating, to be honest.' Jasmine shrugged. 'But that's the way she wants it.' She had decided to leave it all alone; she'd just let it go and let Sally run her own life. And when she met Sally's new man, she'd have to accept him and be happy for them, she thought. Would this man fit in with Sally's plan of staying in Sandy Cove for good?

'Does your dad know about this new man?' Maeve asked, pulling Jasmine out of her daydream.

'Yes,' she replied. 'But still, how is he going to feel when she makes the big announcement?'

Maeve climbed down from the ladder. 'If he knows, then I'm sure he'll be fine. Have they stayed friends all these years?'

Jasmine smoothed the tablecloth she had just put on one of the tables. 'Friends? Not really. But on friendly terms, yes. I know that my father is still fond of Mam, and that she, deep down, feels the same. That's what I've always thought, anyway. I haven't heard from him for a while, though.'

'I'm sure he's just been busy. You'll be able to talk to him properly when he arrives.'

'You're right,' Jasmine said, cheered up by that thought.

Maeve suddenly laughed as Aisling wobbled out of the kitchen carrying three baskets full of bread rolls in her arms. 'That's a big load for you, sweetheart.'

'Yes,' Aisling grunted, 'but we have to hurry up 'cos some of the guests are already here.'

'Are you serious?' Jasmine exclaimed, alarmed. 'It's only four o'clock! And we said five on the invites, didn't we, Maeve?'

'We did,' Maeve said. 'Can't believe people are arriving early. That is not very Irish at all. Who are these guests, Aisling?'

'Cordelia and Declan and Daddy and Turlough,' Aisling said, carefully placing the baskets on the tables. 'And a big van.'

'Oh, phew,' Maeve sighed. 'Not real guests, actually. Cordelia offered to help get everything ready and Declan is going to light the barbecue. Paschal said he'd take care of the delivery from the catering firm. And Turlough is setting up the sound system and putting the loudspeakers out on the terrace. All well, so we can relax and get changed in peace.' She took Aisling's hand. 'Come on, darling. We have to go and make ourselves pretty for the party. You have to put on your dress.'

Aisling smoothed back her hair and looked solemnly at Jasmine. 'Are you putting on a dress, too?'

'No, I'm going to wear pink Capri trousers and a blue top,' Jasmine replied.

'Then I'll wear frousers, too,' Aisling declared.

'It's called trousers and you're not going to wear them,' Maeve corrected. 'The ones you have are covered in mud. Your dress is lovely.'

'But I want to be like *her*,' Aisling protested. 'I don't want to wear a silly dress.'

Jasmine crouched in front of Aisling. 'I wanted to wear a dress, but I didn't have one, so I had to wear the silly trousers. I'm really jealous that you have a pretty dress to wear. What colour is it?'

'Blue and white,' Aisling replied, looking doubtful.

'That sounds really beautiful,' Jasmine said. 'I bet you'll be the prettiest girl at the party and we'll all be jealous.'

Aisling giggled. 'You're joking.'

'Absolutely not,' Jasmine declared. 'It's the truth.'

'That's right,' Maeve filled in, pulling at Aisling's hand. 'You'd better hurry and get into that dress before everyone arrives.'

Jasmine stood up. 'And I'll have to change into my silly trousers. Let's see who's ready first, okay?'

'Come on, Mammy,' Aisling ordered, pulling at Maeve. 'Let's go.'

They all hurried into the house, Maeve and Aisling going upstairs and Jasmine to the downstairs bedroom beside the kitchen where she had left her party outfit. She changed her clothes and ran a brush through her hair which had grown to shoulder length, and secured it in a low ponytail with a blue velvet scrunchie. Then she stood back and looked at herself in the mirror, wondering what her father would think when he saw her. Her earlier sleek Paris chic had been replaced by a more natural look. Her face was tanned and just needed a touch of blusher and mascara and her nails were no longer manicured and lacquered a deep red, but cut short. That Paris haircut was a thing of the past and the longer length made her look younger and less polished. It was quite nice, she thought, less contrived and a lot less manufactured. She didn't need to hide behind a façade any more. And that was all thanks to Aiden. And Sandy Cove. How could she bear to leave it? How did Aiden feel about it? They hadn't really discussed it. But they would, she thought. They had to come to some kind of solution and not give up on living here part-time in some way…

Jasmine smiled at herself, thinking of how her life had been turned upside-down since she left Paris two months ago, her tail between her legs. She would return stronger and happier than ever before, ready to tackle whatever challenges lay ahead. The only sadness left in her heart was her father's unrequited love for Sally. But that was his sorrow, not hers. She had done what she could and failed. He had to go on his own journey to find happiness with someone who might be out there waiting for him. Someone who might be better for him than Sally. *And maybe that's for the best*, Jasmine thought. *You can't force people to fall in love to suit yourself.*

By six o'clock, the party was in full swing. The last guests were just arriving in true Irish fashion and the finger food was nearly devoured. Sally, her new man and Kamal had still not arrived, but Jasmine had just received two text messages: one from Matthieu to say he would be a little late, and one from Sally to say they were on their way and to 'get ready'. Jasmine looked around for Maeve and found her chatting to one of the two Marys at the end of the lawn, one of the twins in her arms. She waved and Maeve spotted her, excusing herself, giving the twin to a smiling Mary. She ran across the lawn, weaving between the guests and finally arrived, panting. 'What's up?'

'They're here,' Jasmine announced, her heart beating faster as she saw the curtains of the living room window twitch and then Sally stepped through the French windows onto the terrace.

Jasmine blinked and stared at Sally dressed in a turquoise flowing kaftan with sequins around the neckline. Her wavy hair fell down to her shoulders, the light blue and pink streaks enhancing her glowing face and sparkling eyes. Jasmine had never seen her mother look so happy, or so stunning. Everyone else seemed to think so, too, judging by the sudden hush across the lawn full of guests.

'Holy Moses,' someone whispered behind Jasmine. 'That is some apparition.'

'She looks incredible,' Cordelia murmured as if to herself.

'Amazing,' Jasmine muttered back, her eyes on the figures she could see behind the window.

Sally clapped her hands. 'May I have your attention, please.' She cleared her throat as everyone stopped talking. 'Thank you all for being at my coming of age party. I'm so touched to see everyone here and I hope you're all having fun. More fun to come, and more food, too. I can smell the barbecue and I'm sure you're all starving. But first, a few announcements. This is not just a sixtieth birthday party I'm throwing to pretend to be brave. Turning sixty and admitting it is not easy for a woman, I can assure you. I've been bellyaching about this birthday for weeks, as my darling daughter can confirm. I was going to just stick my head under a blanket and drink vodka all day and try to deny it was happening. But that was no fun, so I thought why not face it and be that old woman who does what she wants and says what she thinks, giving the finger to political correctness?'

Everyone in the room chuckled, smiling and nodding at one another.

'Sure, you've been like that for years,' someone shouted.

Sally laughed. 'Yeah, I know. But now I'm entitled.' She took a deep breath. 'But enough about my age. There are some exciting things going on in my life right now. Things I never thought would happen. Not at this stage in my life, anyway. But when my darling daughter arrived here a while back, she showed me that age is no barrier to doing things you want and to starting afresh, in business and love. She's the reason you're here today. As we talked and she urged me to own my age and embrace life, I began to see that age is truly just a number. She didn't interfere or try to live my life, but quietly showed me the way forward.'

Jasmine squirmed at the bit about not interfering as that was exactly what she had done at the beginning, before she decided to let go and leave Sally alone.

'Love and business,' Sally continued, 'not together but side by side seem to be happening in my life right now. Of those two, love is the most important by far. But when love and business are combined, then it's the most wonderful thing. So, without further ado. I must introduce you to some very dear men who have turned my life around.' She gestured at the window. 'Please come out and join me, darlings.'

Two men stepped out on the terrace to stand beside Sally, both smiling and putting an arm around Sally's waist.

Jasmine gasped as she stared at the man on Sally's right. What was going on?

Sally beamed and kissed them each in turn. 'Here they are,' she said.

'It's Kamal,' Maeve murmured in Jasmine's ear. 'But who is the silver fox on her other side?'

'It's my father,' Jasmine replied. Tears of despair welled up in her eyes as she looked at Matthieu, dressed not in his usual designer suit but in jeans and a white collarless shirt. His white hair was a little longer, making him look younger than his sixty-three years and even more handsome. His brown almond-shaped eyes, so like her own, sparkled as he looked at Sally. But Sally had turned to Kamal and whispered something in his ear.

'Oh, God, I could kill her,' Jasmine whispered to Maeve. 'She's having a fling with Kamal and starting a business with my father. I think I could kill them both, actually.'

But as Sally spoke again, her heart nearly stopped.

Chapter Twenty-Seven

'But first comes love, as I just said.' Sally stepped forward, taking Matthieu's hand. 'This man made me happy once in my life, when I was very young. Then we parted due to some stupidity on both our sides and we didn't speak for years. And we made our darling daughter very unhappy.' She looked at Jasmine with sadness and contrition. 'But now, so many years later, a whole lifetime, really, our daughter has brought us together again. We realised as we connected through phone calls and email messages, that we truly love each other and have done ever since we broke up all those years ago.'

'Oh my God,' Jasmine gasped, the couple in front of her a blur through her tears. 'Am I dreaming?'

'No, darling,' Sally said, holding out her hand. 'You're not. It's real. It's true and it's wonderful, don't you think?'

'It's fantastic,' someone shouted. 'Cheers for love!' Then there was a general applause and more shouting and cheering while Jasmine stepped up to her parents, standing there in each other's arms.

Jasmine tried to stop crying, but the tears kept rolling down her cheeks. 'Why did you do this?' she asked angrily. 'Why didn't you tell me you were falling in love and getting back together? Didn't you know that's what I have been wishing for all my life?' She turned to her father and switched to French. '*Et toi, nom d'un chien. Qu'est-ce que ça veut dire?* You have lied to me for weeks and told me—'

Matthieu let go of Sally and put his arms around Jasmine. '*Non, chérie*, I haven't lied to you. I just told you to leave your mother alone and let her live her own life.'

'And all this time…' Jasmine paused. 'How could you keep it from me that you were falling in love again?'

Kamal, who had remained silent with a benign smile on his lips, stepped forward. 'Jasmine,' he said. 'Try to see this through their eyes. Try to understand that they were afraid to tell you until they were sure. They didn't want to disappoint you again.' He put a calming hand on her shoulder. 'All is well. Their stars have aligned and the universe has made it all happen. Now you have to be happy for them and live your own life calm in the knowledge that your parents have found each other again, just as it was meant to happen.'

Sally nodded and kissed Kamal on the cheek. 'You're so right. Thank you, dear partner.'

'Partner?' Jasmine asked, staring at them. 'Now what?'

Matthieu laughed and shook his head. 'Calm down, Jasmine. It's about business. We're all going to be partners. And this affects you, too, in a way.'

'It does?' Jasmine asked as Sally clapped her hands again.

'Hello!' she shouted. 'Can you shut up for a moment so I can make an announcement?'

'Another announcement?' someone shouted back from the drinking, chatting mass of people.

'Yes!' Sally shouted back. She put two fingers in her mouth and emitted an ear-splitting whistle, which made everyone stop talking. 'There,' she said, looking satisfied. 'Kamal and I are starting a business right here in Sandy Cove. With my soon-to-be new husband, too. It's going to be a wellness centre and we just got planning permission for an extension to Kamal's yoga studio. There will be a little shop selling herbal remedies, a small tea room where you can drink herbal teas and eat raw food salads, an acupuncture and massage clinic and a meditation room. Yoga classes will be extended to all forms of yoga, and we will hire more staff. Kamal and I will be running it and Matthieu will look after the business end of things.'

The guests stared at her in silence and then broke into applause and whistles.

'Woohoo!' Nuala shouted. 'Great news for Sandy Cove!'

'Fantastic,' Mary O exclaimed. 'This will create more jobs and more business for us all.'

'Sally smiled and waved. 'Thank you all. I knew you'd love it. Now, let the party begin.'

Declan held up his glass. 'Cheers for putting Sandy Cove on the map!' he shouted from the end of the lawn. 'And the meat is cooked and it's all ready to be eaten. Please form an orderly queue here and grab some plates.'

There was a communal cheer and everyone rushed to the back of the lawn to the long table crammed with newly grilled steaks, sausages, baked potatoes, grilled corn on the cob and big bowls of all kinds of salads.

Jasmine, still stunned by what she had just heard, didn't move. Was this really happening? She looked at Sally and Matthieu, deep in conversation with Kamal, and tried to come to terms with it all.

It was good news and everything she had wished for, but she was still confused and so many questions were still unanswered.

Matthieu turned and looked at her, taking her hand. 'Come inside with me,' he said. 'We need to talk. Remember I said this all concerns you, too?'

Jasmine nodded and smiled at him. 'Yes. But of course I'm very happy about you and Mam. And I forgive you for not telling me.'

'Wonderful. But there's more,' he said, pulling at her hand. 'Let's go somewhere quiet so we can talk.'

'We can go into the study,' Jasmine suggested. 'It's next door to the living room.'

Matthieu nodded to Sally and Kamal and let Jasmine lead him through the French doors, through the living room and into the study, where they sat down on two leather armchairs facing each other in front of the small fireplace.

'*Alors*,' Jasmine said when she was settled. '*Racontes-moi.*'

Matthieu nodded and cleared his throat, continuing in French. 'It's about my business in France.'

'The finance consultancy?'

'Yes. I'll have to give it up, of course, now that I'm moving here and starting this venture with Sally and Kamal. We have been discussing this for weeks, and now finally it will be all sorted out. If you agree.'

'Agree to what?' Jasmine asked, staring at her father.

'To taking over the business in Paris, of course.'

Jasmine gasped. 'What? Taking over… But… I mean…' She stopped, not knowing what else to say. Running her father's consultancy firm would be a dream come true. It would mean she'd get back to the career she loved.

'Well, not quite taking over,' Matthieu corrected himself. 'I mean you'd be a partner, as there are two others, as you know. But they have already approved my plan and are looking forward to working with you.'

Jasmine's eyes widened. 'Really? Oh, Matthieu, this is such a surprise. And such a huge responsibility.'

He smiled. 'You don't think you can handle it?'

'Of course I can,' Jasmine exclaimed, slapping Matthieu's arm. 'And you know it.'

'I don't doubt it for a second.' Matthieu sat back, still smiling. Jasmine couldn't believe her ears. 'Sally tells me you've fallen for a gorgeous Irish boy. Someone you've known for years. Do you think you might lure him over to Paris? I don't know how qualified he is, but maybe we could find him something to do in the firm?'

'You don't have to,' Jasmine said, laughing. 'He already has a job in Paris.'

Matthieu blinked, looking surprised. 'Is this true?' he asked, switching to English. 'In that case, I think…how do you say… all your Christmases have come together?'

Jasmine leaned over and hugged her father. 'Yes, my dear papa, they really have.' She jumped up and waved her arms in the air, shouting, 'Yes! Yes, yes, yes!' Then she sank down on the chair again, laughing and crying at the same time. It was all so perfect it frightened her. All this was falling into her lap, except for one thing – Sandy Cove. How could she bear to leave it for good?

Matthieu looked at her with concern. 'What's the matter, *chérie*?'

'No,' Jasmine sobbed. 'I'm fine and I'm happy. It's just that it's too much happiness all at once and it's so hard to accept it. And now I have to leave Sandy Cove forever, and I don't know if I can.'

'Oh,' Matthieu said, looking both uncomfortable and confused. He looked around as they were interrupted by the door opening and Aiden looked in.

'What's going on?' Aiden said, running to Jasmine's side. 'Why are you crying, Jazz?' He pulled her up and wrapped his arms around her. 'I just got here and was told you had gone in here with…' He glared at Matthieu. 'Who are you?' he asked. 'What did you say to her?'

'He's my father,' Jasmine said and stopped crying. She groped for a tissue in her pocket and found a crumpled paper hanky. 'Matthieu, this is Aiden, my boyfriend.'

Aiden stared at Matthieu. 'I see. So you're the dad who left her when she was six and now you've come back to upset her again?'

'Not exactly,' Matthieu started. 'I… Well, maybe I should leave Jasmine to explain. I think you might be less angry with me when she's told you what I just said to her.' He touched Jasmine's cheek. 'I'll see you later, my darling.'

'Okay,' Jasmine mumbled into Aiden's shirt. When her father had left, she lifted her tearstained face and looked at Aiden, telling him everything that had happened and the offer she had had. 'All of a sudden, everything has been resolved and everyone will live happily ever after,' she ended and fell into Aiden's arms again.

'Oh my God, it's like the end of a Disney movie,' Aiden said into her hair.

She looked at him, frowning, suddenly afraid again. 'Exactly. Or it would be if I wasn't so miserable about leaving, and that's why

I was crying. All that's happening seems to be pushing me out of Sandy Cove for good. I know I can come here and stay with my parents for a few days now and then, but I'd have nothing here of my own. I'd just be a visitor.'

Aiden took her by the shoulders. 'Don't worry,' he said. 'I know what you're saying and I feel the same. I don't want to give up on Sandy Cove either.'

'You don't?'

He let her go. 'No. I thought you knew that. Just as I knew how you felt. I was going to keep this as a surprise, but I think I'd better tell you.'

'Tell me what?' Jasmine asked, forgetting about her own sadness.

'How would you feel about buying an old wreck of a cottage and doing it up? There's a little place just outside the village on the way to Waterville that's going for a song. It has a good roof but the whole place is in need of serious work that we'd probably have to do ourselves. But once it's finished, it would be our base here, where we could spend holidays and shorter breaks whenever we can get away from Paris. It would be—'

'Oh yes,' Jasmine exclaimed, tears welling up in her eyes. 'That sounds perfect.'

'It's going to be hard work,' Aiden warned her. 'And we'll have to rough it while we do it up.'

'But it would be ours,' Jasmine said, hugging him. 'Why didn't I think of that? Oh, Aiden, this is nearly too much to take in. So much happiness at once. Something bad is bound to happen to ruin it.'

'When your dreams come true, you can't really believe it,' he said. 'I know all that's happened to you recently must have been terrible for you. And of course, in a way, you're right. Life is never perfect and bad stuff happens all the time. Illness, money problems, people dying, and all kinds of other miseries. It will all happen and we'll have to struggle from time to time. But there is one thing that will never change and that is my love for you. And yours for me, I hope. If we stick together, we'll cope with all the rest. So please try to trust me, at least.'

She looked into his earnest blue eyes and felt suddenly ashamed. What was she doing standing here complaining when she had all she had ever wished for? Her journey since she came here had been full of obstacles, but she had tackled them all and arrived at a place that felt so right. She was a different person to the lost woman who had arrived that cold evening, looking for comfort. She knew he loved her with all his heart and always would. Anything else was unimportant.

'Of course I trust you, Aiden,' she said and gently touched his cheek. 'And I will enjoy all the good luck that has come my way all at once. It was such a shock, that's all.'

'I know.' He took her hand. 'But now I think we should go out there and enjoy the party. I want to meet your dad and say sorry for being so grumpy when we met just now. And I want to say congrats to Sally and dance with you and eat badly cooked steaks and drink wine and all the rest of the stuff you do at parties.'

Jasmine laughed and nodded. 'Me, too. Let's go out there and party all night. And then tomorrow, we'll go and look at that cottage. I can't wait,' she continued, smiling at him. 'I'm sure it's gorgeous.'

'Not really,' he confessed. 'It's a wreck. You might think I'm mad to even think about doing it up.'

'I won't,' she protested. 'We have all the time in the world to make it lovely.'

He laughed and took her in his arms. 'You're just as mad as me.'

'Lucky we found each other, then,' she said and kissed him. 'Who else would have us?'

Epilogue

Jasmine stood on the edge of the cliffs and looked down the slopes leading to Wild Rose Bay. The landscape looked so different to what it had been like in early spring. Then, the sides of the slopes had been covered in bare branches and rough grass, but today, in late June, the wild roses were in full bloom, covering the hills in a riot of dark pink, a beautiful backdrop to the little beach below, where the blue waves lapped the against white sand. The path that led to the beach was clearly visible, as Aiden had cleared some of the dense foliage earlier that week. Jasmine looked around for him and Milou and spotted them further down the path. She had been so eager to get here that she had raced ahead, leaving Aiden and Milou to follow at their own pace. She smiled as she saw Aiden stop to let Milou sniff at something in the bushes. Those two. Such good friends already. Her gaze drifted further out across the glittering ocean and she took a deep breath of the sweet, fresh air. What a wonderful haven this was after the hectic time she had been through as she settled back into life in Paris.

Jasmine had gone to Paris soon after Sally's party to start work and set up the apartment to suit her and Aiden when he took up his job in September. Aiden had come over for a few days to meet his new boss, which had turned into a kind of honeymoon for them as they both got used to big city life, which for Aiden was quite a change. Struggling with French bureaucracy as they had to sort out Aiden's residency status was a huge pain in the neck, which nearly made Jasmine cry as they filled in the many complicated forms. But Aiden had told her that this was just one of those things that made their life a little less perfect, which should calm Jasmine's fear of something terrible happening.

She loved his way of taking everything in his stride and seeing the bright side at all times. Even when they started work on the small cottage they had bought only a month ago. Aiden had to do most of the heavy work when Jasmine couldn't get away from Paris. It was going to take a long time to finish it but they had already moved the four-poster bed there and managed to sleep in the bedroom despite the broken windows and creaking floorboards. But Jasmine couldn't be happier. It was their place that they would keep forever, whatever else happened to them. They would have the buzz of Paris when they were working, and enjoy the peace and tranquillity of Sandy Cove when they had time off. Neither of them wanted to take breaks anywhere else. Sandy Cove was where they wanted to be when they had time to relax.

Life was, for the moment, quite wonderful, Jasmine thought, as she looked at her engagement ring, smiling as she remembered her proposal and Aiden's reaction. He had laughed out loud and squeezed her tight and said he never thought she'd ask. Not long after that, Aiden had given her the most unusual engagement ring she had ever seen. She ran her finger over the smooth green stone set in white gold on her finger. It wasn't a stone at all, but a piece of sea glass, polished by the ocean, that they had found on the beach of Wild Rose Bay. Aiden had brought it to a jeweller in Killarney who had set it in white gold and made it into a beautiful piece of jewellery. The only other jewellery she wore was Siobhan's Claddagh ring on a gold chain around her neck, a good luck charm she never took off. It reminded her of that day when Aiden had rescued her and she had realised she loved him.

How perfect that was, she thought, finding her long-lost friend and then falling in love with him. It was discovering Wild Rose Bay that had really brought them together. The ancient love story had resonated with both of them, feeling a strong connection with the people who had lived there centuries ago. And how wonderful that her parents had also found each other, which, they constantly declared, was all Jasmine's doing, having pushed her father to get in touch with Sally.

How happy they were, Jasmine thought, and how quickly her father had settled into Sally's cottage and the quiet village life. They were busy setting up the wellness centre that would be opening the following year and seemed to have fun looking at plans and setting up the website, bouncing marketing ideas off each other. The people in Sandy Cove had taken the handsome Frenchman to their bosom and they were all looking forward to the wedding in August, when the little church would be packed and the party at the Harbour pub afterwards even more fun than Sally's coming of age last April.

'Here you are,' Aiden said, breathless, as he arrived at Jasmine's side, Milou at his heels. 'I had to put the lead on him as he was running up the mountain. I don't want him to start chasing sheep.'

'That would not do,' Jasmine agreed. 'In any case, he needs to get used to behaving like a Parisian dog again.'

'And I have to get used to being a Parisian man,' Aiden filled in. 'And I look forward to that. Even getting married in that little church near the apartment.'

'Are you sure we shouldn't get married here?' Jasmine asked. 'In Sandy Cove?'

'No. We met in Paris and we're going to live there.' Aiden laughed. 'My mother won't forgive you if you change your mind. You know how she loves dressing up. And so do my sister and my brother's wife. They're all looking forward to telling their friends they're going to a society wedding in Paris.'

'Society wedding?' Jasmine protested. 'Hardly. But if that's what they want to call it, so what?'

She smiled as she remembered their weekend in Dublin with Aiden's family. She had liked his father instantly, but his mother had been a little stiff at first, possibly due to her shyness. It had taken Jasmine the whole weekend to break the ice, but then her future mother-in-law had thawed and they had begun to relate.

'She likes you a lot, really,' Aiden said. 'It'll be all right, don't worry.'

Jasmine squinted against the sun as she looked up at him. 'There you go, reading my mind again.'

'Your face is like an open book,' he replied, squeezing her tight and kissing her on the top of her head. 'Oh, come on. What does it matter? We'll be living in Paris and spending our holidays here. It's not as if she'll be next door, is it?'

'You're right.' Jasmine leaned against Aiden's strong body and looked out over the bay. What a life they would have. Paris and then the little cottage they were doing up together right here in Sandy Cove. The best of both worlds. She touched Siobhan's ring on the chain around her neck and knew that it had brought her the luck the legend said it would.

'That cottage is a gem,' Aiden said. 'It'll take a lot of work to get it liveable, but we have the time and can do it slowly.'

'I want to make it really cosy, so we can live there when we're old,' Jasmine said. 'I can't think of a better place to spend my old age.'

'Me neither,' Aiden agreed. 'But hey, let's go down there for a swim and be young and irresponsible first.'

Jasmine laughed and started down the path. 'Come on, then. Last one in the water is a big chicken.'

They ran down the path together at breakneck speed, Milou behind them, all the way down to Wild Rose Bay.

A Letter from Susanne

I want to say a huge thank you for choosing to read *Daughters of Wild Rose Bay*. If you did enjoy it, and want to keep up to date with all my latest releases, just sign up at the following link. Your email address will never be shared and you can unsubscribe at any time.

www.bookouture.com/susanne-oleary

I hope you loved *Daughters of Wild Rose Bay*. It was such a joy to write. I love going back to Sandy Cove and Kerry, which is such a beautiful place, and so inspirational. Some people think I work for the Kerry tourist board because of my glowing descriptions in my novels, but I'm afraid I don't. But if my book makes you want to go there, you will get a warm welcome from the wonderful people who live there. Even if you can't go there in person, I will take you there in the next two novels that I'm already working on. Many more stories to tell and characters to meet!

If you did like the story, I would be very grateful if you could write a review. I'd love to hear what you think, and it makes such a difference helping new readers to discover one of my books for the first time.

I love hearing from my readers – you can get in touch on my Facebook page, through Twitter, Goodreads or my website.

Thanks,
Susanne

         www.susanne-oleary.com

         authoroleary

         @susl

Acknowledgements

As always, I must thank my amazing editor, Jennifer Hunt, for her hard work and endless support as she applies her magic touch to my stories. Also Kim Nash and Noelle Holten and all the lovely people at Bookouture for all the hard work, support and cheer.

I must also thank my dear friends, Maud, Agneta, Helena and Angelica, who cheer me on, read my books and inspire me to keep writing. Huge thanks also to my husband and the rest of my family, especially my sister Lena. Last but not by all means least, thank you, dear readers, for reading my stories, posting reviews and sending me lovely messages, which I truly appreciate.